sometimes
it happens

ALSO BY
LAUREN BARNHOLDT

Two-way Street

Watch Me

One Night That Changes Everything

sometimes it happens

LAUREN BARNHOLDT

Simon Pulse

New York London Toronto Sydney

ᗯᗯ

SIMON PULSE

An imprint of Simon & Schuster Children's Publishing Division
1230 Avenue of the Americas, New York, NY 10020
First Simon Pulse hardcover edition July 2011
Copyright © 2011 by Lauren Barnholdt

All rights reserved, including the right of reproduction
in whole or in part in any form.

SIMON PULSE and colophon are registered
trademarks of Simon & Schuster, Inc.

For information about special discounts for bulk purchases,
please contact Simon & Schuster Special Sales at 1-866-506-1949 or
business@simonandschuster.com.

The Simon & Schuster Speakers Bureau can bring authors
to your live event. For more information or to book an event contact
the Simon & Schuster Speakers Bureau at 1-866-248-3049 or visit our website at
www.simonspeakers.com.

Designed by Bob Steimle
The text of this book was set in Cochin.
Manufactured in the United States of America
2 4 6 8 10 9 7 5 3 1

Library of Congress Cataloging-in-Publication Data
Barnholdt, Lauren.
Sometimes it happens / by Lauren Barnholdt. — 1st Simon Pulse hardcover ed.
p. cm.
Summary: With help from her best friend, Ava, and Ava's boyfriend, Noah,
Hannah is recovering from being dumped by her boyfriend, Sebastian, but on
the first day of their senior year in high school, Ava learns that Hannah and Noah
betrayed her while she was away.
ISBN 978-1-4424-1314-6 (hardcover)
[1. Interpersonal relations—Fiction. 2. Betrayal—Fiction. 3. Secrets—Fiction.
4. High schools—Fiction. 5. Schools—Fiction.] I. Title.
PZ7.B2667Som 2011
[Fic]—dc22
2010043368
ISBN 978-1-4424-1316-0 (eBook)

For Jennifer Klonsky, for being smart, savvy, and amazing

Acknowledgments

A million thank-yous to:

My agent, Alyssa Eisner Henkin, for being the hardest-working, smartest, most enthusiastic agent in the business. Alyssa, I cannot thank you enough for everything you've done for me.

My sister Kelsey, for being Ally's favorite, our Wednesday sleepovers, and for reading all my work.

My sister Krissi, for her tattoo, our Old Navy trips, and always being there when I need her.

My mom, for her covert Facebook page, being my biggest inspiration, and always believing in me.

The best friends ever: Kevin Cregg, Scott Neumyer, Jessica Burkart, and Erin Dionne.

And of course, my husband, Aaron, for everything. Aaron, you came into my life and changed it one hundred percent for the better. I am so lucky to have you, and I love you with all my heart.

sometimes
it happens

The First Day of Senior Year

I really should *not* be so scared. I mean, I've done this millions of times before. Okay, maybe not millions. But for the last twelve years, on every weekday minus summers and vacations, I've gone to school. And I've never been afraid before. (Well, except for maybe a little bit in kindergarten, but isn't everyone a little afraid in kindergarten? And besides, even then I wasn't freaking out or anything. Not like Layna Hodge, who threw up all over the play box in the corner.)

Today, the first day of senior year, I'm terrified. This is because there is a very good chance that at some point today I will:

a. lose the love of my life,

b. lose my best friend, or

c. have an awkward encounter with the boy who broke my heart last year. (Note: This is a different boy than the previously mentioned love of my life. [See a.])

I take a deep breath and grip the steering wheel of my new car, then pull into a spot in the visitor lot of my high school. I'm technically not supposed to be parked here, but the visitor lot is way closer to my homeroom than the student lot, and since it's the first day of school, I'm pretty sure I can get away with it. Plus it won't be as obvious if I have to peel out of here and make an escape. *Okay,* I tell myself, *you can do this. You are invincible; nothing can rattle you. You have nerves of steel; you are a confident, strong woman; you —*

There's a knock on the passenger side window and I scream, then immediately hit the automatic door locks.

I look over. Oh. It's only Lacey.

She knocks on the window again, and I reluctantly unlock the doors.

She slides into the passenger seat, her long, red curly hair pooling around her shoulders. She smells like coffee and strawberry-mango shampoo.

"Hey," she says, "What's wrong? Why'd you freak out when I knocked on your window? And why are you parked in the visitor lot? It took me forever to find you."

"Nothing's wrong," I say. Which is a lie, of course. But I can't tell Lacey that. She knows nothing about what went on this summer. She knows nothing of the fact that my best friend Ava is coming back today, that everything is different, and that everything is horrible. That I'm going to see Noah, that I'm going to see Sebastian, that I'm going to maybe end up in a mental institution by the end of the day. Although, a mental institution actually might be preferable to going to school, so that might not be such a bad thing, now that I think about it.

"Just normal first day of school nerves," I say brightly.

"First day of school nerves?" Lacey says, like she's never heard of them. Which kind of makes no sense, since Lacey is one of the most nervous people I know. "You need caffeine then," she says. "It will fix you right up." She holds out the cardboard carrier that's in her hand. It's filled with three cups from Starbucks, and one's marked with my fave: a large vanilla latte with Splenda and extra cream.

"Thanks." I accept the huge coffee and take a sip. I don't really buy into her reasoning that I need the caffeine, since it definitely isn't going to calm me down. But maybe it'll give me a shot of energy that will make me so buzzed I'll be all excited to go into school. On the other hand, it's only caffeine, not magic.

"Where's Noah?" she asks. "I brought him one, too." Of course she did. Coffee with a shot of espresso, extra sugar, extra cream. The same drink he had every single day this summer, when the three of us worked together at Cooley's Diner, but we always brought in our own coffee because the stuff at Cooley's tastes disgusting. (Cooley's Diner coffee = mud, only, like, more bitter and tinged with the taste of a dirty cup.)

"Noah?" I ask, trying to keep my voice light. My hands tighten around my coffee, and I almost spill the whole thing all over myself. "I dunno." I shrug, like Noah hasn't even crossed my mind, when, of course, he's the only thing I've been thinking about.

"Didn't you guys drive to school together?"

"No."

"Why not? You guys drove to work together every day over the summer."

"Not *every* day," I say. "And besides, I have a car now." I run my hand over the steering wheel of my new car, the car that took me all summer to save up to buy. It's red (perfect), four doors (perfect), a 2005 (adequate) and has 120K miles on it (not so perfect, but beggars can't be choosers, especially when it comes to transportation.) "And besides," I add, "Noah drives to school with Ava usually."

"Oh, right." Lacey wrinkles up her nose. "I forgot that *Ava's* back." She says "Ava" like it's a dirty word. "Sorry," she says. "I know she's your friend."

"That's okay." If Lacey thinks I'm acting weird, she doesn't say anything, which is a good sign. If Lacey doesn't realize anything's going on, maybe Ava won't either. And if Ava doesn't, maybe Noah won't. And that way we can just forget everything that happened this summer, especially what happened last night. Just push it all under the rug and start fresh. La, la, la, there it goes, like some kind of garbage being taken out to the curb, poof! I start to feel a little better. Maybe everything is going to work out after all. Of course, I don't want to be the kind of girl with a scandalous secret, but sometimes you have to take what you can get and just —

Suddenly, something slams into the back of my car, and my whole body flies forward, my chest hitting the steering wheel.

"Shit!" Lacey says. Her fingers tighten around her coffee and the lid goes flying off, her cappuccino sloshing over the sides of the cup and splattering the front of the glittery silver tank top she's wearing. "Shit, shit, shit!" She swivels her head around, strands of her hair whipping against her face.

I look in the rearview mirror. A red car (something expensive — maybe a Lexus?) has backed into me, and the driver, a girl wearing camouflage capris (doesn't she know those are so five years ago?), comes rushing out of the driver's side, and then peers down at my bumper. She looks like she's about to burst into tears.

I close my eyes for a moment, and then open my door and climb out, Lacey hot on my heels.

"What the hell is wrong with you?" Lacey demands. She pulls the sunglasses she's wearing down off the top of her head and slides them over her eyes.

"Oh my God, I'm like sooo sorry," the girl says. She's younger than us (probably a sophomore?) and she twists her hands into a knot in front of her. Her face is getting all scrunchy, like she really might be about to start crying.

"It's okay," I say, kneeling down and inspecting my

bumper. There's a tiny scratch, about two inches long, running down one side of it. "It looks like it's just a small scratch."

"A *small scratch*?" Lacey yells. She bends down and looks at the car. "You know how much small scratches cost to get fixed, Hannah? Like thousands of dollars!"

"I'm so sorry," the girl says again. She's wearing Converse sneakers, a black tank top, and about three million pounds of black eyeliner.

"It's okay," I say. She's obviously one of those gothy girls who, like, pretends she's over everything, but inside is about five seconds away from crying constantly. Seriously, goth girls cannot handle anything.

"My dad is going to flip," Goth Girl says. "He just got me this car. For a birthday present."

"Oh, God," Lacey says. I'll bet she's rolling her eyes under the sunglasses, thinking of the hours and hours we spent this summer behind the counter at Cooley's, sweating under the broken air conditioner and serving bottomless cups of coffee to the old men who would come in every day, sit for hours, and then tip us a dollar.

"Look," I say to the girl, before Lacey can tear into her again, "Can you just give me your insurance information?" I guess that's what you're supposed to do in these situations. I mean, I'm not completely sure, since I've never actually been in a car accident. Until a few days ago, I never even had a car.

"Right," the girl says. She heads to her car, rummages around in her glove compartment, and comes back. She carefully copies everything down onto a sheet of paper from a brand new black binder that's covered with stickers of bands I've never heard of, then rips it out and gives it to me.

"Thanks, Jemima," I say, glancing down at her name on the paper. Jemima? No wonder she looks so nervous. With a name like that you're probably used to bad things happening to you. Starting, of course, with your parents naming you Jemima.

"Why were you pulling out of a space, anyway?" Lacey asks. "School's about to start. Shouldn't you have been pulling *into* a space?" She looks down at the coffee stain on her tank top. "Does your insurance cover clothing? Because this tank top was extremely expensive." It's a lie, of course. Lacey got that tank top for $12.99 at Old Navy.

"I forgot something," Jemima says, chewing on her bottom lip. "At home. So I was going back to get it. And I'll pay for your tank top. How much did it cost?"

"I hope your dad's, like, a lawyer or something, being able to afford that fancy car. Because, honestly, if I get whiplash or some kind of neck affliction . . ." Lacey rubs her neck, ignoring Jemima's tank top offer.

"Okay, well, bye!" I say to Jemima, shooting her a look that says, *get the hell out of here if you want to save yourself.*

She scampers away obediently before Lacey has a chance to threaten any more litigation.

"Lacey!" I say. "You didn't have to scare the poor girl."

"Sorry," she says. "But Hannah, you have to be tougher on people. What if we were pushovers, and she decided to, like, commit insurance fraud or something so that she wouldn't have to pay for your car."

"Insurance fraud? Lacey, I don't think that's really—"

"Besides," she says, "*I'm* the one who should be scared. I have a bad neck now probably."

"You do not have a bad neck," I say, rolling my eyes. I walk back toward the car and open the door.

"What are you doing?" Lacey asks. "It's almost time for homeroom. The bell's going to ring in, like, one minute, and I need to see what Danielle Shapiro is wearing. I'll bet she has a fake tan with one of those little heart cutout things. You know, like skanky body art?"

"You go ahead," I tell her. "I'll just—"

"Hannah!" Lacey says. "You are coming into school! Forget about stupid Sebastian Bukowski and his dumb friends. You are sooo over him!" She crosses over to my side of the car and puts her hands on my shoulders. "Hannah, you are amazing. You are gorgeous and smart and you deserve someone way better than Sebastian. He doesn't even deserve to be a passing thought through your brain." She looks into my eyes. "Now, we are going to go into school, me and you, and no matter what happens, I'm going to be right by your side, okay? Nothing to worry about."

"Thanks, Lace," I say, giving her a weak smile. I don't

have the heart or the strength to tell her that Sebastian's not even the half of it. That he's not even the *quarter* of it. I don't have the heart to tell her about Ava, or about what happened with Noah last night. And I don't have the strength to argue with her. So when she takes my hand, I don't protest, and when she pulls me across the parking lot, I force my feet to march in the direction of school.

Here goes nothing.

Three Months Earlier, the Last Day of Junior Year

"Seniors, bitches!" Ava declares, then slams her locker shut and whirls around, her shoulder-length blond hair forming a halo behind her.

"Not yet," I say, shifting my bag from one shoulder to the other. I've just cleaned out my locker, and it weighs about a bazillion pounds. Seriously, I'm kind of afraid the strap is going to break. How have I accumulated so much stuff in just ten months? They should totally make a new show on *A&E Hoarders:* "Locker Edition." "We still have a whole summer before we're seniors."

Ava looks at her empty locker. "Goodbye, locker," she says. "Goodbye, hallways. Goodbye, school!" She grabs me and twirls me around the hall. "We'll miss you! And when we see you again, we'll be SENIORS, BITCHES!"

"Don't you think that's a little dramatic?" I say, but I start to laugh even though all the twirling is making me a little dizzy. "We're going to be back here in, like, two and a half months."

"Yeah," she says. "But everything will be different then. We'll be *seniors*." She gives me a look, like being seniors is the most important thing that's ever happened to us. Which I guess it kind of is, since so far in my life nothing too exciting has gone on. But the truth is, I don't really *want* to be a senior. I mean, I guess it's okay, because once senior year is over, I won't have to go to high school anymore, and let's face it, who doesn't want high school to be over? But on the other hand, it means change. I don't do well with change. At all. In fact, I try to avoid it at all costs.

And besides, high school isn't *all* bad. Yeah, there's the getting up ridiculously early, and the learning things you know you're going to have no use for, and the annoying girls who think they're better than everyone, and the worrying about your future every time you have a math test that you don't do so well on, and the boys who break your heart.

But I *like* having classes with Ava and my boyfriend, Sebastian. I like knowing that when I come to school every morning, I can get away with taking sips out of my travel coffee mug that's filled with a vanilla latte, as long as I don't make a big deal out of it. I like knowing how to get out of gym class (say you're having stomach issues), how to get out of dissecting frogs in bio (ethically opposed), and what girls to steer clear of because they'll have no problem stealing your boyfriend and/or talking behind your back (Lynn Mol and Lila Jankowitz). I don't know *any* of those things about college (or, you know, the world at large), which makes it seem scary and overwhelming.

"Hey, guys," Ava's boyfriend, Noah, slides up to us in the hallway, puts his arms around Ava from behind, and nuzzles the back of her neck.

"Noah!" Ava rolls her eyes, but slides back into him. I swallow and try not to feel jealous. Not of Noah. I mean, he's nice and everything, but I don't like him like that. The jealousy is more because of just how close Noah and Ava are. Actually, I guess close isn't really the word. It's more like they're comfortable together. Which is the total opposite of me and Sebastian.

Even after five months together, I still worry that Sebastian's not going to call me when he says he will, and I'm still not completely sure what the rules are when it comes to kissing him in the hall or holding his hand at parties. Sebastian isn't so into PDA. Which is fine, but it makes it kind of uncomfortable when we're hanging out with Ava and Noah. Whenever we go on double dates, those two will be, like, practically making out, and Sebastian and I will be standing next to each other, feeling all awkward. Which would also be fine, if we could talk about it later. Like, if Sebastian would be all, "Wow, Noah and Ava are crazy, I'm so glad we don't have to be all over each other in public to know how much we care about each other." And then I would be all, "I know, right? But maybe we could hold hands sometime at least." And then Sebastian would be like, "Okay, anything for you." But that will never happen. Mostly because (a) Sebastian and I really don't talk about relationship issues that much, and (b) he would never say "anything for you."

"Party tonight," Noah says now. "At Jenna Lamacchia's."

"Ugh, over it." Ava takes a piece of gum out of her purse, chews it a couple of times, then spits it back into the wrapper. She throws the wrapper with the chewed up gum into her now-empty locker. Ava doesn't like gum. She just chews it to make her breath smell fresh. "I hate Jenna Lamacchia, and I don't want to go to a party."

"Why not?" I ask, "It could be fun." It's a lie, and we all know it. The only reason Jenna Lamacchia's house is fun is because her parents are never home. Her parties are always ridiculously loud, there's always a bunch of people in the guest bedroom smoking pot that wafts through the whole house, and you can hardly move because the living room is so small. Plus, it's not even that special anymore since she has a party, like, every night. "Besides," I say, "there's nothing else to do." That part, at least, is true.

"What's going on?" Ava asks, narrowing her blue eyes at me suspiciously. "Why do you want to go to Jenna's so bad?"

"I don't," I say.

"Then why did you just say you did?"

I consider lying, but I know Ava will see right through

it. That's what happens when you've been best friends since sixth grade. "Fine," I say. "If you must know, Sebastian has been MIA all day, so I'm not totally sure, but I'm assuming he probably wants to go." Sebastian loves going to Jenna's house. Mostly because of the pot in the back bedroom.

"You want to go to Jenna's because you know Sebastian wants to go?" Ava asks. "Hannah, that's kind of pathetic."

"Ava!" Noah says. "Be nice." But his tone is teasing and he's biting on the back of her neck.

"Sorry, Hans," Ava says. "But you shouldn't want to do something you hate just because Sebastian wants to get high in Jenna's back bedroom."

"Look, " I say. "I'm not—" And then I see Sebastian, walking down the hall toward me, his long legs encased in the jeans I bought him for Christmas.

"Hey," he says, like it's totally normal we haven't seen each other all day. Like it's totally normal that he didn't meet me outside by the benches before school the way he told me he would, and then never texted me to apologize and/or explain why. He slides his arm around my waist and gives me a kiss. On the top of my head. WTF? I start to freak out a little. Okay, a lot. Sebastian has never kissed me on my head before. In our whole five-month relationship, I have never gotten a kiss on the head. Mouth, cheeks, sure. But head? No. Being kissed on the head is something your parents do to you when you're, like, seven. And I'm smart enough to know that when your sixteen-year-old boyfriend is doing it, it's not a good sign.

"Sebastian," Ava says. "Would you please tell Hannah that you aren't going to break up with her?"

"Ava!" Noah says.

"Ava!" I say. I want to say more, but I can't because then what if Sebastian thinks I really am worried that he's going to break up with me? So I just slide my arm around his waist, look up at him, and force my face into a smile. And when he smiles back, I let myself believe it's going to be okay.

We end up at the party, of course, because there's nothing else to do.

"You totally have to go back to the mall and get that tank top in blue," Ava says as we tromp up the sidewalk toward Jenna's house.

"Why?" I glance down at the long yellow tank top I'm wearing over black leggings.

"Blue just looks a lot better on you than yellow," she says. "I keep trying to tell you that you're a winter, not a warm."

I have no idea what she's talking about. "You've never told me that before."

Ava ignores me and steers me up the cobblestones to the front door, then walks right into Jenna's house. There's a cloud of smoke permeating the living room, and Belle and Sebastian is blaring from the iPod in the corner. You can hardly move because there are so many people. You'd think that, with it being the last day of school and all, someone else would be having a party too, but nooo. It's

Jenna Lamacchia's or nothing. God, my life is boring.

"I'm going to find Noah," Ava says, then disappears into the crowd and the smoke. At least, I think that's what she says. I can't really hear her. I sigh and then slide outside to the back patio to wait for Sebastian. I texted him earlier, but he hasn't texted me back, which probably means he's not here yet. Sebastian's kind of like a girl—he takes forever to get ready and is late for everything. It really doesn't make any sense because it's not like he's some kind of fashionista or anything. He wears jeans and T-shirts almost every single day.

Girls in bikinis and boys in swim trunks are splashing around in Jenna's kidney-shaped pool, but there are no lights out here except for a few of those really cheap plastic ones that stick in the grass. Which is kind of weird. And also super dangerous. What if someone drowns because they can't see anything? I'm somehow able to snag a deck chair in front of a plastic cup of beer that someone's abandoned on the picnic table. And that's when I see him—Sebastian. He's in the pool, holding one of those water volleyballs. Seems like he's ensconced in some kind of game. Nice of him to meet me at the door. Or at least text me back.

I sigh, and think about joining him in the water. I do have a bathing suit on under my clothes—a skimpy, silver bikini, with teeny-tiny straps. Definitely not something I would normally wear, but I bought it last week because Ava said I should, and she was very persistent. We got into a semi-argument about it in the dressing room of Sand Dune

Swimwear (not like a fight-fight, more like Ava was getting exasperated with me because she said my fashion sense wasn't daring enough, and then I got annoyed with her because she was being kind of mean), but now I'm glad she made me buy it. It probably sounds totally anti-feminist, but maybe a sexy bikini is a good way to get the spark back between me and Sebastian.

I stand up, slide my feet out of my sandals, pull off my tank top and leggings, and then, holding my clothes loosely to my chest (partly because there's nowhere to put them and partly because I don't know if I'm quite ready to expose myself in front of all these people), start walking toward the pool. And that's when Sebastian surfaces in the deep end, puts his arm around some girl I've never seen before, and kisses her.

The First Day of Senior Year

"I seriously could have whiplash," Lacey's saying as we walk toward the front doors of the building. "That happened to this woman on an episode of *90210*. The old one, I mean."

"The old whiplash?" I ask, confused. Whiplash is a disease. Or an affliction. An injury? Whatever it is, I don't think there can be a new kind. Unless it's one of those new diseases that keeps popping up, like a couple of years ago when everyone was freaking out about swine flu. It's also possible that the closer we get to school, the more my mental capacities are diminishing, making me unable to understand even the simple intricacies of teen dramas on The CW.

"No, the old *90210*. You know, the one with what's his name in it? The guy with the hair?" I shrug and give her a blank look. "Well, whatever," she says.

She opens the door, and we step inside, which is, like, a totally and completely amazing achievement, considering I was almost hyperventilating in the visitor lot just a couple of minutes ago. Although, now that I'm here, I'm not exactly sure how I should behave. I mean, there are so many people I'm trying to avoid. Should I just keep my head down, hoping I don't make eye contact with anyone who happens to cross my path? Should I scan the halls with an eagle eye so that if I *do* spot one of them, I have time to duck out of the way? Or (and this is the most terrifying choice) should I maybe just stop avoiding them altogether, since the longer I do, the scarier it's going to be, and eventually they might realize what I'm doing and be all, "Hey, Hannah, why are you avoiding me?"

This whole thing is very complicated. *Not as complicated as it's going to be*, a little voice in the back of my head whispers. I do my best to ignore it.

"Um, hello?" Lacey says. "Are you even listening to me? Who are you looking for?"

"No one," I say quickly. I point to the little sign outside of room A3. "There's my homeroom! I guess I'll see you later." I try to turn and walk away from her, but Lacey grabs my shoulder and whirls me back around.

"Hannah," she says. "You were looking for Sebastian, weren't you?" She puts her hand on her hip and taps her foot, waiting for my answer.

"No, I wasn't!" It's not even a lie. Like I said before, at this point Sebastian is the least of my concerns. Although he's definitely someone I'm avoiding. Just not the main person (people?) I'm avoiding. This is really making my head spin.

"Then who were you looking for?" She's looking at me with a mixture of concern and suspicion. Not that I blame her—if I were her, I'd be suspicious too. I mean, I spent pretty much the whole beginning of the summer trying to get over Sebastian. Lacey witnessed me crying a lot, eating a lot, and trying to drown my sorrows in beer. Which didn't work. It only made me sick. Actually, all of those things—the crying, the ice cream, and the alcohol—made me sick. The combination of them probably screwed my stomach up for life.

"No one."

"Hannah, seriously, are you okay?" Lacey asks. She tilts her head toward me, her lips pressed together.

"I'm *fine*," I say again. "Why do you keep asking me that?"

"Hannah," she says and waits. I think about it. I should tell her. I should. This is Lacey, she's my friend, she's not going to judge me for it. She's not going to get all up on her high horse and lecture me or anything. She's nice. She used to volunteer at the ASPCA for God's sake! The girl has a heart. She even hates Ava, which might actually be a plus in this situation.

I take a deep breath. "Okay," I say. "But first you have to promise that you won't (a) tell anyone or (b) judge me."

"I won't," she says, her tone serious.

"All right," I say, "So you know how—"

But the bell rings then, cutting me off, and Lacey bites her lip. "Go on," she says. "Who cares about being late to homeroom on the first day?"

The halls are full now, kids shuffling by us, jostling their bags into my side as they go.

"No," I say. "You should go. You don't want to get in trouble already." Last year, Lacey skipped a lot of her classes, so many that she almost got denied credit. She had her reasons of course (it had to do with a boy—what doesn't?), but try telling that to the people in guidance. They really don't understand how hard it is to hold your mental state together enough just to *get* to school in the first place, let alone when you have some kind of stress in your life.

"I don't care," Lacey says.

"I do," I say. No way Lacey should get in trouble because I made a mess out of my life.

"Fine," she says. "But meet me here after homeroom so we can compare schedules?"

"Definitely."

She turns and disappears into the sea of faces, and I turn and look at the door to my homeroom. Nine minutes. Homeroom is nine minutes. Well, actually, that's not true. Today we're having an extended homeroom for, like, nineteen minutes so we can get our schedules and lockers and everything. But still. Nineteen minutes. I can definitely handle that. *Just get through homeroom,* the little voice in my head says. *And then you can worry about what you're going to do.*

Feeling slightly optimistic since the voice in my head has decided to try and be positive for once, I push past the crowd in the hall and into the room. And then I stop. Because there, already seated in the second to last row by the window, is Ava. She's wearing a purple summer dress and doodling in a notebook, but as soon as I see her, she looks up, almost like she has some kind of instinct that I'm there.

"Hannah!" she says, her face breaking out into a smile. "Yay! I saved you a seat!"

My heart dips and flips, and all of a sudden, I feel like I'm going to throw up. My feet want to turn me around and march me right out of here and back to my car. But I know I can't do that. I mean, she's already seen me. So I take a couple of deep breaths, then force myself to move forward and into the classroom.

The Last Night of
Junior Year

Sebastian's hands are on the girl's face and in her hair and playing with the long strings of the bikini top that ties behind her back. I start to feel all faint and kind of wobbly, so I elbow my way through Jenna's backyard and into the house, where I head straight for the bathroom on the first floor.

I lean over the toilet and wait to see if I'm going to be sick, but once I'm in there, my stomach isn't churning as much, and I start to think that maybe I just had some kind of weird panic attack that made me think I had to throw up and/or faint when I really didn't. I take deep breaths and fill my hands with cold water from the sink, then splash it all over my face. My eye shadow starts to run, and the bronzer I'm wearing comes off and starts staining my hands, but I don't care. I keep putting the water on my face, over and over.

How, how, *how* could this have happened? And why *now*, on the last day of school? Although, I guess that part, at least, is pretty obvious. Probably Sebastian thought it would be better to break up at the beginning of the summer so he could have fun hanging out with whatever girls he wanted, bringing them to the beach and ogling them in their skimpy bikinis, taking them to the huge Fourth of July party he always has up at his family's summer house, and inviting them to hang out by his pool all day, every day without me around bothering him to get a job.

Oh, God. I shouldn't have spent so much time bothering him to get a job! I didn't even *care* if he got a job! It was just his dumb parents. They were constantly on his ass, especially his dad, and I just figured that if he got a job, they'd give him some peace. I thought it was a good trade-off. But obviously I came across as some kind of horrible, nagging wife!

Of course, deep down I know it probably doesn't have anything to do with me telling him to get a summer job. It's probably about sex, because it's *always* about sex, there's no getting around it. But what else did he want from me? I mean, I *know* what else he wanted from me, but, I mean, besides that. We were doing Everything But! I am totally and completely the Everything But girl! I was getting very good at Everything But! I never complained about Everything But. I was constantly and happily ready and willing to give Everything But! Unless . . . oh, God. Am I horrible at Everything But? Supposedly, all you have to do is be enthusiastic, you know? It's kind of like pizza, you can't really get a bad—

There's a knock on the door.

"Just a minute!" I call, slipping my clothes back on over

my bikini and hoping whoever's at the door can't hear in my voice that I'm having a nervous breakdown. "I'll be right out." I look at my face in the mirror. I look horrible. Bronzer is all over my hands and running down my cheeks, mixed with mascara and purple glitter dust eye shadow. I grab a wad of toilet paper and start wiping my face, trying to clean up the mess.

"Hannah, it's me!" the voice says. Ava. Oh, thank God. I pull open the door, grab her arm, and yank her into the bathroom.

"I saw you come running in here and I didn't know what you were—" She sees my face. "Ohmigod," she says. "What happened?" She goes right into Jenna's linen closet and pulls out a clean blue towel, runs it under some warm water, and starts cleaning the ruined makeup off my face. Yikes. I hope that towel isn't expensive.

"I saw Sebastian," I say, my stomach starting to churn again. "In the pool. With another girl."

Her eyes narrow. "Please tell me it was just normal Sebastian stupid flirting behavior? Annoying but ultimately harmless?"

"No," I say, shaking my head. "There was kissing. Lots of it. With tongue." And that's when I start crying.

"That asshole!" Ava says. She looks at the dirty towel in her hand, drops it on the floor, then reaches into the closet for another one.

"Should we be using those?" I ask, as she runs it under the warm water. I grab some toilet paper off the roll and blow my nose. "They look kind of expensive."

"Hannah," Ava says, giving me a look. "This is an emergency. And besides, you shouldn't be worried about that, you should be worried about *you*." She hands me the towel, then reaches into her bag and pulls out her cell.

"Who are you calling?" I ask. I'm still crying, just not as hard.

"Noah." Then, into the phone, she says, "Hey, it's me. Can you come into the downstairs bathroom, we're having an emergency."

"I don't want Noah to know!" I say. "That's humiliating!"

"It's okay," she says. "He's good in a crisis." She looks in the mirror over the sink, checks her teeth, and runs her fingers through her hair. There's a knock on the door. Geez, already? I haven't even had time to acclimate myself to the situation, and now I have to share it with Ava's boyfriend? And how did he get here so fast anyway? Is he some kind of speed walker?

"Come in," Ava says, without even bothering to ask who it is. Noah walks in, looking slightly nervous.

"What's going on?" he asks when he sees me sitting on the closed toilet, sniffling into a stained towel.

"Sebastian," Ava hisses, "is out there making out with some troll!"

Noah looks at me, his eyebrows raised, and I nod in confirmation. "Although she's not really a troll," I tell him, thinking about it. "I mean, I didn't really get that good of a look at her, but she didn't look trollish, she had these really defined arms and her hair was—"

Ava shoots me a look and I cut myself off, square my shoulders, and say, "Sebastian is out there making out with some troll." Ava nods in satisfaction, then whirls around and reaches into Noah's pocket, pulling out his phone. She starts scrolling through it. "Who can we get?" she asks.

"Who can we get for what?" I ask. I rip another piece of toilet paper off the roll and dab my eyes. I knew I should have brought my makeup with me. But the purse that matches these shoes is really teeny-tiny, and I couldn't fit anything in it, so all I have is my lip gloss. Perfect for touching up my lips pre-make-out-with-Sebastian session, but definitely not at all helpful for fixing my face post-seeing-Sebastian-making-out-with-someone-else meltdown.

"There's Chase Parker," Noah says immediately. He vaults himself onto the counter in Jenna's bathroom. She has one of those huge counters that has two sinks, so there's plenty of room for him to sit.

"Chase Parker?" I ask, confused. "What are you guys talking about?" They're not going to try and get Sebastian beat up, are they? Chase Parker could definitely take him. He's huge and built, and there was even this whole craziness last year where Chase was running some kind of illegal steroids ring out of his gym locker. Allegedly.

"Could work," Ava says. She hands the phone out to me. "Call him."

"I don't want Sebastian beat up!" I say. "I just want to go

home." I lean my head against the tile wall and close my eyes. Yes, going home to wallow sounds perfect. I can eat something greasy. Maybe I'll take a couple of Tylenol PMs to help me get to sleep. I think my mom might even have an old bottle of Ambien lying around somewhere from right after her and my dad got divorced. Not that I'm usually into medicinal therapy. But your boyfriend making out with someone right in front of you calls for desperate measures.

"Not beat up," Ava says. "For a rebound." She's leaning into the mirror now, retouching her lip gloss.

I must have a really blank look on my face, because Noah turns to me and says, "You know, like a rebound guy? To hook up with?"

I gasp. "I can't hook up with someone just to hook up with them!" Have they both lost their minds? "Wait a second," I say to Noah. "You think Chase Parker would hook up with me?" I'm kind of flattered. Not that I want to hook up with Chase Parker, obviously. But he's kind of considered a catch. Most girls only care about his sexy washboard stomach, his deep blue eyes, and the fact that he's popular. They don't really care about the steroids, and if anything, that whole scandal kind of just served to make his stock rise. I guess because it makes him seem kind of dangerous.

"Why not?" Noah says. He shrugs.

"Thanks, Noah," I say, wondering if he's just being nice or if he really is that naïve. Probably both.

"So should I call him?" Noah asks.

"No." I lean my head against the smooth tile of the bathroom wall and close my eyes. "I just want to go home."

"You're not going home," Ava says.

"Why not?"

"Because if you go home, you're letting Sebastian win."

"He's already won," I say. "He's the one out there making out with another girl, and I'm the one who's in here, crying and wishing I'd never come."

I start to sob again, and Ava comes over, kneels down on the rug in front of me, and gives me a hug. "Look," she says. "I am going to leave this bathroom, I am going to go out to the party, and I am going to find someone who is willing to hook up with you. And when I get back, you are going to be ready? Got it?"

She turns on her heel and walks out before I can answer, leaving me alone with Noah.

"Sorry," I say, looking up to where he's sitting on the counter.

"For what?"

"For making you waste the best party hours sitting in here with me."

"You're not making me do anything," he says. "And besides, it's not a very good party."

"So if it was a good party you'd be mad at me?"

"Maybe," he says. But I can tell he's joking, and I almost smile.

We sit there in silence for a couple of minutes Awwwk-ward.

I mean, I don't know Noah *that* well. Definitely not enough to know what to say to him while I'm trapped in a bathroom having a crisis. He and Ava have been together for almost ten months so obviously I've been around him a lot. And the four of us—me, Ava, Noah, and Sebastian—hang out once in a while. But Noah and I have never, like, spent time alone or anything. And he wasn't really in our group of friends before he and Ava started dating. In fact, he transferred to our school at the beginning of this year, so I don't even have any, like, funny but forgotten stories I can bring up to him, like about how he threw up on a field trip in fifth grade or something.

The silence stretches on for a couple more minutes, and I try to think of something to say. Something about him and Ava maybe? Or something about our computer class! That's where I first met Noah, before Ava even met him. It was an Intro to Web Design class and only lasted half the year, so it's been over for a while.

Maybe I should ask him if he's going to take Intro to Web Design Two? That would be kind of stupid, since we both agreed the first class was a total waste of time. Maybe I can ask him about baseball. Or I could ask him what he's planning on doing for Ava's birthday, which is coming up in a few months. Well, in September. But still. He's probably going to need pointers way in advance on what to do and how to plan. Guys are completely clueless when it comes to birthdays. For my birthday last month, Sebastian bought me three bottles of lotion from Victoria's Secret and this very trashy lingerie set from Frederick's of Hollywood. I wasn't sure what was more disturbing, that (a) he went to two different lingerie stores, spending God knows how long picking things out in there, (b) he thought I would like anything in a leopard print, or (c) it was a definite hint that he wanted to have sex.

But now that I'm thinking about it, I really should have just worn that leopard-print teddy. Lingerie doesn't mean you have to have sex, it just means you're getting into a sexy mood, like maybe a let's-do-Everything-But kind of mood. I could have worn it, or I could have taken it back and gotten something else, something in a softer pink, maybe, with some kind of lace —

"So," Noah says. "Are you going to take Intro to Web Design Two?"

"I doubt it," I say.

"Me neither."

Silence again. Finally I can't take it anymore, so I stand up and look at my reflection in the mirror over the sink. "So," I say. "Scale of one to ten, how horrible do I look?"

"You don't look horrible."

"I don't look great."

"You look exactly like you should after you just found out your asshole boyfriend is cheating on you."

"Thanks," I say. I blow my nose again and start to feel a little bit better just as Ava comes tearing back into the bathroom.

"Jonah Moncuso!" she yells, waving her phone around. "Jonah Moncuso thinks you're hot, he's thought you were hot since seventh grade." Somehow I find this a little hard to believe since in seventh grade I unfortunately decided it would be a good idea to put blue streaks in my dirty blond hair, and had buck-teeth that took three years of braces to fix. It's more likely that Jonah Moncuso is drunk and figures hooking up with me is better than not hooking up at all.

"I don't know," I say. "I'm not sure if it's a good idea." And by "not sure" I obviously mean "definitely not."

"Of course it's a good idea!" Ava says. She's in Jenna's medicine cabinet now, rummaging around.

"What are you doing in there?" I ask. If she thinks I'm going to take someone else's prescription drugs to loosen up for my rebound, she's definitely mistaken. Taking my mom's Ambien is one thing, but drugs from some random medicine cabinet is another.

"Looking for some makeup for you," she says. "You can't go kissing someone looking like that." She pulls out a bottle of pills. "Wow," she says. "I had no idea that Jenna was on Adderall, did you?"

"Ava!" Noah grabs the bottle out of her hand and puts it back in the cabinet. "You can't just go around looking through people's bathrooms, it's a breach of confidentiality."

"Yeah," I say. Although now that I think about it, the Adderall does explain a lot.

"Oh, relax," she says. "It's not like I'm going to tell anybody." She's setting up a bunch of stuff on the counter, lining up bottles and tubes. "Well," she says, looking at me and then looking at the mess in front of her. "It's not ideal, since you're a lot fairer than Jenna or whoever these belong to, but it'll have to do. We'll just smear the foundation all down your neck and hope for the best."

"I'm not using that," I say. "Who knows what kind of diseases I could get."

"What would you rather have happen?" Ava asks. "Everyone seeing you slumping out of here with your head down and your makeup a mess, or everyone seeing you making out with some other guy, even if there's a slight chance you might get a skin disease?"

"Depends on how bad the skin disease would be," I say. "Like, is it one that eats my flesh? Or just your normal, run-of-the-mill rash?"

"I think we should just take you home," Noah says, jumping off the counter. "Come on, Hannah, you don't want to make out with Jonah Moncuso, do you?"

"Not really," I say morosely.

"Then let's go," he says, "We can stop at McDonald's or something on the way and then I'll drop you both off at Ava's. You guys can watch chick flicks and listen to angry girl rock or whatever it is girls do when they decide they hate guys."

"That sounds good," I say gratefully.

"No way," Ava says. "You're going out there, and you're making out with Jonah Moncuso!" She waves her cell in my face. "See? Here's the text where he says you're hot."

"Ava—" I start. But before I can finish, my own cell

starts to vibrate in my purse. I pull it out. A text from Paige Brokaw, this girl who I'm kind of friendly with, but not really. It says, "S is in pool making out w/ some freshman!!! OMG, WHAT WILL U DO? DID U GO HOME??? CALL ME!"

Well. I guess that makes the decision a lot easier. I can't let the whole school witness my public humiliation. If I leave now, everyone will know why. So even though it's completely and totally against my better judgment, I let Ava make me up with Jenna's makeup. And then I follow her back out into the party, Noah walking reluctantly behind us.

The First Day of Senior Year

"Hannah!" Ava's almost screaming now, and waving her hand around like a crazy person. Which actually kind of makes sense. I did stop after taking two steps into the room and now I'm not moving at all, even though she first called my name, like, ten seconds ago. "Are you coming over here or what?"

"Yes, I'm coming," I say, and shuffle into the room. *Okay,* I tell myself, *new plan.* Just pretend that everything's normal! Which it is, pretty much. If Ava had come home twenty-four, or even, say, twenty hours earlier, what happened last night wouldn't have happened. And she totally could have, too. Come home early, I mean. In fact, she was supposed to, but she decided to stay in Maine a little longer with her camp friends.

Ava leaps out of her seat and throws her arms around me. "Ohmigod, I missed you so much!" She pulls away and grins.

"You just saw me two weeks ago," I say, sliding into the seat next to her. I reach into my bag and get really busy pulling out a notebook and a pen. I wish it wasn't the first day of school, so I'd have books or homework or something to keep me busy. Of course, I wouldn't have homework for homeroom, but I'd have at least something I could pretend I was finishing up.

"Yeah, but that was different. Did you get my text last night? I wanted to see if you wanted to meet up before school."

"Yeah, I was . . . I was already sleeping."

Her eyes narrow in concentration as she studies me. "Did you . . . you didn't cut your hair, did you?"

"No," I say, reaching up and fingering my hair. "I mean, kind of . . . I just . . . I got a few layers." I went with Lacey a couple of days ago to Bellaria, this super swanky salon in Boston. She got her long red curls straightened, and I got a trim and some layers, and then we went shopping for school clothes. It was really fun, although Lacey kept having to stop and fish around in her bag for her hand sanitizer. She doesn't do well with taking public transportation or touching things that a lot of other people have been touching, like doorknobs, clothes racks—you know, pretty much anything.

"You should totally get extensions," Ava says. She tosses her newly long hair over her shoulder. "Don't you think they look totally natural? Long hair is really in right now."

"Totally natural," I agree.

"Maybe after school we can go and get you some clip-ins," she says. "You know, so you can try them out. They're not that expensive, but you should probably get real human hair ones." She giggles, like the thought of real human hair is funny. Which it kind of is. And also kind of gross.

"Yeah, maybe," I say, even though there's no way that's going to happen. First for the aforementioned gross factor, second for the fact that I really love my new haircut, and third because I'm totally and completely broke. "So how was the last day of camp?"

"Amazing," she says. "The girls just grew so much, you know? I really didn't want it to end. I spent the whole car ride home last night bawling."

Ava's been away in Maine, working as a camp counselor. If you knew Ava, you would know that this is not what you would call, um, a good fit. Ava doesn't really like to work, and she's definitely not the outdoorsy type, unless you count lounging around by the pool. So when she told me she was going, I was shocked. Especially since she told me the day after I caught Sebastian cheating on me, which was definitely not the best timing. *Not the best timing*, the voice in my head whispers, *story of your life*.

"That's great," I say, deciding not to get into the fact that from what I saw when I was visiting her there a couple of weeks ago, it didn't seem like Ava had really learned anything. And the girls there seemed pretty much like exactly what they were—spoiled little rich girls, whose parents spent fifteen thousand dollars to send them away for three months.

"Yeah, it was kind of life-changing, you know?" Her smile, while usually vibrant and white, seems even more so today.

"Did you . . . did get your teeth whitened?"

"Yeah," she says, pretending to be embarrassed, but I can tell she's pleased I noticed.

"When did you have time to do that?"

"Oh, you know, on one of our days off last week," she says. "I went with Lulu."

Oh, right. Lulu. Ava's camp friend. Apparently Lulu is super cool because she has ten piercings in one ear and none in the other, and she meditates and Ava thinks that's so super spiritual. The two of them are planning a spring break trip to an ashram where they're going to do Bikram Yoga six hours a day and eat an all-vegan diet. "So listen," she says, "I wanted to say I'm sorry again about what happened when you came to visit, that was . . . I mean, it was kind of . . ."

"Yeah," I say, remembering the weirdness that happened that weekend. "It's not a big deal, really!" I force a smile, hoping she doesn't want to get into it. But I don't have to worry, since Ava doesn't have a chance to say anything. Because at that moment, Sebastian Bukowski comes walking into the room, his eyes scanning the class until they land on me.

"Oh my God," I say, turning my head and looking away. "I didn't know he was in our homeroom." I thought he was in room B3! I asked Jessica Conrad to ask her boyfriend, Blake, who's really good friends with Sebastian, and she told me Sebastian was in B3, and since I'm in A3, I figured I was safe. But I must have gotten misinformation. Damn that Jessica Conrad! I should have known better than to trust her—she pushed me off the swings once in third grade.

"Don't talk to him," Ava instructs, "He doesn't even deserve your acknowledgment. What a jerk-off."

She's right. He is totally getting ignored. Who even cares if he's in this homeroom? It doesn't matter, because that is really of no concern to me anymore. In fact, of all the bad things that could happen today, this shouldn't even rank. La, la, la, not caring.

But then Sebastian slides into the seat next to me, his hair all floppy and cute, wearing his favorite black jeans even though it's about eighty-five degrees outside. He taps me on the shoulder, and Ava's eyes widen in shock.

"Hey, Hannah," he says. "Can I talk to you?"

The First Day of Summer

My phone rings at nine o'clock the next morning, and I reach over and look at the caller ID, wondering if Sebastian couldn't sleep, like me, and is calling to explain/apologize/beg to take me back. But it's only Ava.

"Hellooo," I say morosely into the phone. I've been up all night crying. Big, sloppy, wet tears that pooled on my pillow and made it hard to sleep since my pillowcase became a disgusting, sopping mess. Although I have to admit Ava was right—the making out with Jonah Moncuso did kind of help. And so did the three beers I drank. But definitely not enough to erase the fact that Sebastian never called me to see how I was doing, or to ask me *why* I spent all night making out with Jonah Moncuso, or to tell me why *he* was making out with some other girl, or even to at least break up with me properly. I mean, who does that? He obviously knows that I know that he cheated, and he knows that I was making out with Jonah. Everyone knows I was making out with Jonah. It was kind of creating a buzz at the party, if you want to know the truth.

"I knew you'd be awake," Ava says. "Get out of bed."

"No thank you." I roll over and bury my head into my damp pillow. The sun is streaming in through the windows, and I calculate how much energy it would take to get up and close the blinds. Too much, so I decide to just keep my eyes shut extra tight.

"I'm coming over and taking you to Starbucks," Ava says.

"You *are*?" This is a supreme sacrifice on Ava's part. She hates Starbucks. She thinks coffee stains your teeth, plus her psycho ex-boyfriend, Riker, works there, and sometimes Ava thinks he might, like, slip something into her drink. Like poison or a laxative or something. She thinks this not because she's paranoid, but because one time after she ordered, Riker actually said, "You want some poison or a laxative with that?" She totally complained to his boss, but the boss didn't care. That's because the boss, this college girl named Britney, is having sex with Riker.

"Yes," she says. "And we're going to order breakfast sandwiches and cookies and whatever other overproduced, disgusting, addictive things Starbucks has to offer."

"Will you even get whipped cream on your coffee?" I ask her.

Pause. "Yes."

"Ava, I love you!" Things are suddenly looking up, and I throw the sheets off and jump out of bed, heading to my dresser to pull on a tank top and shorts.

But when Ava gets there ten minutes later, I'm depressed

again. And when we get to Starbucks fifteen minutes after that, I'm really, *really* depressed.

"I loved him," I moan once we're sitting at a table in the back, an assortment of muffins and breakfast sandwiches in front of us.

"No you didn't," Ava says. She's making my coffee for me just the way I like it, with tons of cream and sugar. It's actually making me feel better that she's treating me like an invalid. I'm glad she knows I'm having a hard time and that I need to be coddled.

"Yes, I did," I say, as she slides my coffee across the table to me. "I really did, I thought he was the love of my life!" Even I know this is a little dramatic. I mean, I didn't really think Sebastian was the love of my life. But he could have been. You know, like when he matured. But now I'll never know. It's totally sad.

"Well, you need a new life plan then," Ava says. "And pronto." She hands me a breakfast sandwich, melted cheese oozing out of one side. "Eat," she instructs. I take a bite obediently, and Ava nods in satisfaction. Then she says, "Anyway! I have news!" She claps her hands and looks excited.

I immediately drop the sandwich back onto my plate and look at her. "What?" I ask, my heart soaring. She might be about to tell me that Sebastian loves me after all! That he heard about my hot make-out session with Jonah and now he's realized what he had. Of course, I couldn't take him back after he cheated on me. Could I?

"I'm going to Maine!" Ava declares. She takes a dainty bite of her raspberry cheese Danish, then delicately licks her fingers, all without making crumbs or getting any kind of mess on herself.

"A road trip?" I ask hopefully. I love road trips! It's exactly what I need, too! I'll stay away from Facebook, my phone, and all other communication devices. Like my instant messenger and my front door. (A front door is totally a communication device! What if he decides to show up? You know, to communicate.) "Where in Maine? What should I bring?" I'm standing now, and almost jumping up and down. An old man sitting in the corner is looking at me like I'm crazy.

"Uh, no," Ava says, looking nervous. "Not a road trip. Um, I'm going to Maine. For the summer."

I sit back down. "I'm sorry," I say. "I thought you just said you were going to Maine for the summer." That can't be right. Ava never goes anywhere for the summer. She likes to relax and stay right here. "Wait," I say. "Is your family going on vacation?" If so, maybe I can go with them! Ava's mom loves me. Like, for real. Whenever Ava and I would get into fights in middle school (or, let's face it, high school), she would always email me and be like, "You and Ava should be friends again."

"No," Ava says. "I'm getting a summer job there. I'm, uh, going to be a camp counselor."

"You're *what*?" I ask, looking at her incredulously. "But you and I decided we weren't going to get summer jobs!"

It's true. Ava and I decided we'd rather spend the summer hanging out by the pool, so we didn't look for summer jobs. Ava's philosophy was that we'd have to get jobs *next* summer before we went to college, and probably every summer after that, so it was our last chance at freedom. And even though I kind of sort of wanted to spend the summer working so I could get a car when school started, I figured she had a point. Although the logic *did* seem slightly flawed, because the freedom a car brings is totally better than the freedom of one summer. But whatever, I'm all about the instant gratification.

"Hello, ladies," Riker Strong says, walking over to our table. He's in his Starbucks uniform, and holding a tray of cut up bagels. "Would you two like to try a free sample of our new cranberry vanilla bagels?"

"Sure." I take one off the tray and pop it into my mouth. I guess depression hasn't affected my appetite.

"Hannah!" Ava yells. "Don't eat that!" She holds out a napkin. "Spit it out immediately."

"No," I say, chewing and swallowing. "It's good."

"Ava?" Riker asks, grinning and holding out the tray.

"No, thank you." Ava turns away and refuses to look at him. When he's gone, she looks at me. "You can't just eat things he offers, you have no idea what he's done to them!"

"He didn't do anything to them," I say. "He didn't know what bagel I was going to take. Look, he's over there giving them to the other customers now." I watch as the old guy in the corner who was staring at me earlier takes three samples off the tray and gobbles them down. Geez, talk about greedy. Doesn't he know it's one per customer? "So unless he wants to poison us all . . ."

"He probably does want to poison us all," Ava says. "And besides, I didn't say poison. He could have done anything, like spit on them, or . . ." She trails off, leaving me to imagine all kinds of gross bodily Riker functions that could have been released on or near those bagels.

"Ava," I say, "that's disgusting." But I kind of wish I'd spit it out now, and I take a big drink of my coffee to get the bagel taste out of my mouth. "Now can we please get back to talking about how you've lost your mind?"

"I haven't lost my mind," she says. "My mom's friends with the camp director, and he called her early this morning saying they were one counselor short, and asked if I'd be interested." She shrugs, as if to say, *what could I do?* (Answer: Um, say no because your best friend is heartbroken and needs you here, and besides, even if the aforementioned heartbreaking hadn't taken place you guys still had plans to spend the summer together.) Then she looks at me like she's expecting me to be happy for her.

But all I say is, "We said we weren't going to have summer jobs this year, remember?"

"I know that's what we *said*," Ava says, waving her hand like that was so five years ago, even though we just talked about it last month. She takes off her sunglasses and sets them down on the table, then shakes out her ponytail, letting her long, blond hair pool around her shoulders. "But I couldn't pass this up! This isn't, like, a summer job, Hannah, this is an *experience*."

I stare at her blankly. "But what about me?" I ask.

"We-ll," she says. "I asked the director if you could go too, but they only need one person." She smiles, as if to show how nice it was of her to ask about me.

"No, I mean, what about me? What am I going to do without you?"

"Hannah, you'll be fine," Ava says.

"No, I won't!" I say. "I'll be all alone all summer with no car and no friends and no anything!"

"Hannah," Ava says, "you're acting kind of hysterical. What about Krystal Shepard? You like her, call her up and see what she's doing this summer."

"*First* of all," I say, "I am not acting hysterical." Not really true, but if there was ever a time to be hysterical, this is definitely it. "*Second* of all, Krystal Shepard is going away to some pre-college program in Spain this summer. And *third* of all, Krystal Shepard is not you! No one is!" It's true. I mean, it's not that I don't like Krystal, she's just not a close friend. In fact, besides Ava, I don't really *have* any close friends. In middle school we used to hang out with a lot of different girls, but there always seemed to be fights and drama, and eventually, after girls had been circling in and out of our group for years, our group became just me and Ava. Which, looking back, was actually really stupid since now I'm stuck with no friends for the summer.

"And what about Noah?" I rush on, starting to get really panicked. "How can you just leave him like that?"

"Noah," Ava says. "doesn't rule my life." She takes a bite of her brownie, and then she says, "Hannah, I'm really sorry about the timing of everything. I am. You know I was planning to spend the summer with you. It's just . . . I don't know, I think it would be good for me, to challenge myself. And you can come and visit me anytime you want."

I don't point out that, without a car, there's no real way for me to get to Maine, and I don't bother protesting anymore because I know her well enough to realize she's not going to change her mind. What I really want to do is ask her how she can leave me here all by myself when I'm totally broken-hearted, and what she thinks I'm going to do all summer with my boyfriend hooking up with someone else, and me with no other friends and no car to go anywhere even if I *did have* friends to go places with.

But it won't make a difference. Ava's willing to get up at nine on the morning after a party to take me to Starbucks, and she set me up with a rebound hook up, like, five seconds after I caught my boyfriend cheating. . . . But I know her well enough to know that when she makes up her mind, she makes up her mind. And if she's set on going to Maine, then she's going to Maine.

So I just smile sadly, and tell her I'm going to miss her. Then I try not to think about how horrible the summer is going to be without her.

And three days later, after Ava and I have spent countless hours at Super Walmart, picking out all the things on her packing list, she loads up her car and pulls out of my driveway, on her way to Maine. And I return to my bed, where I stay for the next four days.

The First Day of Senior Year

"Can I talk to you?" Sebastian asks again. He's asking again because the first time he said it, I totally ignored him.

"No, you cannot talk to her," Ava says. "You're not even in this homeroom, so get out of here." She's turned toward him in her seat now, looking vaguely threatening even though she's wearing a very girly purple dress.

"I wasn't talking to you, Ava," Sebastian says. "So mind your own business." Yikes.

"Look," I say. "I don't have anything to say to you." Wait. So Sebastian *isn't* in this homeroom? He came in here just to talk to me? So Jessica Conrad *was* telling the truth. Wow. He made a special trip down from the third floor just to talk to me, even though the second bell's going to ring any second. Not like Sebastian cares about being late for class. But still.

Whatever. It doesn't matter if he's not in this homeroom. I mean, it doesn't change the fact that, when it comes down to it, I really *don't* have anything to say to Sebastian. He's pretty much been ignoring me all summer, except for a couple of weeks ago when he randomly showed up at my house around one in the morning causing kind of a big scene, and then when he showed up at the diner causing an even bigger scene.

"You have nothing to say to me?" Sebastian asks, sounding pissed, and a little bit surprised. "Does this have anything to do with Noah?"

"I don't know what you're talking about," I say quickly, rolling my eyes and turning back to Ava, hoping she gets the point that Sebastian is a raving lunatic who has no idea what he's talking about.

"Is that why he was at your house the other night at one in the morning? And why he almost punched me?" The warning bell rings, signaling homeroom is going to start in one minute, and Sebastian stands up. "I'll wait for you after homeroom," he says to me. He shoots Ava a dirty look, and then takes off.

"Noah almost *punched* him this summer?" Ava asks. *"Why?"* She's turned completely toward me now, her eyes wide and questioning. Shit, shit, shit. Damn that Sebastian. Seriously, what is with him? Like he hasn't ruined my life enough.

"Oh, um, it was nothing," I say. I uncap my pen and open my notebook, trying to look normal and like my biggest priority is writing down any important info we're going to get in homeroom. "Sebastian stopped by the diner, you know, and he was being a jerk as usual."

"And Noah *punched* him?"

"No. I mean, he almost did, but it didn't really come to that." I say it like there's a big difference between actually punching someone and almost punching someone, which I guess there kind of is. I mean, you can't get arrested for almost punching someone, even though the intent is the same.

"Was he messing with Noah or something?" Ava asks.

"No," I say, shifting on my chair. This part, at least, is true. But luckily, I don't have to say that, or explain it, because Mrs. McGovern walks in and starts taking attendance. Which is good. Because there's no way I want Ava to know the real reason that Noah almost punched Sebastian. And that's because of me.

The Summer

"It's definitely broken," my mom says, looking down at our washer with a frown on her face. Ava only left three days ago, and already my life has hit a new low. Friday night. And I'm doing laundry. Although I guess it's not technically night. I mean, it's five o'clock, which is more like evening. And I guess I'm not *technically* doing laundry, because as soon as I put my clothes into the machine and tried to start it, the whole thing made this ridiculously horrible noise with lots of shuddering and shaking and then just . . . died.

"Maybe it's unplugged or something," I say hopefully. I look behind the washer, but the cord is plugged right into the wall outlet. It stares back, taunting me. I think it might be pissed off. The washer, I mean. It could probably sense that it wasn't going to get much use this summer, since in my depressed state my hygiene habits have so far taken a backseat to other, more important endeavors, like stalking Sebastian online.

"Honey, it's broken," my mom says. She sounds like she's

trying to break it to me gently. I can't really blame her. The other day she told me there was no more vanilla ice cream, and I burst into tears right in the middle of the kitchen. She obviously knows I'm fragile.

"But I need clothes!"

"Well," she says. "I'll drive you to the Laundromat on my way to the hospital." My mom's a veterinary technician, and she works nights at the emergency animal hospital in Grafton, which is about forty minutes away. She wants to be a veterinarian though, which means that when she gets off her shift, she takes classes at Tufts' veterinary school. Which means she's never around. Which means I should be throwing lots of parties and having fun and kicking people out all panicked when my mom pulls in the driveway unannounced. But I can't do that since Ava's not here and I have no boyfriend and I'm too depressed to clean my clothes, let alone plan and throw a whole party.

"The Laundromat?" The only thing worse than spending your Friday at home doing laundry is to spend it at the Laundromat doing laundry. "Forget it." I close the lid of the washer, leaving the clothes in there. "I'll just find something else to wear." What, I don't know. Everything I have is dirty, but I'm sure I can figure out something. Maybe I can make a dress out of a garbage bag. Lady Gaga wore that meat dress to the VMAs, so I should be able to dress in garbage bags. I'll get black ones, to symbolize my current state of mind. Like performance art or something.

"Come on," my mom says. "I'll help you get everything ready."

"No." I head out of the laundry room and into the great room, where I lay down on the couch and pick up the remote, getting ready to turn on the TV and pick up my *Friday Night Lights* marathon right where I left off. Tim Riggins is so hot.

My mom follows me. "Hannah," she says from the doorway, "do I need to call your father? Maybe you should go and spend some time with him since being here obviously isn't making you feel better."

I glare at her. It's an empty threat (she would never send me to stay with my dad, and my dad wouldn't want me even if she did), but it's enough to get me going. The last thing I need is my dad calling, asking me how I'm doing. To put it bluntly, my dad is kind of an asshole. My parents got divorced when I was ten, and my dad lives, like, two hours away, but he hardly ever calls or sends money or anything. Which is probably why I'm so depressed about Sebastian. I clearly have issues with abandonment.

"Fine," I say. "But we're getting the washer fixed."

"Of course," my mom says. "And then maybe this weekend we can sit down and talk about you possibly getting a job."

Geez. So much for her knowing I'm fragile. I ignore the part about the job and make a big production of heading up to my room to get the rest of my clothes together. I mean, if mom thinks a job is going to cure my depression, she really couldn't be more wrong.

❊ ❊ ❊

There are actually a ton of people at the Laundromat, which is kind of annoying because almost every machine is full. I already can't wait to get out of here, and it's going to completely suck if I have to wait for a dryer. Don't people have anything better to do on a Friday night? Oh, well. Judge not lest ye be judged, or whatever.

I heft my two garbage bags of clothes (one for whites and one for darks) up onto an empty washer. I couldn't put them in laundry baskets because I'm going to have to walk the twelve blocks home and there's no way I can do that with baskets — as it is, I'm worried about doing it with bags. Then I feed one of the twenty dollar bills my mom gave me into the change machine.

It roars to life and eighty quarters come tumbling out. Most of them collect in the metal compartment under the dispenser, but a few of them bounce out and roll all over the floor. I try to stomp on them with my flip-flop as they go by, but two of them go rolling under a dryer. Ugh. This is turning out to be a disaster already and I haven't even put my clothes in a washer yet.

I turn to the guy who works there, a middle-aged man with an overgrown beard. He's wearing a green plaid coat (in summer?) and tinkering with a washing machine. "Excuse me?" I ask. "Do you have a plastic cup or something I could use for my quarters?"

"No," he says in a really unfriendly way, then goes back

to working on the machine. Wow. Talk about bad customer service.

I decide not to worry about the two that went missing, and scoop up a handful of quarters from the metal compartment, not sure where I'm going to put them. What a pain in the ass this is turning out to be. I am so hitting up the vending machine on the way out and getting one of those so-disgusting-they're-good chocolate Yoo-hoo drinks, so that I have fuel for the walk home. I definitely deserve it after all this.

I'm just about to try and stuff as many coins as I can into my pockets and maybe just leave the rest, when a hand reaches down next to me and scoops up the rest of my quarters. Like, seriously scoops them all up. In one smooth motion, like one of those giant claw machines that you use to try and win crappy stuffed animals.

"Hey!" I say to the anonymous hand. "What are you—"

"Sorry," Noah says. "I saw you were having a little bit of a problem."

He reaches into his pocket, pulls out a Ziploc bag, drops my quarters in, closes the bag, and then hands it to me. I just stare at him. What the hell is *Noah* doing here? And why does he have Ziploc bags with him?

"Do you need some help?" he asks. He gestures to the ground, where my trash bags are now sitting.

"Hey!" I say, looking at them. "How did those get on the floor?"

I turn around and see a woman wearing a black-and-white-patterned wrap dress calmly loading her clothes into the washer that, just a few seconds ago, had my clothes on top of it. Apparently she thought it was okay to just move my stuff onto the floor. "That woman," I say to Noah, pointing and not caring if she hears me, "stole my washer!"

"You snooze you lose," Noah says, shrugging, like I have no idea what goes on in a Laundromat. If he's freaked out by the general disheveledness of my appearance (I haven't really been sleeping or, ah, grooming so well, so I'm wearing cotton pajama pants, a tank, and my hair is pulled back in a messy ponytail), he doesn't say anything. Noah, on the other hand, looks fresh as a daisy, in khaki shorts and a black T-shirt. Probably he has fun plans later tonight. "So you do need some help then?"

"No," I say. "I don't." The last thing I want is to hang out with Noah. Nothing against Noah, I'm just not feeling all that social. I kind of hate people lately. In fact, this whole Laundromat thing was obviously a mistake. I'm definitely not ready to be out of the house. "I was actually just leaving."

"You were?"

"Yeah."

"Then why were you putting money into the coin machine?"

"Oh, that." I wave my hand like the answer should be evident. "I wanted to get a Yoo-hoo out of the vending machine and it doesn't take twenties." I roll my eyes, like it's completely ridiculous that a vending machine wouldn't take twenties. When you think about it, it kind of is. I could totally spend twenty dollars in a vending machine.

"The vending machine?" He sounds amused. And also like he doesn't believe me.

"Yes," I say. "It's the only one in a five mile radius that has Yoo-hoo." I have no idea if this is true, but I cross my arms over my chest, daring him to challenge me.

"Yoo-hoo?"

"Yeah, you know, Yoo-hoo? It's kind of like chocolate milk in a can?" Doesn't he know better than to question my beverage choices? Most normal people would take one look at me, realize I'm insane, and then go on their way. Plus, how can you not know what Yoo-hoo is? It's like, one of the best drinks ever. In a disgusting, I-can't-believe-I'm-actually-drinking-this, kind of way.

"Yeah, I know what Yoo-hoo is. I just didn't know people actually drank it."

"Well, they do," I say. I so don't need this. I mean, I honestly have enough problems. I scoop up my bags from where they're sitting on the floor, and turn on my heel, heading for the door. Unfortunately my garbage bags have ripped open (WTF? Probably that washer stealer's doing), and my clothes are kind of falling all over the place. "I have to go," I tell Noah, peeking over the pile of fabric in my arms. "So, um, bye."

"Do you need some help?" he asks again, and then starts

to follow me as I try to navigate my way through the crowd.

"No, thanks," I say. "I'm totally fine." A pair of yoga pants drops through one of the holes in the bag and falls onto the floor. Someone steps on them as they walk by, leaving the imprint of their sneaker on one of the legs. Why the hell are there so many people here? I mean, really. I'm glad I'm leaving. I definitely need to find a place to do my wash that's a little less crowded.

"Watch out!" Noah yells as I bend down to pick up the pants and almost crash into a little boy playing with a Matchbox car. On the floor of the Laundromat. Talk about a lawsuit waiting to happen.

"I'm *fine*," I say to Noah, successfully dodging the kid, but in the process dropping a bunch of shirts and stuff on the floor. And when I stoop down to pick *those* up, a bunch of other stuff goes tumbling to the ground. Shit, shit, shit.

"You don't look fine." Noah crouches down next to me and starts picking up the stuff that fell. Thank God it's not bras or anything. He probably wouldn't be used to seeing the kinds of underwear that I have. Except for the lingerie Sebastian bought me, most of my underwear is from Target. I don't wear granny panties or anything, I just don't usually wear the kinds of things that Ava does (sheer, lacey, and flimsy). Of course, I'm not having sex like Ava is, either, so that probably has something to do with it.

"Well, I *am* fine," I say, doing my best to sound huffy. "I just need to get my bearings."

"Hey," Noah says, holding up a white T-shirt with an ice cream stain on the front. "These clothes are dirty!"

"No they're not," I say, snatching the shirt out of his hands. I drop it back into the whites pile. Well, what used to be the whites pile. Now it's just kind of a . . . well, an all-kinds-of-clothes pile. I'm definitely going to have to sort these again.

"If they're not clean," Noah says, picking up one last pair of yoga pants and setting them on top of the pile that I'm holding, "then why are you leaving?"

"*Because*," I say, "I don't like the customer service in this place." Which isn't even a lie.

"Right," Noah says. And then, before I can stop him, he takes the clothes right out of my hands, and heads over to the row of washers in the back.

"Hey!" I yell, running after him. "What do you think you're doing?" Is he crazy? You can't just go around grabbing someone's clothes! That's, like, complete and total thievery.

"Washing your clothes." He drops them into a machine, adds some powder from a big box that someone's left sitting on the counter, then inserts some quarters into the slots, and starts it up.

"Now," he announces as the washer roars to life. "We sit and wait for them to be done."

"We sit and wait for them to be *done*?" I ask, staring at him incredulously. "No, we most certainly do not. And you totally just stole some soap from someone!" I open the top of the washer, but it's too late. All the clothes are already wet. I turn around and glare at him, even though I'm actually not that mad about him hijacking my clothes. I mean, they did need to be washed. What I'm mostly mad about is that he obviously did it because he thinks I'm incapable of looking after myself. He thinks I'm some kind of sniveling, broken-hearted mess who can't even handle a trip to the Laundromat. Whether it's true or not is completely beside the point.

Noah ignores me. He just sits down in one of the plastic orange chairs against the wall, then slides his messenger bag off his shoulder, and sets it on the ground. The edge of a Macbook case peeks out of the top.

"Do you want a magazine?" he asks politely, gesturing to a few that are on the table in front of the chairs. "There's *People* or *Good Housekeeping*. Your pick."

My phone rings before I can tell him where he can shove his magazines, and I pull it out of my purse. Ava.

"Ava!" I say. "That's so weird, I just ran into Noah at the Laundromat. In fact, he's here right now." I give him a smug look and then sit down on the chair next to him. Now he'll be in for it. I'll tell Ava exactly what he's been up to, and she'll give him a piece of her mind for treating me like some kind of invalid. Maybe she'll even break up with him, and then he'll have to beg me to get her to forgive him.

"Oh, thank God," Ava says. "I told him to go to the Laundromat and keep an eye on you."

"You did?" I called Ava when the machine broke to

complain about how I had to go to the Laundromat tonight. But what does that even mean, she told him to keep an eye on me? Ohmigod. She probably called him and told him I'm a mess! That I'm unable to function on my own, that she's afraid I can't even do a simple thing like my own laundry. (Which, when I think about it, is kind of true.)

I'm not sure if I should feel special or offended. I guess it was nice of her to be concerned, but who wants to have to have an eye kept on them? It makes me sound like a child who can't be left alone. Which is kind of ironic—my mom has basically abandoned me for the summer, and my best friend is asking her boyfriend to babysit me. Sigh.

"Yeah, I told him you would probably be having a hard time, and that he should go and make sure you were okay." She says it all breezy-like. "Anyway, I'm calling because I need you to google something for me."

"Google something for you?"

"Yeah. Can you find out who the girl that plays the daughter in *Californication* is? We're watching it and we know she looks familiar, but we're not near a computer and—" in the background, I can hear the sounds of voices and a television, and then Ava says, "Lulu, quiet, I'm on the phone!" I roll my eyes even though she can't see me. But before I can say anything, she says, "Never mind, Hannah, we figured it out! I'll call you later, and tell Noah I'll call him, too. Bye hon, miss you."

She clicks off, and I put my phone back in my purse and

glance at Noah, who's suddenly very engaged in his *Good Housekeeping* magazine. Probably because he knows that I know that he wasn't really coming to the Laundromat to wash clothes. Which I really should have figured out in the first place. I mean, a boy in the Laundromat with a laptop and no clothes on a Friday evening? Very suspect.

"So you were checking up on me?" I ask.

"No," Noah says. He puts a faux-shocked look on his face, then turns back to his magazine, pretending to be engrossed. I take the magazine out of his hand and toss it back onto the table.

"That's good," I say, "That you weren't checking up on me. Because I'm totally fine."

"I know." He shrugs.

"And I *don't* need to be checked up on."

"Definitely not."

"I'm perfectly capable of taking care of myself."

"Perfectly."

"So we agree."

"Yup."

"So then where are your clothes?"

"What?"

"Your clothes," I say. "Where are your clothes? You came to the Laundromat so you must have some clothes." I fold my arms across my chest and wait.

"Oh, my *clothes*," he says, giving me an easy grin. "I didn't come down here to do laundry."

"Oh, really?" I say. "Then what were you here to do?"

"I was here," he says, rolling his eyes like it should be obvious, "so I could go across the street to Cooley's and check my schedule for the week."

"And you just happened to see me coming into the Laundromat?"

"Exactly," he says. "And I thought I'd say hi."

"Good try."

"You don't believe me?" He sounds wounded, like the thought of me not believing him makes him incredibly sad.

"No."

"Then come with me," he says. He unfolds his long legs and stands up. "To Cooley's. You'll see they just posted the schedule. If I'm lying, I'll buy you a chocolate shake."

"And if you're not?"

"Then I'll still buy you a chocolate shake." He grins at me again, and I'm about to tell him no thank you. Even though it's a totally lame charade, this whole thing we're doing, it's actually kind of fun keeping it up and seeing who's going to crack first. But in the end, the promise of chocolate wins out (although it's definitely helped out by the sketchy-looking guy in the corner who's wearing a T-shirt that says "BEEN THERE DRANK THAT" and eyeing Noah's seat), so I get up and follow him out the door.

When we get to Cooley's, there's a girl with long red curls and fair skin wiping down the counter, and as soon as she sees us, she looks up. "Hey, Noah," she says cheerily. "The schedule's posted in the back, and you're not going to be happy."

Noah shoots me an *I told you so* look. "You set that up!" I say, even though I know it's not true. "You told her to say that you were coming in to check your schedule." I look at the girl, checking her out for any signs she's in on this. She's still wiping the counter, not looking particularly guilty. But she could just be a good actress.

"And when would I have done that?" Noah asks.

"I don't know, you probably covertly texted her on the way over here or something."

"Lacey will hook you up with a milk shake," Noah says, ignoring my accusation and setting his messenger bag down on one of the stools. I look at the girl with red hair. She looks at me. "Lacey, Hannah. Hannah, Lacey," Noah says.

We nod at each other, even though now I realize that I already know her. Well. Not *know her*, know her. She was in my history class a couple of years ago. She always seemed friendly enough, but we never really talked. In fact, I really don't talk to that many people at school, which is another reason I don't have many friends besides Ava.

"Hey," Lacey says, giving me a smile once Noah disappears into the back of the diner to check his schedule. "What kind of shake do you want?"

"Chocolate," I say. "Please."

"Coming right up." She turns around and heads toward the ice cream case that lines the back wall, and I take a second to inhale the scent of French fries that's permeating the air. God, they smell good. I wonder if it would be way too over the top to order some fries too.

My eating habits haven't been all that great lately, but with all the stress from the break up, I figure I deserve to eat what I want. Besides, the eating-disordered, stick-thin Paris Hilton body is so five years ago. Not to mention the whole string bikini thing definitely didn't work out so well when it came to getting Sebastian interested in me. Although I guess, technically, he never saw me in it. But still. What's the point of depriving yourself to be skinny if it doesn't even make a difference?

I'm about to call out to Lacey, and let her know I want to add to my order, but before I can, she's walking from the ice-cream cooler and back to where I'm sitting at the counter. And she doesn't have my chocolate shake.

"So," she says, holding her hair up off her neck and turning her head to the side. "This might be kind of weird, but, um, does this look strange to you?"

"Does what look strange to me?" I ask. I glance around, hoping she's not talking about me. I mean, I wouldn't say I look *strange* exactly, just extremely disheveled.

"This," she says, and leans over the counter, pushing her head closer to me.

I'm still not sure what she means. So I just say, "Yeah,

wow, you have very pretty hair. Is it natural?" I kind of want to ask her why she's not wearing it up—the last thing I want is hair in my milk shake, eww—but she might be some kind of wacko, so I keep my mouth shut.

"Not my hair," she says. "My neck."

"Um . . . you have a very pretty neck?" I try. It's not even a lie. She has great skin, really smooth and fair.

"No," she says. "The spot."

"What spot?" I ask, deciding to try a different tactic and get some clarification.

"The one behind my ear."

I peer closer. "Oh, yeah," I say. "What about it?" There's a tiny, miniscule little spot behind her ear. Looks like a freckle. It's kind of cute, actually.

"Are you sure?" Lacey asks. She rushes back to the mirrors on the wall and starts twisting all around, trying to get a better look at it. "I just noticed it when I bent down to get your ice cream and . . . it's not bleeding or anything?"

"Um, no," I tell her. "It's just a very small orange freckle."

"Orange," she repeats. "Hmmm." She's muttering to herself (something about checking out Web MD on her break) as she heads back over to the ice cream, and I watch her closely as she scoops a bunch of chocolate ice cream into the blender.

Noah comes out from the back then, looking dejected.

"Told you it was bad," Lacey says sadly. She pours a bunch of milk into the blender and then adds chocolate sauce and a few scoops of some kind of powder. I hope she's making it malted, and the powder isn't arsenic or something she pulls out when she gets all worked up about orange spots that are probably just mosquito bites.

"Yeah, it's bad." Noah plops down onto the stool next to me.

"Why, what's wrong?" I ask as Lacey sets the glass down in front of me.

"I just have a lot of hours," Noah says. "Like, forty-five this week." He sighs and starts twirling a ketchup bottle back and forth between his hands.

"Isn't that good?" I ask. "More hours equals more money?"

"Yeah, except it ruins your whole summer. It's better to have a balance—about thirty hours is good money, and then you still have time to have fun."

"So you're kind of lazy," I say. "Got it. Do you want some of my milk shake?" I'm doing it to be nice and cheer him up, but secretly I'm hoping he says no. Not that I want to be all selfish, but I really do need the chocolate.

"Thanks," he says, leaning over and taking a long pull from the straw.

"No problem," I say, watching him carefully to make sure he doesn't take too much. When he's done, I take the glass back and take my own sip, letting the chocolately goodness explode in my mouth. Ohmigod. It's amazing. So amazing that when Noah reaches for another sip, I pull the glass away from him.

"No way," I say. "One sip is all you get. Have Lacey make you your own."

"Sure," Lacey says, "You totally deserve it if you're going to work forty-five hours next week."

She gets to work making the shake, and I glance around the diner. There's, like, hardly anyone in here. One college-aged kid sitting in the corner, reading a book and sipping some coffee. And one old man, over in the back booth, slurping down a bowl of soup and looking out the window.

"It doesn't seem that busy in here," I say. "Why does everyone have to work such long hours?"

"Well, right now's the dead time," Noah says. "See, for breakfast and lunch this place gets crazy. But then after, say, two o'clock, it's pretty dead until we close at seven."

"You guys close at seven?" How ridiculous. I mean, that's like, the prime time people go to dinner. You can never get a reservation anywhere for seven o'clock. One time Sebastian and I tried to get into this Italian restaurant in the North End for our anniversary, and they were so booked we had to make our reservation for nine. And that place wasn't even that popular. Thinking of Sebastian causes a knot to form in my throat, and I quickly take another sip of my shake.

"Yeah," Noah says. "Most of the, uh, dinner crowd is

out of here by then." It takes me a second to realize what he's talking about, but then I get it. Old people. The majority of their customers must be old people, and everyone knows old people are done with dinner by six and in bed by, like, eight thirty.

"Right," Lacey says. "And Cooley doesn't want to hire any more people, because everyone wants the day shifts so they can make good tips. So he just schedules me and Noah to stay, for, like, ever." She rolls her eyes and then gathers her long red hair up into a ponytail with a hair tie that she picks up from behind the counter. "I keep telling him he needs to hire more people. Especially since it's probably, like, illegal for him to make us work so much since we're minors. But does Cooley care about that? Nooo. He just wants the hours covered." She looks at me nervously. "Are you looking at my freckle?" she asks.

"Uh, no," I say, quickly averting my eyes. "Definitely not." I *was* kind of staring at her, but not at her freckle. Just her hair, which is gorgeous. My own hair is kind of . . . greasy, if you want to know the truth. Shampooing and conditioning has not been high on my list of priorities. Like, at all.

"Hey!" Noah says. "Hannah, why don't you work here?"

"Me?" I almost choke on my shake.

"Yeah," Noah says. "You'd be perfect. And Ava said you wanted to get a summer job, right?" Is Noah blind? Does he not see that I am completely incapable of doing even the most mundane tasks, such as, you know, showering and doing laundry? How am I supposed to work? Not to mention interact with people. I hate people right now.

"No, thank you," I say. I decide not to mention the fact that my mom would love it.

"Why not?"

"Because I don't want to spend my summer in some super greasy, hot diner."

That seems like an acceptable answer, but apparently not to Noah, because he says, "You'd rather spend it in bed eating ice cream?"

"I'm not going to spend it in bed eating ice cream," I say. "What makes you think that?"

"Because you're wearing pajama pants with ice cream stains on them," Lacey says. I look down. Sure enough, there's a stain of chocolate ice cream on the knee of my cotton GAP pants, along with some kind of cheese smear. Probably from the whole box of Cheez-Its I inhaled. My face burns with embarrassment. Oh. My. God. What have I become? At the rate I'm going, I'll probably end up being a four-hundred-pound shut-in. I saw a special about it on Discovery Health. People get depressed and don't leave the house for a few days, then it turns into a few months, then it's a year, and finally they have to lift you out with a crane so they can take you to the hospital.

"I'm *fine*," I say to Noah for what feels like the millionth time.

"Then take the job," he says. He raises his eyebrows, challenging me.

And that's how it starts.

The First Day of Senior Year

It turns out that Lacey's in my first period math class, but after we meet in the hall to compare schedules, she sends me ahead and into the math room, because she "has something to take care of." So I go in and find a seat, and a few minutes later, she comes breezing in, chatting into her phone.

"Yes," she says, "three thirty would be perfect, thank you so much for seeing me on such short notice." It takes me a second to realize what that probably means, since I'm focused on trying to catch my breath (I sprinted here from my homeroom in an effort to avoid Sebastian. People thought I was crazy. Or maybe a freshman.)

"Who was that?" I ask Lacey as she slides into the seat next to me. Even though of course I already know. I should have put a stop to this right after she supposedly hurt her neck in the car accident, but I was too distracted by my own drama.

"Dr. Friedman," she says. She's off the call now, but still

on her phone looking up some directions on Google Maps.

"And who is Dr. Friedman?"

"My new doctor," she says.

"Lacey!"

"What? I need to get my neck checked, and they just happened to have an appointment available after school."

"What happened to Dr. Ferguson?"

She slides into the seat next to me and gets really busy pulling her notebook out of her bag. "Lacey?" I prompt.

"She . . . um . . . Dr. Ferguson and I aren't seeing each other anymore."

"You're not *seeing* each other anymore?" It's not like they were dating. You can't just not be seeing your doctor anymore. Unless you're a total hypochondriac like Lacey, who goes to the doctor for every little thing, and then doesn't believe said doctor when they tell her she's fine. "What does that mean?"

"It just means that I've decided to go in a different direction." She pushes a stray red curl behind her ear.

"A different direction?"

"Yeah, you know, with my medical needs."

"So basically Dr. Ferguson told you you couldn't come back?"

"Well, she was kind of difficult," Lacey says. "I mean, whoever heard of a doctor that turned people away? I have insurance *and* I'm a good patient! It's really not a good business practice when you think about it."

"And this would have nothing to do with the fact that when your blood test for anemia came back normal, you demanded a retest, saying you didn't trust the phlebotomist or the lab?"

"Nothing whatsoever," Lacey says, obviously lying.

But I don't have time to push her on it, because at that moment, Noah walks into the room. Heat and longing rush through my body, and tears prick the backs of my eyes. I quickly look away, even though it feels like torture to take my eyes off him. He looks amazing. He's wearing a green sweatshirt, because the classrooms on this side of the school are always kind of cold, and without even having to see it, I know he probably has a T-shirt on underneath, one with the name of an indie band on it. Baggy jeans, his hair still floppy because he was supposed to get a haircut last night until we ended up—

He walks right by me, not saying anything, and the tears that pricked my eyes threaten to spill down my cheeks, so I squeeze my eyes shut tight, and tell myself there will be no crying, no matter what. Not here, not in school. Of course, I expected this a little bit, I knew that he might not want to talk about what happened, but I at least figured he'd be friendly, say hi. Keep up *some* kind of appearances. But apparently not.

"What's up with Noah?" Lacey asks. She's leaning forward in her chair, and we both watch as Noah takes a seat on the other side of the room, his long legs sliding under his desk.

"What do you mean?" I ask, hoping that I sound like it's totally normal for Noah to be ignoring us, even though it's so totally not.

"He walked right in and didn't say hi to either one of us. Did we do something to piss him off?" She's playing on her phone, her fingers flying over the keyboard as she checks her Facebook page.

"I don't know," I say, shrugging. "You know how boys are, he probably thinks he's too cool for us now that school started back up." I roll my eyes and laugh. "So tell me about this Dr. Friedman, is she any good? Did you look her up on Rate My MD dot com? Because—"

But before I can stop her, Lacey leans over the aisle and yells across the room, "Hey, Noah! We're over here, come and sit with us."

He hesitates, I can *see* him hesitating, even though it's probably not obvious to anyone else, including Lacey. I know he's weighing what would be worse—having an awkward interaction with me by coming to sit with us, or tipping Lacey off that something's going on by not coming. But then finally, he gathers up his stuff and walks over to our side of the room, settling into the seat in front of Lacey. He puts his books on the desk and swivels around so he's facing her, his back to me.

"Long time no see," Lacey jokes, even though, of course, we both just saw him yesterday.

"Yeah," he says, then turns slightly in his chair. "Hey, Hannah," he says to me.

"Hi," I say. The longing washes over me again, and it's so overpowering that I look down at my desk and try not to let it completely overtake me. I force myself to take deep breaths, to not give in, wondering if this is how it's going to be from now on, if Noah is always going to have this kind of effect on me, if I'm ever going to be able to be normal around him again. *You have to,* I tell myself. *You have to do it, somehow you have to figure out how to do it.*

"I hate math," Lacey says. "Are either of you any good at it? Because I might need help."

"I'm not bad," Noah says.

"I'm pretty good, too," I say. I cannot believe the three of us are talking about math! It's enough to drive me crazy, just the fact that the subject is even being brought up! I mean, math! How ridiculous! How did this become my life? Seriously, I cannot even take it anymore.

"Oh, look," Lacey says, looking out the door of our classroom. "It's the car smasher." On the other side of the hall, the girl from this morning, Jemima or whatever, is loading her books into her locker. She turns around when she hears Lacey's voice. "Hi, Car Smasher!" Lacey says. "How's your morning going? Have you gotten embroiled in any more lawsuits?"

Jemima opens her mouth to say something, then thinks better of it and scuttles away.

"Lacey!" I say. "You have to stop scaring that poor girl."

"Why?"

"Because!"

77

"Lawsuits?" Noah asks, looking confused. "What are you guys talking about?" He's looking at me, his eyes locking onto mine, and for a second, I'm afraid I won't be able to speak.

"That . . . she hit my car this morning," I say.

"More like slammed into the back of it without even looking," Lacey says. She holds her phone out to me. "That's Danielle Shapiro's vacation house," she says. "Isn't it ridiculously ostentatious? I can't believe she posted a picture of it."

"Jesus," Noah says. "Is your car wrecked?"

"No," I say. "It's just a little scratch. But that girl is freaking out about it for some reason."

"She's probably afraid you're going to try and get revenge," Noah says.

"Revenge for what?"

His eyes crinkle in the middle and get all serious, and suddenly, I feel nervous. Probably because I can tell I'm not going to want to hear whatever he's about to say. Besides, "revenge" is one word I do not want to hear today. Like, at all. "Hannah, that was Jemima Marshall."

"Yeah?" I ask. "So?"

"So you know she's the one that was hooking up with Sebastian that night, right? In Jenna's pool?"

I slide my head down onto my desk. Just when I thought this day couldn't get any worse.

The Summer

Honking. Outside my bedroom window. At five forty-five a.m. That's, like, earlier than I get up for school. Well, not always. During the three-month period I was hoping Sebastian would ask me out, I got up at five every day. It took me a while to get ready: I had to shower, deep condition, shave my legs, blow-dry my hair, and then coordinate my purse with my outfit. I was always tired and broke due to the fact that I was getting no sleep and spending all my money on clothes and makeup. So eventually that madness had to stop.

Now I grab my bag, shove my feet into my black Sketchers, take one more look at myself in the mirror, and run out to the driveway.

"Hey," I say, sliding into Noah's beat-up old Corolla.

"Hi." He indicates the cup holder between us, where there are three steaming cups of coffee. "I remembered that you like lattes," he says as he pulls out of my driveway. "But I didn't know how you take it, so I got you tons of Splenda and sugar on the side. Oh, and there's a bag of muffins in the back."

"Muffins?" I ask, reaching behind me and grabbing the bag.

"Yeah," Noah says, "Lacey likes to have muffins in the morning."

"Perfect," I say. "I'm starving." I pull out a carrot muffin and take a bite, wondering how this whole thing happened. I mean, one minute I was sitting in the Laundromat, not sure I even had the mental capacity to wash my clothes, and the next I somehow had a job at Cooley's. The whole thing was actually pretty painless when it comes to job interviews.

Not that I've had that many job interviews. In fact, I've had zero. But last year in Home and Careers we did a whole unit on how to act in an interview, and they made it seem super complicated, with all these smart things you were supposed to do, and we practiced questions like, "what makes you an ideal candidate for this job?" It was actually pretty pointless, since all the answers they told us to give were complete and total bullshit. Plus we had to role-play with other people, and it was hard to imagine that my partner, Kristin Wiggins, was some kind of high-powered executive interviewing me, since she's a total alcoholic and I'd just seen her puking in the bushes outside of Jenna Lamacchia's the day before.

Anyway, when it came to getting a job at Cooley's, there

was hardly even any kind of formal interview. Noah and I just hung out at the diner that day, talking to Lacey, and eating fries until Cooley showed up about an hour later.

"This girl wants a job," Noah said to Cooley. Which wasn't exactly true, but I'd learned enough from my Home and Careers training to know better than to appear ambivalent.

"Hmm," Cooley said, looking me up and down. He's a huge man, at least six three, with a lot of chest hair and gold chains that he wears over an open white shirt and tight white pants. He's very scary, because he looks like a drug lord or something. So even though I didn't really want the job in the first place, I was nervous.

Cooley reached behind the counter and picked up two soda glasses. "You," he said, pointing at me with one beefy finger. "Feel these with soda for Cooley."

"Feel these with . . ."

"He means fill," Noah whispered.

"Oh, okay." I grabbed the two cups, put one under the Sprite, one under the Coke, held them there until they were full, and then put them on the counter. I thought about adding, "have a nice day" or "would you like fries with that?" to, like, be impressive and show him I was thinking ahead, but before I could, Cooley said, "You're hired. You start Wednesday, six a.m."

It was that easy.

Of course my mom was thrilled. She was, like, almost hyperventilating and kept beaming and telling me how amazing it was and how proud she was of me, and then she made me check my alarm clock five times since she was going to be at work when I left. And even though it was totally over-the-top, typical mother behavior, it actually made me feel kind of good.

But now, sitting next to Noah in the car and nibbling on my carrot muffin, I'm starting to get a little bit anxious. I try to calm myself down, but Cooley's isn't that far away, so by the time Noah pulls in a couple of minutes later, my stomach is still flipping all around.

"How do I look?" I ask him, smoothing down the khaki shorts and white Cooley's T-shirt we have to wear.

"Like you're going to have a great day," he says. It's super cheesy and he knows it, but it makes me feel better.

"What if I screw up?" I say. "Does anyone ever get fired from Cooley's?"

"Hannah," Noah says, turning off the car. "You're going to be fine."

"How do you know?"

"Because you passed the two-cup test."

"The two-cup test?" I ask, pulling down the visor and smoothing my hair down in the mirror. I really should have gotten up earlier and put on makeup or something. How am I supposed to get good tips if I look like a mess?

"Yeah, in your interview? When Cooley asked you to get those two sodas?"

"That was a test?"

"Yeah," he says. "If you fill the two glasses at the same time, you pass. If you fill them separately, you fail. It's like an efficiency exam."

"I had no idea," I say. "Why didn't you warn me about that?"

Noah grins. "I had to make you earn it at least a little bit."

"Thanks," I say and roll my eyes. "How nice of you to make me earn a job I didn't want in the first place."

"If you didn't know it was a test," Noah asks, "then why did you think you were hired?"

"I thought Cooley was just crazy." I want to ask Noah if Cooley's maybe a drug lord, but somehow that doesn't seem appropriate. I swallow a big sip of coffee, take a deep breath, and then smooth my hair one more time.

"Hannah," Noah says, reaching out and squeezing my shoulder. "You're going to be fine, seriously. Come on, you can hang with me for the first half hour, and I'll show you around." He unbuckles his seatbelt and steps out of the car, and a second later, I follow him.

But as soon as we get inside, Lacey pops up from behind the counter, seemingly out of nowhere, then grabs my arm and pulls me into the bathroom, leaving Noah standing by the door, holding the bag of muffins and looking confused.

"What are you doing?" I ask. "Why are we —"

"Shhhh!" Lacey hisses. She pushes the bathroom door shut behind us, locks it, and then leans against it and presses her arms out to the side, like she's afraid someone might follow us in. "Did you see that girl out there?" she asks.

"No."

"You didn't?"

"No. You didn't give me a chance before you grabbed my arm and almost wrenched it out of its socket." I rub my shoulder, which is all sore from her pulling on it.

"Sorry," she says, looking sheepish. "But there's a girl out there, a very horrible girl." She wrinkles up her nose. "Her name's Danielle, and she used to be my best friend, until she had sex with my boyfriend behind my back."

"Ouch," I say. At least Sebastian had the decency to hook up with some girl I didn't know. Imagine if he'd hooked up with *Ava*? That would have been a huge disaster, much more so than him hooking up with some random sophomore with toned arms. Also, I'm kind of relieved that this has nothing to do with the spot behind Lacey's ear. I am so much better at helping with relationship drama than I am with dermatalogolical conditions.

"I know," she says. She studies her reflection in the mirror over the sink, which is super streaky. Someone really should clean in here. Hopefully that's not the new person's job. Not to sound snobby, but cleaning toilets on my summer vacation might be enough to really make me lose it. "So, anyway,"

Lacey says, whirling around, "you have to wait on her."

"Who?"

"Danielle!" Lacey says, throwing her hands up in exasperation.

"*Me?*"

"Yes, you."

"But I don't know what I'm doing!" I just got here five seconds ago for God's sake! I haven't even had time to . . . I don't know, whatever it is people do when they first get to work. Drink coffee, catch up on coworker gossip, ease into things.

"It's not that hard," Lacey says. She spins me around, puts her hands on my back, and starts pushing me toward the door. "Just go and write down what she wants, then take the ticket and stick it on the counter in the back, so Noah can make it."

"But—"

"Please," she says, her green eyes pleading. "I can't go out there and face her! It might give me an anxiety attack, and I'm out of Xanax."

Ugh. "Fine," I say, sighing. "Whatever." How hard can it be? Take the girl's order, and give it to Noah to cook. Easy peasy, right? Lacey grins at me and hands me her order pad and a pen. I walk out of the bathroom and over to a table in the far corner of the diner, where a small blond girl is sitting. She's wearing wire-rimmed glasses, and her hair is all messy. Traces of last night's mascara are smudging her eyes. "Um, hello," I say. "Welcome to Cooley's Diner. My name is Hannah, may I please take your order?"

"I seriously doubt it," she says, and looks me up and down in a really snotty way. "Where's Lacey?"

"Lacey? Um . . . Lacey's in the back, working on something." A lie, but not really. I mean, Lacey *is* working on something—not coming out here and having to face Danielle.

"I want Lacey," Danielle says, folding her hands on her menu and looking up at me expectantly.

"Yes, well, I'm Hannah and I'll be happy to wait on you." I poise my pen over my pad and give her my best smile. "Can I recommend the home fries? They're our specialty." I have no idea if that's even true, but I have to say something. And home fries seem like a good bet. Diners are always known for their home fries, aren't they?

"No," she says, then closes her menu. "Lacey."

Okay. Apparently now she's not even talking in complete sentences. I contemplate going into the back and telling Lacey she has to come out here and wait on this girl. But then I glance over my shoulder and see Lacey peering out from the bathroom door, her eyes looking serious and scared. Then I remember what she said about having an anxiety attack, and how she freaked out over that tiny little mosquito bite/mole/freckle/whatever-the-hell-it-was behind her ear. Who knows what will happen if Danielle starts upsetting her? Lacey doesn't seem like the type who should be out and about in the world without her Xanax.

So I turn back to Danielle and say, "Look, Lacey's not

available. So you can either order, or get out of here." I pick up her menu, like I'm going to take it back behind the counter. "What's it going to be?" Her jaw drops open, like she can't believe I'm speaking to her like that. (Which, let's face it, *is* kind of unbelievable, especially since it's my first day. I don't think Cooley wants me talking to the customers like that, even if he is a drug lord.)

Danielle recovers quickly, and then says simply, "I guess I'll get out of here." She stands up, picks up the glass of water that's sitting in front of her, and then very slowly and deliberately pours it on the table. "Oops, sorry about that." She smiles sweetly, then turns around and leaves, the bells on the door tinkling as she walks out.

"Where's she going?" Lacey asks, running out of the bathroom. She slides into the booth Danielle just left and peers out into the parking lot.

"She's leaving," I say. "I guess she didn't want to order without you. And she spilled a whole glass of water all over the table. On purpose."

"That little brat!" Lacey says. "I knew it! You wouldn't believe what she—"

"Hello!" a middle-aged man in the corner yells. "I've been waiting for someone to take my order for fifteen minutes." Lacey rolls her eyes, then shoves a pad in my hands. "Take it away," she says.

So much for training.

❈ ❈ ❈

The day flies by even though Cooley has us all working a double, so by the time seven o'clock rolls around, I'm exhausted.

"You guys go ahead," Noah says, wiping down one of the booths and then flinging the rag over his shoulder. "I'll stay and close up."

"Are you serious?" Lacey asks, shaking her long red hair down and collapsing into one of the booths. "You're going to stay and clean up? By yourself?" She bites her lip. "That's awesome, but are you sure?"

"Yeah," he says. "You take Hannah home, okay?"

I think about protesting, about saying I can walk, but it's twelve blocks and I'm exhausted. So as much as I don't want to be the loser without a car who needs rides from people, it's better than having to walk home in the heat.

We're halfway to Lacey's car when I realize that I don't have my cell phone. "Forgot my phone," I tell her. "Be right back."

When I get back inside, Noah's behind the counter, sitting in front of his laptop, a look of concentration on his face. He must be doing some ordering, or whatever it is restaurant people do on computers before they clean up for the night.

"Hey," I say. "I think I left my cell in here somewhere. Have you seen it?" I'm down on my hands and knees now, looking behind the counter. But no phone.

"Let me go check the lost and found," he says. "A lot of times, if there are keys or phones lying around, they end up back there."

"Thanks," I say gratefully, straightening up and plopping down in his chair. The laptop in front of me is open to a word document, and on the screen is a page of what looks like a script. It's called "Midsummer." "Scene One," it says "Int. Car, At Night. Laura Watson, seventeen, sits in the passenger seat. She is beautiful but complicated, with a—"

The laptop screen snaps shut. "What are you doing?" Noah asks. He's looking down at me with a scowl, his eyes dark and angry.

"Um, nothing," I say, my face turning hot. "I just—"

"You just what?" Noah's lips tighten into a line.

"Nothing," I say. "I mean, I'm sorry. I shouldn't have looked at that. I mean, I *didn't* look at it, I didn't really see anything, it was just . . . um, did you find my phone?"

He slaps it into my hand.

"Thanks," I say. But he doesn't say anything back, so I rush out of the diner and back to Lacey's car.

"Something really weird just happened," I say to Lacey once I'm in the passenger seat. I pull my seat belt across my body and click it in. "So I went back in there to get my phone, right? And Noah was—"

"I'm about to do something bad," Lacey says, cutting me

off. She's staring straight ahead, a look that's somewhere between fear and excitement on her face, and her hands are tight around the steering wheel.

"You are?" I'm intrigued. Intrigued enough to forget about the whole weird interaction Noah and I just had. I mean, what's a little fight over looking at someone's computer when Lacey's about to do something horrible?

"Yes." She pulls the rearview mirror down and starts to fiddle with her hair. "I'm going to drive past Riker's house before I go home."

"Riker *Strong*?" I ask incredulously. "Why would you be driving by Riker's—Ohmigod! *Riker Strong* is your ex-boyfriend? The one Danielle had sex with?" How did I not know this? Probably because once Riker and Ava broke up, we spent most of our time totally avoiding him. So it would make sense that I never really knew who he was dating next. Still, you'd think I would have heard *something* about it, or at least remember seeing him in the hall with Lacey or something. I wonder if she knows how obsessed he is with Ava. Hell, I wonder if *Danielle* knows. She probably wouldn't be too pleased if she knew her boyfriend was still practically in love with someone else. Probably she'd do a lot worse than just spill a cup of water.

"Yeah," she says. "Why?"

"He used to date my friend Ava." I want to tell her that he stalked her after she broke up with him, but something tells me Lacey wouldn't want to hear that. So all I say is,

"Lacey, I don't think that's a good idea. To drive by his house, I mean."

"Oh, come on," she says. "Like you haven't driven by Sebastian's house?"

"Nope," I say. "I prefer to barricade myself in my room and stay away from everyone." I can't help feeling a little bit smug about this. Maybe I've gained a few pounds and maybe I wasn't the best about showering and maybe Ava had to tell Noah to keep an eye on me because she was afraid I was going to spike my Coke with arsenic, but besides spending a little too much time on his Facebook page, I never stalked Sebastian the way Lacey's obviously done to Riker.

"Then how are you supposed to know if he's hanging out with other girls?" Lacey seems confused.

"Lacey," I say. "I saw him kissing another girl right in front of me. I'm kind of assuming that he's hanging out with other girls."

But as I say it, my voice starts to falter just a little bit. I've had a good day, a busy day, a day where I made a lot of money (one hundred and fifty dollars, which is not a lot of money to some people, but is definitely a lot of money to someone whose bank balance is two dollars and sixty-three cents, aka me) and felt like I was actually doing something instead of being completely unproductive and consuming my weight in ice cream. (Which, let's be honest, was only going to get harder and harder as my weight went up.) But now the day is over and all I have to look forward to is going home, lying in bed, and watching DVDs . . . And then I have to get up early again tomorrow and go work at my shitty diner job, doing the whole thing over and over, every day, for the rest of the summer. Pathetic.

"Well, I'm driving by Riker's," Lacey says. She starts the car up, then glances at me out of the corner of her eye, like she's giving me one more chance to stop her. But I don't have the energy. "Do you want to come?" she asks. "Or should I drop you off at home first? Either way is fine, I don't want to make you feel uncomfortable by having to go on my stalker mission with me."

I hesitate for a second, but then I say, "Okay, I'll come." I take a deep breath. "But, um, can we drive by Sebastian's house too?"

Lacey smiles.

We go to Sebastian's house first, because his house is closer. Riker actually lives right around the block from me, and when Lacey finds this out, she almost has an orgasm. "This is perfect!" she screams. "I can pretend I'm hanging out at your house and then we can go for walks around the block or something. He's always outside, he likes to work on cars and play basketball in his driveway."

I don't even tell her it's pretty rude for her to imply that she would use me for my geographical desirability, and I definitely don't tell her that if Riker sees us walking by his house twelve times a day it's probably going to seem a little suspicious, and/or cause him to get a restraining order. But she must be reading my mind, because she quickly adds, "Not that I would use you for your house. And not that I would make it obvious or anything."

"Oh, totally," I say, mostly because she seems really excited, and I don't want to be mean. Besides, if Riker did get stalked, it would serve him right for stalking Ava. Plus, we're getting closer to Sebastian's and I'm trying to brace myself for whatever I'm about to see.

"That's his house," I say, pointing at the white colonial with blue trim on the corner. Lacey slows the car down.

"Don't slow down!" I yell. "What if he's outside or something?"

"Just duck down," she instructs me, like she's done this a million times before. (Which she probably has.) Although, I don't know how she can duck down while she's driving. That definitely doesn't seem all that safe.

I slouch down in the seat, peeking out the window. "There's his truck," I say, exhaling in relief. He's home! Of course, him being home at seven o'clock on a weekday doesn't mean that he isn't going out later. But still.

I feel a squeeze in my chest. Sebastian kissed me for the first time in that truck. He was driving me home from school, and it was this really electric moment, where I was really hoping he was going to, but not knowing if he definitely was, and then, just when I thought he wasn't, he leaned over and—

Wait a minute. Whose car is that?

"Whose car is that?" Lacey asks. "It's super cute." There's a pink Jeep with the top down parked on the street, right in front of Sebastian's house.

"I don't know," I say. A pink Jeep? Sebastian's mom drives an Accord, and his older sister has a black Hyundai that she got as a graduation present a couple of years ago.

And then, when we get closer, I see the bumper sticker on the back of the Jeep. "Granbury High Sophomores Do It Better" it says.

Lacey must see it at the same time I do, because she speeds up and drives off. We sit in silence for a few seconds. "Maybe his mom got a new car," Lacey finally says. "A lot of people have midlife crises and get pink Jeeps. I know this girl whose mom—"

"I saw the sticker," I say. I look out the window, not saying anything.

"Maybe it was one of his sister's friends?" she tries.

"One of his sister's friends who's still a sophomore at our school?"

"He's a jerk, Hannah."

"Yeah." I keep my face turned toward the window, my eyes filling with tears that turn the houses into a blur of colors as we go by. Everything looks all smudgy, and it feels fitting and reinforces how I've felt these past few weeks— like my life is one big smudge.

When we get to Riker's house, his car isn't there.

Lacey doesn't even blink, she just lets me direct her to

my house and then pulls in the driveway. "Are we pathetic?" she asks.

"Yes," I say. But something about having her with me, having a partner in all of this, makes it seem less pathetic. It's nice to have someone that's going through the same thing I am. It makes me feel like I'm not that crazy.

"New pact," Lacey says. "We are never driving by their houses again." She puts her hand out. "Deal?"

"Deal." I shake it.

It's an easy deal to make really. I mean, this is why I've kept myself hidden away these past few weeks. Because even though I've driven myself a little bit crazy thinking about what Sebastian's been doing or what he might be up to, at least they were just fantasies. A fantasy is something that, when it's horrible, even if it might be true, you can say, "Oh, I'm sure that isn't really happening, it's just my imagination running away with me." I mean, my imagination runs away with me all the time, about all sorts of things.

But your imagination running away from you is a lot different than a pink Jeep with the top down and a very inappropriate bumper sticker staring you right in the face. To add insult to injury, it's probably true. Sophomores probably *do* do it better. Definitely better than me, since I've never even done it.

"Do you want me to stay?" Lacey asks. "I mean, I have a late doctor's appointment, but I could cancel it. We could hang out and order Chinese or something."

"No," I say. "I'm fine, really. I'll see you tomorrow."

I slide out from the car and head inside, where I call Ava and leave her a voicemail. "It's me," I say. "Something really horrible happened, and I need to talk to you. Call me back as soon as you get this message. I don't care how late or how early it is."

I hang up the phone and head for the ice cream in the freezer.

The First Day of Senior Year

How was I supposed to know that the girl who hit my car is the sophomore who does it better? I mean, I've only really seen her once, when she was making out with my boyfriend in a pool, and her back was to me. And at that time, I was having a traumatic moment and was completely under duress. And it's, like, a proven fact that people who are in a traumatic moment and completely under duress are unable to remember pertinent details. They did a whole study on it and everything. Of course, it had to do with witnesses and crimes, not people whose boyfriends are cheating on them, but still. The principle is totally the same.

"I guess she was telling the truth when she said that she got a new car," I say to Lacey as we navigate through the hall on our way to our third period class. "She must have traded her pink Jeep in for a red BMW."

"Honestly," Lacey says, "I think you should sue her."

"Just because she hooked up with Sebastian?"

"Yes," Lacey says. "And also because she really hurt my

neck." She rubs it like she's trying to show just how screwed up it is.

"Are you going to have to wear one of those foam collars?" I stop at my locker to drop off the books I've collected in my first two classes. Lacey stops with me.

"I never thought of that," Lacey says. "But probably."

"You can get everyone to sign it, like a cast."

"Not funny," Lacey says. "You shouldn't make fun of me, because someday, sometime, there really *is* going to be something wrong with me, and then you'll—"

"Hannah!" Ava comes running down the hall, her brown platform sandals flapping against the tile floor. She flings herself at me, accosting me with the scent of her perfume.

"Whoa, whoa, whoa," I say, reaching out and grabbing her before she can go hurtling into my locker. "What's wrong?"

"I need to talk to you." Her face is pale and her dark eyeliner, which looked perfect this morning, is now really smudged and giving her a kind of weird, vampire look against the paleness that is now her skin.

"What's wrong?" I repeat. *She found out*, I think. She knows what happened last night. I don't know how, but she does. And now it's going to happen; she's going to start screaming and yelling and maybe even hit me. *How does she know?* I wonder. Did someone see us? Is there a rumor going around? Did Noah tell her? Is that why he was acting so weird? Thinking about Noah telling her makes me happy.

It shouldn't, I know it shouldn't, but a lot of things that shouldn't have happened have. I let the feeling wash over me for one second and then I push it back down before I can start hating myself for feeling it.

Stay calm, I tell myself. *She doesn't know. If she knew, she wouldn't have just tried to hug you and she wouldn't sound like she wants you to make her feel better.*

"I need to talk to you," Ava says again. It's a whisper this time, and her eyes flick over to Lacey.

"Fine," Lacey says, "I have to get to class anyway." But her tone is slightly clipped, like she can't imagine she'd be interested in hearing any of Ava's drama anyway.

Ava grabs my hand, then pulls me into the bathroom in the math wing. There are two other girls from our class, Ivy Defalco and Charlotte Sylvain, doing their makeup at the sinks, and they nod to us as we come in. Ava says hi, but in a really fake cheery voice that I've heard her use sometimes on parents or when she's in trouble. And when she says it, her hand tightens around mine.

She pulls me into a stall. The same stall. Great. Now, not only do I have to worry about a Noah rumor, I have to worry about those girls out there spreading some weird rumor about how Ava and I are lesbians. Not that I care about being thought of as a lesbian. In fact, it's way better than a rumor about me and my best friend's boyfriend.

"Ava," I say. "What. Is. Wrong?"

She holds her finger up to her lips, and I stay quiet. The

sound of the bell ringing reverberates through the bathroom, signaling that we're both late for third period, but it doesn't really matter because this is more important. Plus, it's pretty easy to get away with being late on the first day of school—you just say you were in guidance or you read your schedule wrong.

Once the bell stops ringing, it's like some kind of switch flips inside of her, and Ava kicks open the door to the stall and stomps over to the sinks. "I'm a mess!" she raves. She reaches into her buttery leather tote and pulls out a huge makeup bag. She starts washing her face off with some sort of makeup remover-towelette thing, then flings it into the garbage can forcefully. Okay, then. I guess she's feeling violent.

"It's Noah," she says, almost spitting out his name. She looks at me, her brown eyes huge. "Hannah," she says. "Is there anything you want to tell me?"

I can hear the sound of my heart beating. I can literally *hear* it beating, throbbing really, and the sound of the blood rushing through my body vibrates in my ears, even though I know I'm just being paranoid. If Ava knew, she'd be screaming at me in the hall, not bringing me into the bathroom for a talk. "What do you mean?" I ask.

"I mean," she says, turning back to the mirror. "That if there's anything you want to tell me about what happened this summer, then you should tell me. *Right now*." I look into the mirror, seeing our reflections, the two of us standing

there side by side, as we've been every day on the first day of
school for the past six years, everything the same but completely different.

"What kind of thing?"

"Anything!" She pulls out another towelette and starts
scrubbing the makeup off her eyes.

"Anything having to do with what?"

"Anything having to do with Noah and another girl! You
guys spent like all summer together, right? Did you see anything? Were there any suspicious girls that would come into the
diner all the time?"

The breath I've been holding in goes whooshing out of me
in one big rush of air. "Why are you asking about Noah and
another girl?"

"Because," she says. She throws another towelette into
the garbage, then looks at herself in the mirror. I watch as her
reflection says, "He just broke up with me."

"He just *what*?" This I wasn't expecting. "What do you
mean he just broke up with you?" My head feels all light, and I
look around for someplace to sit, but of course there's nowhere.
It's the bathroom in the math wing, not the bathroom in Blair
Waldorf's house.

"Just what I said," Ava says. "He. Broke. Up. With. Me.
God, Hannah, I'm so upset." Her face crumples and I reach
out and put my arms around her. I can't believe that on the
last day of school, Ava was comforting me, and now I'm here
comforting her.

"I'm so sorry," I say. "I just . . . I can't believe it." This part, at least, is true. "What did he say?"

"Well." She sniffles, then plops herself down on the floor of the bathroom and looks up at me forlornly. "I kept having to follow him around all day, you know? And you know me, Hannah, I do *not* follow people."

"I know," I say. It's true. Ava doesn't follow people. She's always the one getting followed.

"But he was just acting so weird all morning, and I had no choice, you know? He, like, seemed like he didn't want me around." She sniffs again. "So finally, after second period, I was like, 'are you going to tell me what's going on?' And then he was all, 'I didn't want to tell you this in school, Ava, I wanted to wait until after.'"

She stands up now and returns to the mirrors where she starts relining her eyes in a sparkly plum liner that's different from the one she was wearing this morning. I guess maybe she decided that a dramatic morning calls for a more dramatic makeup look. "And then he said he felt like we'd grown apart over the summer, and he didn't think it was a good idea for us to keep seeing each other."

"Wow," I say. I'm leaning against the sink, not sure what to do, what I should say, how I'm supposed to feel. The one thing I do know is that I feel horrible for Ava.

"And the worst part," she says, "is that he acted like it was my fault that we grew apart."

"Well, you weren't really around that much this summer," I say carefully.

"Like you can blame me?" she says. "I was away following my dreams. And besides, being apart for a summer isn't enough reason to break up with someone." She pauses, like she wants me to say something, but I don't. Mostly because I don't know if she really *was* following her dreams. Ava's never expressed interest in any kind of career path. In fact, she always kind of acts like even talking about things like that is stupid. She's never said she wants to be a teacher or a counselor, or even that she wants to work with kids. And it wasn't like she got some great internship in Paris that she'd been wanting. She got a last minute summer job as a camp counselor in Maine.

We're silent as Ava finishes her makeup. Then she takes a deep breath, squares her shoulders and gives herself a big smile in the mirror. "Getting my teeth whitened," she says, "was so the right choice."

She starts to walk toward the door.

"Where are you going?" I ask.

"To class," she says.

"You're going to go to class?"

"Hannah," she says. "I'm not going to ruin my senior year grades because of some guy." And then she pushes through the door and slips out into the hall, not even waiting for me to follow. I wash my hands in the sink, then take a piece of spearmint gum out of my bag and pop it into my mouth. I leave the bathroom and start walking to my own class, my footsteps echoing through the empty hallway and my mind racing. Did Noah break up with Ava because of me? Is he going to try and talk to me now? Was he just waiting to talk to Ava before he came up to me? How upset is Ava really? Is there a chance she might get over it pretty quickly? Does she even—

I round the corner toward C-wing and almost smack right into Noah.

"Oh!" I say. I reach out to steady myself and end up grabbing his shirt, and for a second, I'm afraid I'm going to pull him close to me, but I don't. I take a step back. "Sorry," I say, "I didn't . . . I wasn't watching where I was going."

He's so close that I can see the curve of his collarbone, the top of his T-shirt, the way the hood of his sweatshirt is twisted a little bit in the back. "It's fine," he says. I take a breath and look up at him and his eyes meet mine. Tingles rush through my body and I wait for him to say that he broke up with Ava, that we should meet up after school to talk about everything, that we should figure everything out together.

But all he does is brush by me as he goes down the hall. And so I blink back my tears and head to third period.

The Summer

"What are you doing?"

I look up from where I'm sitting on the front porch (well, technically sprawling since I'm laying on my back with one arm and one leg hanging over the side and onto the cobblestone path that leads to our driveway). I haven't moved since Lacey dropped me off an hour ago. Actually, that's not really true. About a half an hour ago I realized I had to go to the bathroom, so I did. And then I wandered into my bedroom for a second, where I did something very stalkerish that had to do with Sebastian and Facebook. (It totally didn't violate the agreement I made with Lacey, since that was limited to driving by people's houses. Even so, I still feel a little guilty.) But then I came right back to the porch. Talk about a complete and total regression.

I look up to see who's talking to me—Noah. Probably here to yell at me for looking at his computer. Whatever. There's nothing he can say that can make me more upset than I already am.

"Nothing," I say. "I'm just . . . sitting."

"But you're not sitting," he says. "You're laying."

He sits down next to me on the steps, right near my head. I look up at him, then turn toward the yard so that he can't see my face. The whole situation is suddenly too shameful for words.

"Then I'm just laying," I say. "What are *you* doing here?"

"What are *you* doing here?"

"I live here," I say, rolling my eyes. Duh.

"Yeah, but what are you doing here, out on the porch, just laying?"

"Isn't it obvious?"

He looks me up and down. I'm still in my Cooley's uniform, my eyes are wet and my body is lethargic.

"Not really," he says.

"I'm depressed." God, do I really need to spell it out for him? I thought Noah was supposed to be smart.

"About what?"

"About what? Are you seriously asking me that question?"

"I know about what," he says. "I just meant has anything new happened? Because you seemed fine a little while ago."

"Yes," I say. "There was a pink Jeep in Sebastian's driveway." I look up at him from under lowered lashes, gauging his reaction to this critical piece of information.

Obviously, he's too dense to get the ramifications, because his response is to look confused and then repeat, "A pink Jeep?"

"Yup," I say, turning back to look out into the yard. "A pink Jeep." A mosquito lands on my leg, probably to suck my blood and give me a huge itchy bite and maybe even some West Nile. But I'm too upset to move, and so I just let it do its thing.

"Is Sebastian . . . is he . . . I mean he's not . . . he isn't gay now, is he?" Noah asks.

"No!" I smack his leg. "Are you saying I could turn a man gay?"

"No," he says. "I just heard pink Jeep and Sebastian and it was the logical place to go. Besides, there's nothing wrong with being gay."

"The pink Jeep," I say, "Belongs to *her*."

"Her?"

"The sophomore," I report. "And," I rush on before he can say anything else, "she has a bumper sticker that says 'Sophomores Do It Better'." I sit up then, fast, and my head goes a little woozy because I've been lying down for so long. "Is that true?" I ask him. "Do sophomores really do it better?"

"God, no," Noah says. I lie back down, satisfied.

"So what are you doing here?" I ask.

"Ava said you left her a message sounding kind of upset, so she asked me to come over and check on you."

I sit up again. "Are you *serious*?"

"Yeah." He uncrosses his legs.

"I can't believe her!" Suddenly, I'm fuming. "Why would

she send you here when I left her a message? She couldn't call me or text me?" I pick up my phone and check it. "Nothing!" I say. "Not one call. Not one voice mail. Not one text, not even an email or a Facebook message!"

"She didn't have that much time," Noah says weakly.

"What. Ever." I'm so upset, that I burst into tears.

"Hey, hey, hey," Noah says calmly. "No crying." If he's startled by the fact that I'm now sobbing, he doesn't show it.

"I'm sorry," I say. "I just . . . I just . . ."

"Come on," he says, standing up and holding out his hand. "We're going for ice cream."

I stop crying. "Any kind I want?"

"The secret to a great ice cream," Noah says fifteen minutes later, as we stand in line at The Big Dip Ice Cream Stand, "is crunch coat."

I look at him, aghast. *Crunch coat?* Oh, Noah darling, you are so wrong." I almost wish I hadn't heard that, it's so upsetting. He gives me a look, like he wants an explanation. I sigh. "Everyone knows that you ruin ice cream by putting crunch coat on it," I say. "Crunch coat isn't even peanuts, it's . . . I don't know what it is, some kind of weird, synthetic . . ."

"Crunch coat?" he offers.

"Exactly." The line shuffles forward, and we shuffle with it. The line's pretty long, but I guess I shouldn't be surprised. It's eight o'clock on a gorgeous summer night — one of those nights where it's warm, but not humid, with a nice breeze that rustles the leaves and makes the smell of fresh-cut grass and smoke from the grill waft through the air.

"Crunch coat," Noah says, "is delicious. And besides, I'm supposed to be taking advice from you?"

"What's that supposed to mean?"

"You listen to Lady Gaga."

I gasp. "How do you know that?"

"I've heard it pounding out of your iPod when me, you, and Ava hang out."

I consider telling him that I only listen to Lady Gaga because she's on my workout mix or something, but then I think better of it. I mean, I'm not embarrassed. "Lady Gaga is fast-becoming a cultural icon, the likes of which we haven't seen since Madonna," I report.

"Is that right?"

"Yes, that's right." The line moves forward again, and I move with it, enjoying the last few minutes of sun on my face. "And besides, the fact that I listen to Lady Gaga has nothing to do with my knowledge of ice cream."

"What about the Jonas Brothers? Does the fact that you listen to them have anything to do with your knowledge of ice cream?"

"I don't listen to the Jonas Brothers!" This one, I definitely have to lie about. Lady Gaga is one thing, but Joe, Kevin, and Nick are another altogether. "And even if I did, they're very popular with the kids. And they wear purity rings."

"My ten-year-old cousin thinks the Jonas Brothers are over."

"All right, smart ass," I say. "What should I be listening to?" I bend down to scratch my newly formed mosquito bite.

"Are you serious?"

"Yes, I'm serious."

"You could be listening to Paramore, or The Beatles, or Sting."

"Sting? Isn't he, like, old?"

Noah blinks his blue eyes at me, then shakes his head and buries it in his hands. He peeks at me between two fingers. "You're kidding, right?"

"Of course." I roll my eyes and take a step forward. A little girl comes walking back from the order window holding a huge cone with two scoops of butter pecan, one of which promptly falls onto the concrete. She reaches down and picks it up, plops it back on her cone, and keeps walking.

"Wow," I say. "Did you see that? That girl just—"

"Oh my God," Noah says. "You're not kidding. You're not kidding at all! You don't know who Sting is." He's staring at me like I'm the eighth Wonder of the World or something.

"I know who Sting is," I say. Which isn't really true. I mean, obviously I've heard of Sting, he's a rock star. I'm just not completely familiar with his music. "He's the one with the wraparound sunglasses." I shuffle a few more steps forward in line, proud of myself.

"The wraparound . . . oh my God, are you . . . are you

talking about *Bono*?" Noah's looking at me like his head might explode.

"No," I scoff, even though now I realize I totally am. And Bono's in U2. That much I know. U2 has some very good Sebastian-was-making-out-with-someone-else-and-now-I'm-lying-here-depressed-and-feeling-sorry-for-myself music.

"Oh, geez." Noah feigns that I've shot an arrow into his chest and falls to the ground. "You're killing me, Hannah, you're killllllinnngg mmmee." A few kids around us turn and look, and then giggle.

"Get up," I say, but I'm laughing.

"Only if you promise to let me introduce you to some real music."

"Fine," I say. "But only if you promise to tell me what you were doing on your laptop." I say it in a teasing voice, but he stands up immediately, the smile dropping off of his face.

"It's nothing," he says.

"Well, it's not *nothing*, obviously, since I saw something on there, and then you freaked out and slammed the computer shut."

"I didn't freak out."

"Okay," I say, shrugging. I know I should drop it. I mean, whatever he's doing on his computer is his business. I don't really have any right to know. Although, he *has* kind of been all up in my business. I mean, not only did he accost me at the Laundromat, he kind of bullied me into getting a job at his work. Not to mention showing up at my house today and being all, "Oh we have to go get ice cream, tell me about the pink Jeep. Oh please, oh please."

Well. It didn't exactly go like that. It was more like he was trying to be nice, and of course I volunteered the stuff about the pink Jeep. He didn't even really ask about that. And he did bring up the idea of ice cream, which is my favorite thing in the world. But still.

So I decide to drop it, and a few minutes later, we get to the front of the line. We order our ice cream (he makes me get vanilla with crunch coat, and I make him get a peanut butter cup flurry with cream-cheese ice cream), and I'm not sure if it's just that I haven't had crunch coat in a while or that it's ice-cream stand ice cream as opposed to the stuff out of the carton I'm used to eating, but it's really, really good. Like maybe the best ice cream I've ever had.

Later, when he brings me home, he asks if he can come in.

I say okay, mostly because I don't want to be alone, even though I know he's just asking because he promised Ava that he would watch out for me. Despite the fact that we just had ice cream, I make fruit slushies in the blender out of strawberries and fresh orange juice that I picked up at the farmer's market on the corner (I'm confined to buying groceries at places that are within walking distance, so it's been a lot of produce, Costco, and diner food), and we sit out on the deck in the dark.

"What's that?" he asks when I bring the pitcher of slush-ies out.

"Slushies," I say. "I told you I was making them, remember?" I wanted to put tequila in them, but Noah said that would just be numbing my feelings and that I needed to learn to deal with the pain. Which sounded a little bit like bullshit to me, but I decided to humor him. And also to never tell him about my mom's Ambien.

"No, *that*," he says.

"What?"

"This," he says, picking up my journal, which I must have left out on the deck. I wrote in it last night, staying up late and letting the words pour out of me, about how I felt about Sebastian, about missing Ava, everything. I would have written in it today when I was having my mini-meltdown, except I was too lazy to go into the backyard and get it.

"Nothing," I say, trying to stay calm as I reach over and pluck it out of his hand. "It's just a notebook."

"It looks like a journal," he says. He reaches over and pours some slushie into his glass and then takes a sip.

"Well, it's not." I plop down next to him on the couch.

"Okay." He leans back against the squashy deck furniture and looks at me like he could care less. Suddenly, for some reason, I feel offended. I mean, it's so obviously a journal. You'd think he'd at least be a little bit interested in reading it. Aren't guys just dying to read journals and diaries?

Does he think my secrets are lame? I have many scandalous secrets, thank you very much.

"That's it?" I pick up the notebook and shake it in his face. "This is obviously not just a notebook, it's obviously a journal." It's pale green with a sparkly gold butterfly emblazoned on the front of a hard, metal cover. I mean, all it's really missing is the word "journal" stamped across the front.

"I know it is." He shrugs and takes another drink of his strawberry slushie.

"So aren't you going to push me, make me admit it?"

"Nope."

"No?" I stare at him incredulously. "Aren't you curious about what's in there?"

"Look, Hannah, if you don't want to tell me that you have a journal, if you're *embarrassed* by something you shouldn't be embarrassed about, that's something you need to work out with yourself." He shrugs again, then drains the rest of his slushie. "Good slush," he says. "Can I have another one?"

But I'm angry now. "What the hell is that supposed to mean? That I need to work it out with myself?"

"It just means," he says, "that if you're worried about what I'm going to think of you because you keep a journal, then that's something you need to deal with." He shrugs. "You got any snacks?"

"No, I don't have any snacks," I say. Which is, of course, a lie — I absolutely have snacks. Like, Costco-box sizes full of them. Cheez-Its, Oreos, those delish Keebler cookies that are shaped like elves. I even have a huge pre-packaged veggie tray with tons of gourmet dips to go with it. Not to mention pretzels, chips, and ice cream. But no way is Noah getting any of it. Not with that kind of attitude. "And I don't *keep* a journal. I just write in it once in a while."

"You don't have snacks?"

"No."

"But weren't you just telling me about how much you've been eating snacks lately?"

"Are you calling me fat?"

Noah looks at me. "Are you seriously asking me that?"

"Yes."

"You're asking me if I'm calling you fat? You know I'm not calling you fat." He looks at me. "Hannah, is this because I don't care about what's in your journal?"

"No!"

"Yes, it is."

"No, it isn't."

"Yes, it is."

"No, it isn't," I say. "It's not about you caring what's in my journal, I don't even *want* you to care about what's in my journal." This is sort of true, sort of a lie. I don't necessarily want him to care or know what's in my journal, but seriously, why isn't he the least bit interested? Like, maybe I've written tons of stuff in there about all the hot, sweaty sex that Sebastian and I were having. I haven't, of course, since we weren't having any hot, sweaty sex. But I did write some stuff down about all the Everything But that we were doing. Does Noah think I'm completely and totally lame? So lame that I don't even have an interesting journal?

"Is this because you think that I think that your journal is lame?" Noah asks.

My jaw drops. "No."

"Look, I don't think your journal is lame, I just figure that if you can't admit it's a journal, then that's your business." His stomach grumbles loudly. "You hear that?" he asks. "I really need snacks."

"I can *admit* it's a journal," I say. "If you can admit what it was I saw today on your computer. " I raise my eyebrows at him. "But if you can't, well then, I guess that's something you're going to have to work out with yourself, Noah."

He looks at me, and for a second, I think he's going to make some stupid joke and drop the whole thing. But he must change his mind because finally he just nods and says, "Okay, fine. But if we're going to talk about that, then I'm definitely going to need snacks."

I stand up and head to the kitchen.

When I get back to the deck, I'm armed with a tray of potato chips, dip, tortilla chips, salsa, and a whole Keebler cookie sampler.

"Wow," Noah says. "You don't mess around."

"Not when it comes to snacks," I say. We move over to the patio table, and I set all the food down, then reach over and flip the switch on the sparkly deck lights that are wrapped around the railing.

"Now tell me," I say.

"What?"

"You got your snacks. Now tell me what it was you were working on."

"Already?"

"Yes, already," I say. "You said you would, now do it."

"Fine," he says, shrugging. He takes a tortilla chip and dips it into the salsa. "It's a screenplay."

He just says it, like it's not a big deal. Which it is and isn't at the same time. I mean, from the way he was acting, you would have thought he was running some kind of prostitution ring off his laptop or something. On the other hand, writing a screenplay is a pretty major and cool thing to do. So why is he all of a sudden acting like it's no big deal?

And then I get it. He wants me to ask him about it, to be all "Ohmigod that's so cool what's it about ohmigod." Kind of like how I wanted him to be interested in my journal. Well, two can play this game.

"Oh," I shrug. "That's cool, you should have just told me." I pick a cookie up off the tray and take a bite. "I'm going to get a super sugar crash after this," I say. "Especially since we just had ice cream. And slushies." Wow. I really have to stop eating.

"Don't you want to know what it's about?" Noah asks.

"I guess," I say, then give a half-shrug.

"You know what?" he says. "Never mind. I should really get going." It's so abrupt that for a second I think he's joking.

So I say, "Okay, I'll walk you to the door." But when he stands up, I realize he's serious. "Wait, you're serious?"

"Yeah," he says. "I gotta go."

"Okay," I say, deciding to drop the charade. "Out with it."

"Out with what?"

"What's the deal with you and the screenplay?"

For a second, I think he's going to tell me I'm crazy, that there's no deal with the screenplay and he really does just have to go. But instead, he sits back down. "There's no deal. It's just that no one knows I'm writing it."

"Why not?" I ask. "Is it, like, . . . Is it, ah, erotica or something?"

The side of his mouth twists up into a half-smile. "No," he says. "It's not erotica. It's just that I don't want everyone asking me about it. You know how as soon as you tell someone you're doing something, they want to ask you tons of questions about it?"

"Yeah," I say.

"Well, I don't want to deal with that. Plus, it's like—Okay, I know it sounds dumb, but it's serious for me, you know?"

"You mean, you want people to take it seriously, but most people are still going to act like it's just some dumb thing you're doing and ask you about it in the way people do when they don't think you're ever going to finish what you started?"

"Exactly." He pops a cookie into his mouth. "Damn, these things are good."

"Keebler," I say.

"Don't ever underestimate the power of the elves."

"I think it's great you're writing a screenplay," I say. "What's it about?"

"Relationships," he says. "Well, one relationship. You know, drama, first love, that kind of thing."

"Sounds right up my alley," I say. "Is there a sophomore in it? Maybe one who does it better?"

"No," he says with a straight face. "In my screenplay the seniors do it better. Always."

"That's good," I say, nodding my approval. "And you're lucky that you have something you're excited about, something you're interested in. I have no idea what I'm interested in." I take another chip. "Except maybe trying to figure out how much junk food I can eat before I burst."

"You'll figure it out."

"I hope so."

"You do?" He sounds surprised.

"Yeah," I say. "Doesn't everyone?"

"Not Ava."

"Yeah, well, Ava . . . she's a special case. Ava doesn't have to worry about that stuff, because she can do anything."

"Yeah," he says. He leans back in his seat, then puts his

feet up on the table and pushes his chair back, balancing himself. "Ava's one of those people who's totally unpredictable. I wouldn't be surprised if she was a lawyer who made partner by twenty-five, or one of those women who end up marrying a rich doctor and staying home with the kids."

"You want to be a doctor?" I say, confused. But then I get it. He wasn't talking about Ava marrying *him*. He was talking about Ava like they weren't going to end up together. And suddenly, I'm aware of the fact that it's late, I'm home alone with a boy, and that the boy is my best friend's boyfriend.

I get an uncomfortable feeling in my stomach. And I'm not sure if Noah gets one, too, but suddenly, he's standing up.

"I should probably get going," he says. "It's late."

"Totally," I say. "Well, um, thanks for the ice cream."

"You're welcome." I walk him as far as the kitchen, and then he walks himself the rest of the way down the hall and out the front door. I lock it once he's gone, and push my face against the window, watching his car until it disappears around the corner.

The First Day of Senior Year

Last night, my mom had the night off from work, and so she went through the bag I'd packed for school. She's done this every year since I was little, even though I keep trying to tell her that I don't need her to anymore. I mean, it's one thing when you're seven and need to remember your crayons, it's another when you're seventeen and able to be left alone for the whole summer.

Anyway, she slipped a travel-size thing of tissues into my bag, obviously thinking it was super necessary that I had them. She didn't seem too concerned with anything else, like notebooks or pens or paper or a laptop or the special graphing calculator that costs about three bazillion dollars that I need for calculus. Tissues. Out of everything, that's all she seemed to care about. I thought that went to show just how completely and totally out of touch she is, since I'm pretty sure no one's brought tissues to school since like the fourth grade.

But now I can't help but wonder if maybe she had some

kind of weird motherly instinct, because right now these tissues are totally coming in handy. Otherwise I'd definitely have to excuse myself to go to the bathroom or something, because there's no way I could control the amount of snot that's pouring out of my nose. I know, so disgusting. But I've been sniffling quietly to myself for the past twenty minutes, ever since I passed Noah in the hall and got here late.

If I didn't have my tissues, I'd totally have to leave English. And then people would know that I left class, and maybe it would get back to Ava, and then she would want to know exactly *why* I had to leave class and why I was crying, and then I'd have to make something up. And there's a pretty good chance it *would* get back to her, especially in a school this small, where no scandals ever really happen. Like, me leaving in the middle of class crying would be the big deal of the day. Of course, people would probably think it had something to do with Sebastian, but —

"Pssst!" I look out into the hallway, and there's Ava standing by the door, trying to get my attention. She makes a miming motion like she's talking on the phone. I guess she means for me to check mine.

I reach into my bag and pull it out. Three new texts.

All from Ava.

"Meet me in the bathroom" the first one says. "Where r u?" says the second one. And then, "Hannah, I m having a complete & total meltdown here, my life is over, now get ur ass into the second floor bathroom RIGHT NOW."

Oh, God. I quickly type a text back. "Can't leave 4th period, Mr. Cummings doesn't give passes." What happened to her not skipping class for some guy? And besides, we were just *in* the bathroom.

The reply comes super fast. "Get ur ass out here now."

Shit, shit, shit.

"We're going to the diner," Ava declares a few minutes later, after I've told Mr. Cummings I'm having a bathroom emergency and begged him to let me out of class. I'm definitely going to get written up. I mean, I was late to begin with and now I asked for a pass and am not going to be coming back. It's one of those big, wooden block passes, too, with the room number written on it in black Sharpie, which is totally unfortunate, since I'm going to have to bring it back to him at some point. Awww-kward.

"Ava, we can't ditch on the first day," I try, following her down the hall and knowing there's no way she's going to listen to me.

"Yes, we can," she says.

"What happened to you not ruining your senior year grades for some guy?" I ask. She's walking a lot faster now, and I double my pace, trying to keep up with her. I'm half-expecting someone to stop us, to ask us where we're going, and why we're in the hall and headed for the front door, but no one does. I think it has to do with the way Ava's walking. It's like she's on a mission.

"He's not some guy, and it won't ruin my grades," Ava says, as if what she said just twenty minutes earlier meant nothing. Which I guess isn't really that crazy. If there's one thing I've learned about breakups, it's that things can change by the second.

"Fine." I'm not looking forward to sitting with Ava while she goes on and on about how much she loves Noah and how completely devastated she is, but she *is* my best friend, and I'm the one who's put myself in this position. I need to be there for her.

So twenty minutes later, we're sitting in Cooley's and I'm looking around, wondering if there's any way there could be signs of what happened here last night. Like if Noah and I forgot to lock up, or if we somehow left something behind, or if some previously unknown hidden security camera taped us. Oh my God. I never even thought of that. A security camera! I've never noticed one before, but who knows if Cooley has one? He always seems to be getting into shady situations, so maybe he felt he needed a camera just in case anything bad happened here. The thought's too disturbing to even consider, so I quickly push it out of my brain.

"Do you get some kind of discount or something?" Ava asks, scanning the menu. "Because let me tell you, being a camp counselor does *not* pay that well."

"Um, not really," I say. "I mean, I get free fries a lot, depending on who's working." Last week Cooley hired two women to work the day shift when Noah and Lacey and I went back to school. He made this huge fuss about it, and even implied that maybe it would be better for us all to drop out of school and work for him full-time. He made it seem like seventeen was way too old to be going to school and living at home. It definitely reinforced my idea that he's a drug lord. Drug lording seems like the kind of profession you get into when you're young.

"Fries sound good," she says. "We'll order fries. And iced tea." She flips her newly-long hair behind her shoulder and looks at me seriously. "You're my best friend, right?"

"Right," I say, taking a sip of the ice water in front of me. *You are a horrible person*, the voice in my head says.

"And you would never lie to me, right?"

"Right." *More than horrible.* I take another sip of water, the ice cubes hitting my lips as the liquid slides around them.

"Good," she says. "Now tell me everything you know about Noah and what happened this summer. Everything, about any girl, and don't leave anything out, even if it seems like the smallest detail, like, ever."

I look at her, at the way she's looking at me, and think about the way she pretended to be over the whole Noah thing when I knew she wasn't. I think about how she acted like it wasn't a big deal, about how she pretended she was going right back to class only to show up outside my English class, like, fifteen minutes later. I think about the night Sebastian cheated on me, and how Ava was there for me, how she took care of me and made sure I was okay. I think about how she was the only one that I wanted to be there for me that night, and now, when the tables are turned and her heart is broken, I'm the only one she wants to be there for her. And that's when I know. I have to tell her. I have to tell her about last night, about what happened here. I have to tell her that I slept with Noah.

The Summer

I totally thought that after Noah told me about his screenplay that night at my house, that things would be a little awkward between us. But surprisingly, they're not. In fact, it's kind of the opposite — over the next couple of weeks we settle into a comfortable routine of him picking me up every morning before work, and the three of us (Noah, Lacey, and me) working double shifts at the diner.

Spending my days working at Cooley's actually isn't that bad, even though I'm usually super exhausted by the end of the night. Of course, this means I don't have too much energy to spend thinking about Sebastian. I'm not sure if it's because I have less time on my hands, or because I'm just naturally getting over him, but it seems like every day I think about him less and less. Where before, I would come home every night and wonder what Sebastian was doing; now I find myself in bed, watching TV or painting my nails or reading a book, and all of a sudden I'll look at the clock and be like, *Wow, I haven't even thought about Sebastian since this morning.*

Lacey and I have totally stuck to our pact, and she seems to be doing better, too.

Until one particularly hot day in July (seriously it's like ninety-seven degrees) when the air conditioner at the diner breaks at around seven a.m. We call Cooley immediately, and he comes in and promises to fix it, but then disappears and is still nowhere to be found even though it's now lunchtime. For a diner owner, Cooley is actually really irresponsible. I mean, he's, like, hardly ever around. Seriously, we're pretty much running the place, which is ridiculous since we're only teenagers. You'd think he'd be a little more concerned. It totally reinforces my idea that he's a drug lord, and the diner's just a front for the feds. Or whoever it is that's in charge of drug crimes.

Anyway, Cooley put Noah in charge, and Noah keeps getting these cryptic phone calls that are supposedly from the AC repair guys, but so far they haven't shown up, leading us to believe that they are actually from Cooley's brother, *pretending* to be the repair guy.

I try to say there's no way he would lie to us like that, and that it really serves no purpose other than to piss us off more, but Lacey insists that he would, that Cooley hates confrontation, and that it reminds her of the time that Cooley sent in a bunch of his friends who pretended to be regular customers so that he could grade the employees on their customer service. Which, personally, I don't think is that big of a deal. I mean, all the big companies send in secret shoppers.

Anyway, Lacey says I'm not allowed to defend him since I didn't work there then, and I didn't have to deal with this one man sending his iced tea back, like, five million times because it wasn't sweet enough. Which I don't think sounds really all that bad, like, in the grand scheme of things that customers could complain about, but Lacey claims it was horrible, that she had to open over fifty sugar packets, and that the guy was a real asshole about it.

So it's sweltering hot, and I'm standing in front of the fryer because some weirdo has ordered chicken nuggets with extra fries instead of, you know, a salad or a turkey sandwich or a milk shake like any sane person would order on a ninety-seven degree day, when Noah grins at me through the opening between the kitchen and the area behind the counter.

"Hi," he says.

"Hey," I grab some frozen nuggets from the bag and plop them into the fryer basket, then settle it into the hot oil. Steam rises up, making it even hotter than it already is, and I push my hair out of my face. Ugh. I'm all sticky and gross.

"So I think the AC guys really are on their way," he says. Noah's wearing his white Cooley's T-shirt and a pair of crisp black pants, and he somehow looks fresh and put together, even though it's like a million bazillion degrees in here.

"What makes you think that?" I ask.

"Well, they—"

"Hannah!" Lacey yells, rushing behind the counter. Her red hair is a frizzy mess around her head, and the strands that aren't flying every which way are plastered to her fore-head. She grabs my arm.

"Lacey," I say. "Please don't grab me, it's way too hot for that." I take a bottle of water out of the cooler, uncap the top, and down a quarter of it. One of the perks of working here is free cooler drinks and fountain sodas, which totally comes in handy on a day like today.

"He's here," Lacey says, her face all flushed from the combination of heat and excitement.

"Who's here?" I'm confused.

"Who do you think?" she says. "Riker! He's here!"

Noah and I give each other a look, an *oh my God, this could definitely be bad* kind of look. I glance over Lacey's shoulder and peer around the corner of the kitchen. There, sitting in a booth, is Riker. He's wearing tight black skinny jeans and a black Ed Hardy T-shirt. "God, what a poser," I say. "Not to mention, I think Ava bought him that shirt."

"Complete tool," Noah agrees, "His jeans are so tight his balls are probably going to be rendered useless."

"Can that really happen?" Lacey asks, sounding inter-ested. I shoot Noah a look. He should know better than to get her going on illnesses. At least it's one that can only hap-pen to a guy. Otherwise she'd totally start to think she had it.

"Anyway," I say. "So do you want me to go out there and wait on him?"

"Yes," she says. "Would you? I would do it, you know I would, but—"

The door opens then, the tinkling of bells echoing through the restaurant, and I look up to see a girl who looks kind of familiar walking into the diner. She's wearing really short denim shorts and a flowy pink top. Her platform sandals are super high, and she has a pair of sunglasses perched on top of her head. She looks around, then heads toward the back of the restaurant, and slides into the booth with Riker.

"Uh-oh," I say. "That's not . . ."

"Danielle!" Lacey says, her eyes narrowing. "I cannot believe she had the nerve to come here with him."

"Don't worry," I say, reaching over and squeezing her shoulder. "You just stay back here. Have Noah make you one of those apple walnut salads you love."

"Stay back here?" Noah asks, sounding panicked. "For how long?"

"Until they're gone." I grab two menus from behind the counter, not bothering to wipe them off. Danielle definitely doesn't deserve to have a clean menu. She can put up with something a little bit sticky, since she stole Lacey's boyfriend. Not to mention that the last time she was here, she gave me attitude and poured a whole glass of water on one of our tables. A whole glass of water that *I* had to clean up. Not that it was that hard. But still.

"Until they're *gone*?" Noah says. "But that could be, like, an hour. How are we supposed to work with just the two of us? It's almost lunchtime!"

"You cook and I'll wait tables," I say to him, rolling

my eyes. "It'll be just like it always is, except we'll pretend Lacey's on a break."

"For an hour during the lunch rush?"

"Make it work," I say, just like they do on *Project Runway*. I give Lacey's shoulder another little squeeze, then slide out from behind the counter and march over to Riker's table.

"Oh, hello," I say, sliding the menus down in front of them. "Welcome to Cooley's." I turn to Danielle. "I'm Hannah. I think I've waited on you before."

"Thanks." Danielle takes the menu and looks kind of bored. She's totally pretending that she has no memory of our little interaction a couple of weeks ago. Talk about passive-aggressive.

"Hey, Hannah," Riker says, giving me a big grin. "How are you?" I narrow my eyes. What is wrong with him? I mean, seriously. He has to know that I know that he stalked Ava. He knows we're best friends. He knows that we were just in Starbucks a couple of weeks ago, and Ava was getting totally creeped out by him. Not to mention the fact that he cheated on Lacey with her best friend. So why does he think it's okay to say hi to me?

"What can I get you two?" I hope my tone conveys that they deserve each other.

"I'll have peach pie with vanilla ice cream," Riker says.

"Just a Diet Coke for me," Danielle says.

"Great," I say, forcing false cheer into my voice. So basically the whole bill will come out to about seven dollars, and they'll probably leave me, like, a fifty cent tip. Also they're taking up an entire booth that can seat up to six people, and they're only a party of two. So annoying.

"What did they say?" Lacey demands once I'm back behind the counter.

"They said they're both scum-sucking assholes."

"No, seriously." She bites her lip and her green eyes are serious.

"Nothing." I shrug. "He ordered peach pie and she ordered some Diet Coke."

"Oh." Lacey's eyes get all watery, and I realize she was hoping they had said something about her.

"Look," I say, grabbing a glass and sliding it into the ice cubes, then sticking it under the soda fountain. I hit the button for Diet Coke, and the soda comes shooting out into the glass. The fryer behind me beeps, and, without missing a beat, I swing around and pull up the fry basket, letting it drain for a minute. "You shouldn't be wasting even one second of your time on them." I look her in the eye. "Listen to me: They are dead to you."

"Okay." She doesn't look so sure. The bells over the door tinkle again, and I look up to see three repairmen coming into the store, dressed in dark blue overalls. They're either the AC repairmen, or a bunch of random repairmen coming in to have lunch. At this point, I don't really care. If they're random, they're going to have to work for their lunch by fixing the damn air conditioner.

"Now listen," I say to Lacey. "I'm going to send the AC guys back here, and you're going to show them where the air conditioner is, okay?"

"Okay." Lacey nods, like she can handle this.

"I'm going to work on the lunch rush with Noah, and once Riker and Danielle are gone, you're going to come out and help, okay?"

She nods again.

"And then later, we're going to talk about this. Got it?"

"Got it."

I redo my ponytail, slice a piece of peach pie, plop some ice cream on top, grab the Diet Coke, and head back out into the dining room.

But it doesn't really work out. My whole plan to talk Lacey through her trauma, I mean. She gets so upset that she can't come out of the back room, and then one of the repairmen gets really nervous because she won't stop crying, and so finally Lacey has to go home. The rest of the day is completely crazy with me as the only waitress. (Seriously, at one point I look at the amount of people waiting for their orders to be taken, and consider just bursting into tears and/or walking out the door.) Noah and I are kept so busy that we don't even have time to eat, so once we close, he makes us French fries, cheeseburgers, and onion rings and we sit down at the counter with our feast.

"So this," Noah says, "is Sting. Do you like it?"

"What's Sting?" I ask. I sniff the air around him, assuming it's some kind of scent. You know, like, Sting by Tommy Hilfiger or something. Noah's not the type that wears cologne. Not that I know what type he is or anything, I've just never known him to wear cologne before, but maybe it's something new he's trying out. I get really close to him and smell his neck. But I don't smell cologne. I just smell laundry soap and shaving cream and boy.

"Sting," he says. "You know, the musician? The one you thought wore wraparounds?"

"Oooh," I say. I realize he's not talking about some new cologne, but about the song that's playing. Ever since that day at the ice-cream stand, when he found out that I actually have Lady Gaga and the Jonas Brothers on my iPod, Noah's been on a mission to get me interested in "better" music. He even brought in his iPod and a dock, which he hooked up to the diner's speaker system, and now, whenever we're cleaning up after all the customers have gone home, he makes me and Lacey listen to what he thinks is "good" music. Although, Lacey's not as bad as me when it comes to music. She listens to bands that sound familiar but I've never really heard, like Modest Mouse and Hole and The Ting Tings. Their names alone make them sound trendy. And let's face it, nothing is as humiliating as The Jonas Brothers.

"Sting's the one in U2, right?" I ask, then take a sip of my drink. Of course, now I know that Sting was in the Police, but it's fun to tease Noah and watch how pained he gets. It's like every musician or song I don't know is an attack on him.

"Oh, God," he says. He stands up. "All right, I didn't want to have to do this, but I think I'm going to have to use tough love on you now."

"I thought you already were by making me listen to this stuff."

"This *stuff*?" He drops his head onto the counter, as if he can't take it anymore. "This *stuff*," he says, "is some of the best music to, like, ever exist. You do realize that, right?"

"You can't dance to it." I shrug. "And you can't really sing along, and, like, it's not that sad."

"Sad?"

"Yes," I say. "I'm very into sad music right now, for obvious reasons." But as I'm saying it, I realize it's not completely true. I *am* into sad music right now, but at the same time, I haven't had a really bad day since Lacey and I drove by Sebastian's house. In fact, every day since then has gotten a little bit better. I'm actually kind of proud of myself.

"Okay," Noah says, stroking his chin thoughtfully. "I think I understand the problem now. We're obviously going to have to ease you into this."

"Ease me into what?"

"This whole music thing." Noah reaches over me and snags a fry off my plate, then pops it into his mouth. I swallow. Hard. Something about the way he did that, the way he just reached over and grabbed my food like that. . . . It felt . . . almost intimate. Suddenly, I'm super aware of his closeness, the way his hair flops over his eyebrow, the crispness of his T-shirt sleeve where it hits his bicep.

Stop it, I tell myself. *He's Ava's boyfriend, and he took a French fry off your plate. It's nothing to get all freaked out about.* In fact, it's perfectly normal, probably. And the fact that my stomach is flipping all around now means nothing, except I'm obviously starved for male attention. I wonder if I still have Jonah Moncuso's number in my cell. He never called me after that night we made out, but maybe he'd be up for hanging out again.

He reaches over and takes another French fry off my plate. See? Just two friends, sharing French fries, la, la, la.

"You're obviously not ready for Sting or anything like that," Noah's saying.

"I am so ready for Sting!" I mean, I think I am. I want to be, at least.

"No," he says. "You're not." He reaches into his back pocket and pulls out a wrinkled piece of paper, which he unfolds and sets on the counter. "Now I wasn't going to go to this, because I'm exhausted and hot and sweaty and I still need to write tonight, but this . . . this is a drastic circumstance."

I peer down at the paper. "'The Spill Canvas,'" I read. "'Tonight, at The Middle East.'" I look at Noah. "It's a band?"

"Yes," he says. "Now, they're not on the level of Sting, or anything even remotely like that, but for our purposes, they'll do. They play a lot of really sad music," he explains.

"But they're actually a great group, and you wouldn't have to be embarrassed about having them on your iPod."

"Who's embarrassed?" I say, shrugging and eating another fry. "So you're going to put on some of their music?"

"No," he says. "We're going to the concert."

I stare at him incredulously. Is he crazy? "No we're not," I say. "I'm exhausted, and I have to be back here at six a.m." The only places I'm going are the shower and my air-conditioned bedroom.

"You're kidding, right?" Noah says.

"No."

"Hannah, you're a teenager. You're not supposed to be too tired to go to a show."

"But you just said *you* were too tired to go."

"That's different."

"How come?"

He hesitates, like he doesn't really want to say what he's about to say, but thinks I might need to hear it. "Hannah," he says gently. "How much have you gotten out this summer?"

"I get out," I say defensively.

"I don't mean watching TV with Lacey," he says. "I mean out-out."

I open my mouth to protest, but then close it. I realize he's right. I'm young. It's summer. I should be out and about, living my life.

"Fine," I say, popping the last fry into my mouth. "But you're driving."

❅ ❅ ❅

"Over there," I say, bouncing up and down in the passenger seat and pointing to an empty spot on the street. "Right there, right there!"

Noah expertly navigates the car into the space that's just opened up a couple of blocks from The Middle East. Which is totally lucky, since we're in Cambridge, and it's, like, impossible to find a parking spot here at this time of night.

"Good eye," Noah says, shifting the car into park and cutting the engine.

"It's one of my gifts," I tell him, shrugging and pretending to sound modest. I unbuckle my seatbelt. "My hidden talents are instinctively choosing the most horrible music and being able to spot open parking spaces from a mile away." I look down at what I'm wearing. "Are you sure this is okay for a rock concert?"

Noah sighs, and then puts his head down on the steering wheel, the same gesture he made back at the diner when I asked if Sting was in U2. "It's not a rock concert," he says, his voice muffled against the steering wheel.

"It's not?" I frown. "I thought you were taking me to a rock concert."

"It's not rock," he says. "It's more like . . . I don't know, emo, alternative, that kind of thing."

"I guess," I say doubtfully. "But anyway, is what I'm wearing okay?"

I insisted that Noah take me home to change before we

headed to Cambridge to see the show. He told me there was a chance we would miss the first opening act, but I wasn't too concerned about that, since I'd obviously never heard of them. I mean, I'd never even heard of the headliners. Plus, when I went to see a Justin Timberlake concert once, the opening act was pretty horrible, some Disney girl-band that everyone booed.

So Noah took me home and waited in the car while I changed into dark jeans, boots, and a low-cut black T-shirt that's tight around my boobs. I darkened my eye makeup and tied a bandana in my hair to make it look kind of like a head-band, leaving my hair down and flowing. I look cute. Edgy. But not too edgy.

"You look great," Noah says. He reaches over me and opens the door. "Door's broken," he says. "You have to jiggle it just right." His arm brushes against mine as he pulls back, and I feel that same rush of energy that passed through me earlier. *Stop*, I tell myself. *You're just tired. And Noah's a boy, and you're broken-hearted and obviously going a little bit crazy.*

I step out onto the sidewalk, and as if on cue, my phone rings. Ava.

"It's Ava," I say, holding it up.

"Oh." Noah looks at me over the top of his car, where he's still standing in the street. He gets a weird look on his face. "Um, could you not tell her you're with me?"

"How come?"

He slams his car door shut and comes over to stand next

to me on the sidewalk, stepping close to avoid all the people that are passing by. I inhale his scent again, then take a small step back so I don't give his closeness another chance to mess with my head.

"It's not a big deal," he says, "I just—" He's trying to explain before the phone stops ringing, but it's too late. Ava goes to voicemail, which will almost definitely piss her off. Ava hates getting sent to voicemail. She says everyone always has their cell phones with them, so if she gets someone's voicemail, she knows that person just doesn't want to talk to her. Turns out, she's right.

"Are you going to call her back?" Noah asks. We're still standing awkwardly on the sidewalk, emo kids filing by us on their way to The Middle East, their voices blending together and getting swallowed up by the other sounds of the city.

"No," I say. "She'll want to talk for a while, and we're . . . I mean, we're going into the concert, right?"

"The show," Noah corrects. "And yeah."

We don't move for a second. I'm waiting for him to explain why he didn't want Ava to know he was out with me, and something passes between us that I'm pretty sure both of us can feel, even though neither one of us says anything. It's not any kind of attraction, even though I've been feeling that on and off all night. This is something different.

We have a secret now. A secret from Ava. He still doesn't say anything, and I think about asking him again why he didn't want her to know, but I have a feeling doing that would lead to more questions and a whole long conversation, and right now I just want to have fun.

So when Noah finally says, "You ready?" I push all my misgivings aside and follow him toward the club.

Three hours later, we emerge from The Middle East. My hair's a mess, I'm a little buzzed from the beer I convinced someone with a wristband to buy me (and when I say convinced, I mean I paid them twenty dollars, but it was so totally worth it), my ears are ringing (but in a good way), and I feel completely high.

"That," I say. "Was awesome." I twirl around in the cool air, which feels nice after how hot it was in there.

"Whoa, watch out, Mustang Sally," Noah says, as I almost go careening into a girl who's coming out of the club with her mom.

"Sorry," I say to the girl.

"No worries," she says, and gives me a big smile. I love it! It's like we're all in this together! Just two girls, out and about, going to emo shows, hanging out in Cambridge. It's like we're real hipsters or something!

"So you liked the show?" Noah asks as we walk toward the car. "Or is that the beer talking?"

"No, it's not the beer talking," I say indignantly. And it isn't. Yeah, the beer definitely helped a little bit, but the way I'm feeling now has nothing to do with beer, and everything to do with the fact that, for the first time in a long time, I'm having fun. For the past few hours, I wasn't worried about Sebastian, or what was going to happen when I got back to school and saw him, or what he was doing with the pink Jeep girl. In fact, it was the last thing on my mind. And it wasn't because I was zoned out in front of the TV or busy at work. It was because I was actually enjoying myself.

Although, if I'm being completely honest, even when I was *with* Sebastian, I was always worried: worried he might break up with me, worried I would say the wrong thing, worried he wouldn't like what I was wearing, worried we wouldn't stay together. And tonight, for a few hours, I wasn't worried about *anything*. I just danced and drank and had fun.

"That really was amazing," I say as I climb into Noah's car. My bandana headband is wet with sweat, so I take it out of my hair and reach into my bag for a hair tie, then pull my hair up into a ponytail.

"I'm glad you liked it," Noah says, giving me a smile. It's one of those smiles you give someone you think has been sheltered, the kind of smile a mom would give their kid the first time they give them ice cream or something.

"Hey," I say as Noah gets ready to start the car.

"Yeah?" he says, pausing before he turns the key in the ignition. He looks at me.

"Thanks," I say.

"You're welcome." He smiles at me again, and my stomach does the same flip it's been doing all night. But this time I'm in too good of a mood to care.

* * *

I oversleep, of course. Noah and I didn't get home until almost two a.m., and since we have to be at work at six, sleeping through my alarm was kind of a given. So when he pulls into my driveway the next morning at five forty-five, I'm not even close to being ready. I yell out the window, "Just one second!" then quickly pull on yesterday's shorts and scramble around for my Cooley's T-shirt. I spritz some perfume on myself, run a brush through my hair, wash my face, and smear on some foundation and cover-up.

"Sorry," I say when I'm finally in Noah's car. I settle into the passenger seat and he holds a coffee out to me wordlessly. "You actually stopped at Starbucks?" I ask incredulously and take it. I figured Noah would be way too tired to even think about getting us coffee. I know it only takes a few minutes to stop, but when you're dead-tired, even those couple minutes of sleep are precious. Seriously. Sometimes, during the school year, I can totally notice a difference in my mood based on how many times I've pressed the snooze button.

"Of course I stopped," Noah says, "I knew you'd kill me if I showed up without your latte." His voice sounds a little bit hoarse, and there's stubble on his cheeks, but besides that he looks great. His hair is slightly rumpled, but more in an adorable kind of way, not an "I was out super late at a concert and now I'm late for work" kind of way. God, boys have it so easy.

I gulp down the coffee, letting it warm my body and start to wake me up. I don't even care that it burns my tongue, since it seriously might be the best thing I've ever tasted.

"So how'd you sleep?" Noah asks as he pulls the car out of my driveway and into the street.

"For the whole three hours? Okay. You?"

"I slept great." Figures. Of course he did. Although I'm starting to feel a little more awake already. There's a slight headache behind my eyes, but even that's pretty mild compared to what it could be, and my ears are a little clogged up from the loud music, but it's not horrible or anything.

And then I remember something about last night, something that makes me blush. When we got back to my house, I invited Noah inside. Like I said, it was first time in a long time that I'd actually felt really happy, and I just didn't want the night to end.

The whole way home, I'd been singing along with the Spill Canvas album Noah had downloaded to his iPod, and I guess I was getting caught up in the moment. And so when he went to drop me off, I turned to him and said, "Slushies?"

And he was all, "What?" and so I was like, "Slushies. Do you want to come in for a slushie?"

And he got this kind of weird look on his face, the same kind of weird look that he got when he looked at me over the top of his car last night and told me not to tell Ava we were together. And then he said, "Not tonight, it's late."

So then I said, in this super teasing voice, "But Noah, we're young, remember? Come on, I'll even let you have some Keebler cookies."

"I really can't," Noah said. He said that he needed to get to sleep, which made total sense at the time. But now I'm thinking that maybe he said no because he thought I wanted him to come inside so that we could . . . Oh, God. There's no way he could have thought that, right? Especially if he slept great last night. If he thought I wanted to seduce him, he would have been up all night, tossing and turning, wondering how weird it was going to be when he had to tell me that not only was he not interested in me like that, but that he was going to have to tell Ava about what I'd tried to do.

Ava! Ohmigod, I completely forgot about her! I never called her back last night! I pull my phone out of my purse. One lone bar of power stares up at me, along with ten missed calls from Ava, and three texts asking where I am. Damn. She's going to want to know what I was doing last night. Why doesn't Noah want me to tell her we were hanging out? And can I *still* not tell her?

I fire off a quick text even though I know Ava's probably not awake yet, telling her I'm sorry and to call or text me as soon as she wakes up. I want to ask Noah what I'm supposed to tell her when she does, but something tells me it's probably not a good idea. So I lean back in my seat, take another huge sip of my coffee, and decide to look on the bright side.

The bright side being that at least I'm not obsessing about Sebastian anymore. I really am totally getting over him. And it didn't even take that long! Yay!

And then we're pulling into the parking lot of the diner, and like some kind of terrible joke, there's his truck. Sebastian's. Right by the front door, parked in the first parking space. It really is just like a horrible prank. Like fate or God or whoever decided to look down at me and say, "You think you're over him, huh? Well, we'll show you!" and then zapped his truck right into the diner parking lot.

"What the hell is *he* doing here?" Noah asks, pulling his car into an empty spot and peering through the window. Sebastian's standing by the front door of the diner, smoking a cigarette, one hand shoved in his pocket.

"I don't know," I say. "Coming for an early breakfast?"

But it doesn't seem that way. Because as soon as he spots us, Sebastian walks over to Noah's car and leans down so that he's looking right at me through the open passenger window. "Hey, Hannah," he says. "Can we talk?"

The First Day of Senior Year

"There has to be someone else," Ava says. She's picking through her salad, which she tried to order with organic salad dressing and organic carrots. Apparently carrots are more likely to be genetically engineered than other vegetables, so it's super important that you only eat organic ones. It's something Lulu taught her, and it makes no sense to me, but whatever. I'm trying to give Ava the benefit of the doubt, since I know how it is when people get their heart broken. They kind of lose their minds. I ate ice cream and refused to wash my clothes; Ava has apparently decided to obsess over vegetables.

"Why do you say that?" I ask.

"Because," she says. "He wouldn't just dump me out of nowhere." She looks at me across the table. "So you still haven't answered me. Did you notice anything this summer? Who was he hanging around with?"

"No one," I say honestly. "I told you, he was working the whole summer."

"It was probably someone he works with then," she says. She takes in a huge breath through her nose. "Some little trollop who paraded around and, like, mopped the floors for him so he could get out early with her and they could go to some dumb party."

"We do a lot more than mop the floors around here," I say, not that loud.

"What?"

"Nothing." I eat another fry, even though I've totally lost my appetite.

"I hope it's not that Lacey girl," Ava says. "Did you know that she was going out with Riker? And was, like, devastated when he dumped her? She must be really bad in bed."

"Lacey and Noah are not together," I say, my hands gripping the sides of the table.

"I should hope not," she says. She leans closer to me and motions me forward. "I heard she has some kind of weird anxiety disorder, one that makes her keep wanting to sanitize her hands."

"It's not an anxiety disorder," I say, rolling my eyes. Although, now that I think about it, it probably is. You don't become convinced that you have every disease in the book without having *some* kind of anxiety disorder. But still. It's the way Ava says it, like Lacey is totally crazy instead of just a little bit of a hypochondriac. So what if she sanitizes her hands? And so what if she's always at the doctor? It doesn't make her a bad person. It just makes her a little . . . different.

Besides, Lacey's getting a lot better. And Ava shouldn't be so judgmental.

"Whatever." Ava looks down at her salad and takes another dainty bite. "I'm just so glad that I'm back now, and that me and you are together. I missed you so much, I should never have gone away for the summer. I mean, Lulu was nice, but she wasn't you. No one is you."

"I missed you too," I say. I take a sip of my soda, suddenly confused. This is what Ava does to me. One second I want to kill her, and the next second she's being sweet and making me miss her.

"Now that I'm back, we're going to get things normal again," she says, her eyes all determined. "I'm going to find out whoever this slut is that Noah thinks he wants, and I'm going to have a talk with her. Noah and I are going to get back together, and then we're going to find you someone, and then things will be great again." She smiles.

"Sounds good," I say weakly.

"What's wrong with you?" she demands. "You're acting weird."

"No, I'm not."

"Yes, you are."

"I'm probably just tired," I say. "I worked, like, fifty hours this week."

"Ugh, you have to quit this ridiculous job." She looks around the diner, like she can't believe that anyone would voluntarily spend time here. Which makes sense. The diner is kind of gross. And hot. But let's face it, this place kind of saved me this summer.

"I'm not quitting," I say a little too quickly, panicked at the thought. If I quit, when would I see Noah?

"Yes, you are," she says. "We can't have a fabulous senior year if you're at work all the time. Besides, you already got your car, and wasn't that the point?"

"I'm not quitting my job," I say. "I like it."

Ava rolls her eyes. "Don't be ridiculous," she says. "You don't like this job."

"Yes, I do."

"No, you don't."

"Yes, I do." I pop another French fry into my mouth to keep myself from blowing up on her and saying something I shouldn't. "You wouldn't really know," I finally say. "What I like and what I don't. Because you weren't here this summer."

A look flashes across her face for a split second, like she can't believe I brought up the fact that she took off and left me for the summer. But she doesn't look guilty. It's more like shock. Which makes sense, because I never really bring this stuff up with her, figuring it won't do any good. Seeing things from other people's points of view has never been one of Ava's strengths.

"You only liked the job this summer because I wasn't around," she jokes, reaching over and taking one of my fries, probably as a gesture of apology since she's suddenly so into eating only organic. "And now that I'm back, you won't need to kill time here."

"That's true," I say, before I realize I'm falling right back into our old pattern, where Ava makes me think that whatever it is she wants me to do is right, and I go along with it, because . . . I don't know why. Because I don't trust myself to know what I want? It's like that night I made out with Jonah Mancuso. I didn't really *want* to do it, but Ava said it was a good idea. So I did. And now it's the same thing. She's trying to get me to quit my job, which I don't want to do, but she's making it seem like it's the best choice.

"And seriously, you probably only liked this job because you were trying to get over Sebastian," she says. "You were trying to bury yourself in your work. Only usually when people do that, they're, like, high-powered lawyers or something, not waitresses." She laughs, but I don't.

I just take another fry and eat it.

"We should do something fun tonight," she tries. "We could go to Cure. Noah could probably get us in."

I stare at her. "But you and Noah broke up," I say. Has she forgotten the last few minutes, the last hour? Is she crazy?

"Yeah, but we'll be back together by the end of the day." She says it with such certainty that, suddenly, my blood is boiling. It's like a switch—one second I'm on a low simmer and the next I'm at a full-blown boil, like one of those stoves that can boil water in thirty seconds.

"No you won't," I say quietly. And it's not even that I believe it, even though I do. And it's not that I feel the way I did a few minutes ago, and think I need to tell her what happened because she's my best friend. It's that I want to hurt her, to let her know that she can't just come back here and pretend like everything is the same. *She* left us this summer, *she* pushed me to do what I did last night, and *she's* the one who should be feeling horrible about herself.

"Yes, we will," Ava says confidently. But there must be something in the way I'm looking at her that makes her nervous. Because she looks at me and asks haltingly, "Why wouldn't we be?"

"Because," I say, relishing it. "Noah did meet someone over the summer. And that someone was me."

The Summer

Sebastian's wearing a pair of jeans and a T-shirt that looks soft and worn from being washed so many times. And even though I just said that I was over him, that it was the first day in a long time I hadn't thought about him, when I see him here, so close, my heart catches in my throat, and suddenly, I feel like I can't breathe.

"Um, yeah," I say. "We can talk, just . . . wait for me by the door, okay?"

He nods, and then heads back toward Cooley's. I watch him go, his strides long and easy, and I remember how I would see him coming from down the hall, down the street, from far away, wherever, and I could recognize him just from his walk.

Noah leans down in the driver's seat and looks out the passenger-side window, watching as Sebastian walks away. "You okay?" he asks.

"Yeah," I lie. "I'm fine." A rush of emotions are pulsing through my body, and suddenly I'm back at Jenna's party, remembering what it felt like that night when I was standing there by the pool in my bikini with my clothes in my hand, watching Sebastian kiss another girl.

"You sure?" Noah asks. He reaches over and squeezes my hand, and another pulse of electricity goes through me. I pull my hand back like it's on fire. What the hell is wrong with me? How can I be getting all crazy thinking about Sebastian kissing another girl one minute, and then freaking out when Noah takes my hand the next?

"Yes," I say. "I'm okay. I . . . I better go talk to him." I open the door to the car and walk right past Sebastian into the diner. He follows me, like I knew he would, and Noah stays in his car, I guess to give us some time alone. Lacey must be here, but she's probably in the back cooler getting stuff ready or outside talking on her phone, which she does a lot in the morning, especially if she's trying to arrange an appointment with a specialist.

"Hannah," Sebastian says.

I whirl around. "Do you want a table?" I ask, suddenly not really in the mood to hear his bullshit. "Because we don't really open for another fifteen minutes, so technically you should probably be waiting outside."

"No," he says, shuffling his feet on the floor. "I don't want a table. I came here to talk to you." His eyes seem sincere, but I'm too smart for that.

"Why?" I ask. My voice is somehow strong, which surprises me since my whole body feels like it's about to break out into shakes any second.

"Because we never talked. About what happened."

"There's nothing to talk about," I say. I turn my back on him, walk behind the counter, and start filling the salt and pepper shakers that are in front of each stool. I've imagined this moment so many times. Sebastian coming to talk to me, Sebastian coming to tell me he made a mistake, that he wants me back. And now that it's about to happen, I'm not feeling any of the things I thought I'd feel, like relief, or happiness, or contentment. All I'm feeling is angry.

"Yes, there is," he says. He takes a couple of steps behind the counter then, which is so totally against the rules. Cooley is always telling us that no one is allowed behind the counter except for employees. Something about liability and how if someone gets hurt back there, they're not covered by his insurance.

Which sounds like a load of bullshit to me, but I would totally pay right now for Sebastian to, like, slip on a banana peel or something. Which is actually almost impossible since we don't serve that many banana-flavored dishes. Unless you count banana splits, but hardly anyone ever orders those. Maybe I should offer one to Sebastian. Or maybe I should just injure him myself. I wonder if *that* would be a liability.

"I'm sorry," Sebastian says. "I didn't want things to end like this. I didn't want things to end at all."

"Is that what you told the girl you were with in the pool that night?" I say, which is totally bitchy. I'm kind of proud of myself for saying it, actually.

"That's over," he says simply, and shrugs. Like he can just move on from it like it's nothing.

"Sebastian, you cheated on me," I say, just in case he forgot.

"No I didn't," he says. "Not really. I mean, we only kissed. And it was only that one night." He's lying, obviously, because I saw the pink Jeep parked in front of his house that day. Of course, I can't tell him that, since that would tip him off that I'm a stalker. Which I'm not. At least not anymore.

"Hannah, are you okay?" Noah asks from the door. He takes a step into the diner, toward the counter, and Sebastian's eyes flick over to him.

"Yes," I say. "I'm fine."

"Are you done talking?" Noah asks, setting his jaw in a straight line and looking at Sebastian, even though the question is directed at me.

"No," Sebastian says.

"Yes," I say.

"Dude, you should leave," Noah says. His tone is slightly threatening, but more in a we-can-all-handle-this-without-any-problems kind of way. But underneath you can tell he really means *without any problems as long as you do what I say*. And of course Sebastian loves problems and hates doing what people say. My stomach clenches, and I take a deep breath to try to slow my heart rate down. But it isn't working. And I think it's because part of me is really excited that Noah is sticking up for me.

"I'm talking to Hannah," Sebastian says.

"She said she's done talking to you," Noah says, taking a step closer to the counter.

"Yeah, well, I'm not done talking to *her*." Sebastian takes a step away from me and toward Noah even though he just said he wasn't done talking to me. I guess he isn't done arguing with Noah either.

"Yes, you are," Noah says, then takes another step.

"Says who?" And now Sebastian is taking another step toward Noah and they're only a few steps away from each other. The whole thing is totally surreal, like some kind of weird gangster movie, or something, where you just know something is about to go down. Are they going to fight? Is Noah going to punch Sebastian? Is Sebastian going to punch Noah? Is one of them going to get really hurt? Should I try to break it up?

Adrenaline is coursing through my body, and I'm so tense I feel like I could explode. I'm not sure how I feel about this—about Sebastian being here, Noah barging in, and all of us standing here waiting to see what's going to happen. It's a strange feeling, to be completely on edge, your heart pounding, and really having no idea what you feel about anything.

"What's going on?" Lacey asks brightly, as she comes out of the back. "I didn't even hear you guys come in, usually you're so loud and . . ."

She trails off when she sees Sebastian. But something about her presence suddenly diffuses the tension in the room, and Sebastian turns away from Noah to look at me. "I'll call you later," he says, and then pushes past Noah, brushing against his arm angrily as he goes out the door.

"Ohmigod, ohmigod, ohmigod," I say. I rush around the counter, collapse onto one of the stools, close my eyes, and take deep breaths.

"Are you okay?" Lacey asks, rushing up to me and giving me a hug. "What was that asshole doing here?"

"He came to talk to me," I say.

"Are you serious?" She pulls back and looks at me incredulously, then reaches out and gives me another hug. "What a jerk! I cannot believe he would come to your work like that. And first thing in the morning?"

"He was probably out all night, partying and/or drinking." I turn around and look at Noah. "Thanks," I say.

I expect him to look at me and give me some kind of indication that he'll always have my back when it comes to Sebastian, or to at least say you're welcome or something like that, but all he does is nod and then heads into the back room without saying a word.

And he doesn't say a word to me for the rest of the day. Not when I'm giving him my orders. Not when someone finds a piece of burnt potato in their corned beef hash that they insist is a fly and I have to bring it back to him. Not when Cooley comes in and holds an employee meeting about food safety. And not when the people at table five send their meals back three times until Noah gets their burger perfectly medium-well.

By the end of the night, I'm starting to get a little nervous that Noah might be mad at me for some reason. And then I have a horrible thought: What if it has nothing to do with what happened with Sebastian? What if Noah knows what I was thinking last night? Or about how my body had a weird reaction this morning when he took my hand? But that's impossible, right? Unless Noah knows my secret thoughts, how could he tell? And if he's weirded out by it, why did he pick me up this morning and act like nothing was wrong?

Unless he just did it to be polite. Maybe he even told Ava about it, and she told him he should be nice to me, because I'm obviously broken-hearted and deluded. But then at some point, he realized he couldn't do it anymore, so he decided to just ignore me.

I think about this all day, and I'm still thinking about it after we close and I'm resetting the tables for the next day with napkins, forks, and knives.

"Those people really might have found a fly in their hash," Lacey's saying as she works next to me. "Because I have bug bites all over me."

"Flies don't bite," I tell her.

"Yes, they do. Not common houseflies, I don't think, but, like, pinscher flies."

"Pinscher flies?" I ask, setting a knife down next to a spoon and making sure the ketchup bottle on the table is full.

"Yeah, you know, pinscher flies?"

"No," I say. "I've never heard of them."

"Well, look at this," she says, pulling up her sleeve. "That's a pinscher fly bite if I ever saw one."

"That's a mosquito bite," I tell her firmly. Then I go behind the counter to start rinsing out the coffee pots. I've learned that the best way to handle Lacey when she's like this is to be forceful and tell her there's nothing wrong. If you show even a little bit of weakness, she'll freak out and start googling. And once she starts googling, forget it. She starts getting all sorts of worked up.

My phone starts vibrating, and I pull it out of my pocket to look at the screen. Ava. I send it to voicemail, deciding I'll call her back as soon as I'm done here. It's been so busy that I haven't had a chance to talk to her even though she's been texting me all day.

I think about how different my summer would be if she was here. We'd be at her pool every day, hanging out and reading magazines, gossiping about celebrities, and listening to music. Maybe we would have even prank-called Sebastian a couple of times, or spray-painted something on his lawn. I wouldn't be here in the sweltering diner, listening to Lacey talk about her bug bite, and wondering if Noah is mad at me or if Sebastian is coming back.

My phone rings again. Ava. Again. She tends to do that—keeps calling if it goes to voicemail, hoping that you'll think it's an emergency and pick up the phone. Whenever I do give in and pick up, she always just says, "It's about time" in a really annoyed voice, and then I get annoyed with her *and* with myself for falling for her trick. But what if she did talk to Noah? What if Noah told her how weird I was acting, and now she's calling to yell at me? What if it really is an emergency this time?

No, I tell myself again as firmly as I told Lacey her spot is just a bug bite. That's crazy. I send the call to voicemail, but the phone starts ringing in my hand almost immediately. I sigh.

"I have to take this outside," I say.

"Sure," Lacey says. "Take your time, I got it in here." Noah, of course, shows no sign of hearing me.

"Hey," I say into the phone as I push through the door of the diner and go outside to the sidewalk. I force myself to sound bright and cheerful, like *haha, nothing to see here, I wasn't fantasizing about your boyfriend*. "What's going on? How are you? I miss you?" The last one comes out as a question, which sounds weird, even to me.

"Why are you being weird?" Ava asks.

"I'm not being weird." I plop down on a bench, then reach down and roll up the shorts I'm wearing so that they're a little shorter than they already are. If I thought it was hot in the diner, it's about a million times hotter out here.

"Yes you are," Ava says. She sounds exasperated. "You're being all falsely cheerful, what's wrong?"

"Nothing," I say.

"You're lying," Ava says. "Noah told me all about it."

"He did?" I croak. I blink hard a few times, my vision getting all spotty from the hot sun that's beating down on me. For a second, I wonder if I'm going to faint, and I put my head down between my legs.

"Yeah," she says. "About how Sebastian showed up there this morning, completely blindsiding you." Oh, thank God! She's asking about Sebastian, not Noah. Which means that she doesn't know, which means that Noah might not know. But if he doesn't, then why is he ignoring me? Unless he knows and just didn't tell Ava? Jesus, this is horrible. What the hell am I going to do? *Nothing*, I tell myself. *You're going to do nothing*. Big deal that you had a weird moment with Noah. Well, a couple of weird moments. A couple of weird moments that included him telling me about his screenplay, him telling me not to let Ava know that we were hanging out, and me getting completely turned on when he took my hand. Not to mention how I felt when we were sharing French fries last night. Wow. That's really a lot more than a couple of moments.

"Hello!" Ava yells. "Are you there?"

"Sorry," I say, trying to collect my thoughts. "Um, yeah, Sebastian showed up here this morning, saying he wanted to talk to me." I realize that with all my Noah-obsessing, I haven't properly obsessed about Sebastian. What did he want exactly? Does he really want me back? Does he know I drove by his house? Does he know that I called him three times and hung up right after we broke up? (I totally *67'd my number to block it, but with technology these days, you never know when someone's going to invent a way to get around that. Nothing's private anymore, you know?) Do I even care?

"What happened?" Ava asks. "Tell me everything."

"I sent him away, of course. In fact, I gave him a total attitude." I feel like Ava should be proud of me for this, that she should tell me I did a great job, that she can't believe how strong I am. I mean, when she left I was a complete mess, just days off of my meltdown in Jenna Lamacchia's bathroom. Now here I am, sending Sebastian away. It's like I'm a completely new woman.

But there's just silence. Then, "Are you going to call him or anything?"

"No," I say. "Why would I call him?"

"Don't you want to hear what he has to say? Just in case he wants you back?"

I frown. What the hell is she talking about? All Ava has been saying since the night of Jenna's party is how much of a jerk Sebastian is, how I'm way too good for him, how I need to move on and upgrade, and blah, blah, blah. "No-ooo," I tell her. "I don't want to hear what he has to say. Besides, I thought you said that I hated him. That *we* hated him."

"We do," she says, "I mean, we did. When he dumped you. Now that maybe he wants you back, it's kind of a different story."

"Why?"

"I don't know," she says, sounding uncomfortable. "It just is." It sounds kind of like she's implying I'm not going to do any better. So as long as Sebastian broke up with me, it was fine to say he was a loser, but now that he might want to get back together, I should go for it because I'm not going to do any better.

"Are you saying that I can't do better?"

"Hannah, don't be ridiculous," she says. "I would never say that." But she doesn't deny that she's thinking it.

I'm about to press her on it, when Lacey comes running out of Cooley's. "Hannah!" she yells. "I have to go to the hospital!" I roll my eyes and am about to tell her that I really cannot deal with her freak-outs right now, but she shoves her arm in my face. Her bite, which just a few minutes ago was the size of a dime, is now the size of a half-dollar, with an angry red border all around it.

"That doesn't look so good," I say honestly.

"I know!" she says, panicked. "Noah said I should probably have it looked at."

"Does it hurt?"

"No," she says. "But it kind of itches." She looks confused. "In fact, my whole body kind of itches." She lifts up her shirt and starts scratching.

"Who's that?" Ava asks. "And what did she say about Noah?"

"It's Lacey," I say. "She works with us."

"Lacey Adams?" Ava says. "Ugh, the one who can't get over Riker? I can't stand that girl."

"I have to go," I tell Ava. Lacey's still scratching, only now, her stomach is covered with angry-looking red bumps.

"Wait!" Ava says. "Can you tell Noah that—"

"Ava," I say. "I have to go." And for the first time in my whole life, I hang up on her.

The First Day of Senior Year

Ava laughs. A big, loud laugh that echoes off the walls of Cooley's. I've just told her that I'm the one who's been seeing Noah, and she's laughing. Of course, *seeing* isn't really the right word, I guess. Neither is "sleeping with" since that implies it's been going on for a while, and it wasn't. But it was building all summer, and although I'm probably not the reason he broke up with her, I must have at least had something to do with it, even if I was just a symptom of some problem they were having.

"What did you say?" she asks finally, when she realizes I'm not laughing back.

"I said," I tell her quietly, "that Noah and I were together this summer. Not, like, the whole summer. We just . . . it happened last night." Last night, in the back, here, up against the counter, on the floor, Noah's hands in my hair and on my back, and . . . I take a deep breath and hope Ava can't hear how fast my heart is beating from just thinking about it.

"Tell me," Ava says, gripping her fork, "that you're joking."

"I'm not."

A look comes over her face then, one I haven't seen since the sixth grade when Ava found out that Andrea Benson's mom was trying to make a move on Ava's dad. She found Andrea on the playground and started screaming at her, calling her mom a slut and a whore. She had to go to the school psychologist for the rest of the year, that's how crazy it was.

"I see," Ava says quietly. "Well. I guess that explains what happened when you two came to visit me this summer."

"Nothing was going on then," I say. Now that I've said it, that I've put it out there, I want to take it back. But now that I've told her, that I've done it, I can't. It's like, in the one moment I wanted to hurt her, I've ruined everything. I feel sick to my stomach, the French fries I just ate churning around and making me nauseous.

"Nothing was going on then?" She's talking really quietly, which is unnerving for some reason. I want some kind of yelling or screaming. I want her to ask me why, to call me a bitch and a traitor, something, anything other than talking quietly.

"No," I say. "Nothing is even really going on. It just . . . Last night something happened."

"What?" she asks. I don't answer, just look down at my napkin. "What happened?" she says again, this time her voice rising.

"We . . . we were here," I say. "At the diner. We were closing down, it was late, and . . . one thing led to another." I swallow and hope she doesn't ask me what I know she's probably going to ask me.

"Did you guys . . . Did you *sleep* with him?"

For a second, I think about lying. I wanted to tell her, I did, but now all I want to do is take it back, and so my first instinct is to do damage control and stop what I've started. But something inside me tells me that if I lie, it won't really matter. The damage is already done, and now the best thing I can do is get it all out there and hope that she can maybe forgive me.

"Yes," I whisper, looking her right in the eye. Ava looks back, her eyes blazing. And then she reaches across the table and slaps me.

The Summer

I never realized how scary hospitals were until now. I mean, I don't think I've ever really been in a hospital unless you count when I was born. Of course we're not actually in the *hospital*, we're just waiting in the emergency room, which for some reason actually seems scarier. I mean, the hospital at least has people who are already sick and diagnosed. The room out here is for people who have no idea what's wrong with them. Like, it could be *anything*. Or nothing, which I guess is the better way to look at it.

"What do you think's taking them so long?" Lacey asks from the seat next to me. Her leg is jittering up and down, and I reach over and put my hand on it. Lacey reaches out and squeezes my arm.

"Well," I say, "they obviously don't think it's a big deal or they would have carted you right back there."

"Or," Lacey says, "they probably know I'm going to die and so they're leaving me out here because they need to help the people who actually have a chance."

"Lacey," I say. "Did you see them bringing in the guy who was bleeding profusely from the head?"

"Yes," she says.

"If that guy has a chance, then you definitely do."

"True," she says. "Still, I feel like I'm going to faint." She puts her head down between her legs, and the tips of her red curls brush against the floor, which is definitely not sanitary. Who knows what kind of blood and guts have been on this floor.

"Sit up," I say. "Don't you want to watch *Judge Judy*?" I point toward the corner, where a flat-screen plasma TV is mounted on the wall. "You love her."

"I do love her," she agrees, fixing her eyes on the TV. But I can tell she's still nervous. I wish Noah were here. He went to park the car after dropping me and Lacey off in front so we could sign in and get seen as soon as possible. Not that there's that many people here. Besides the man with the gaping head wound (which was so not the visual we wanted when we first got here, let me tell you), the place is pretty dead.

The nurse comes out and looks at Lacey. "Lacey Adams?"

"Yes," Lacey says, twisting her hands in her lap nervously, and then standing up. "Yes, that's me."

"Should I come with you?" I ask.

"No," she says. "I'm okay. I'll text you if I need you." Then she kisses me on the top of my head and follows the nurse to the examination room.

I pick up a *Parents* magazine that's sitting on the table in an effort to distract myself from the yuck hospital smell, and page through an article about how to throw the perfect birthday party for your toddler. Which is completely pointless, since I don't have a toddler. I don't even know any toddlers. But you never know when that kind of thing could come in handy (and honestly, a lot of the sweet-sixteen parties I've been to have been almost like toddler parties, what with the crazy cakes and streamers and people pitching fits), and I kind of like that the emergency room has such fun reading. It's like they want you to be happy and keep your mind off everything, which I can totally appreciate even though Lacey probably just has hives or something. But if that man with the gaping head wound has any relatives that show up, I'm sure they'll appreciate the cheerful reading material.

"Hey," Noah says, loping into the waiting room. "Is she okay?"

"I don't know." I set the magazine back on the table as Noah slides his keys into his pocket and sits down next to me. "They took her to the back."

He nods, then reaches down and picks the magazine up. The same one I was just reading. Which is kind of rude, when you think about it. I mean, he doesn't know for sure that I was done with it. Maybe I was just taking a reading break.

"There's a great article in there about how to throw a birthday party for a two-year-old," I tell him.

"Oh yeah?" He keeps reading. And doesn't laugh.

"Yeah," I say. "You could throw one for a toddler you know, like if you had a little cousin."

"Thanks." Still reading.

"Are you mad at me or something?" I ask, because I don't really want to sit out here not talking, and also because I'm sick of driving myself crazy wondering if he's mad and what I did that's so bad he won't even say a word to me until we're in the waiting area of an emergency room.

"No," he says. But his eyes shift to the clock on the wall, like he's trying to figure out how long he's obligated to talk about this before making his escape. "Why would I be mad at you?"

"Because you've refused to talk to me all day."

"No, I haven't."

"Yes, you have." I wait, and when he doesn't say anything, I give up. If he's going to be a total asshole about this, then I'm done. I grab another magazine and start to read angrily. Well, I'm not sure you can really read angrily. But you can make it clear that you're upset by sighing a lot and ruffling the pages. Which is what I'm doing now.

"I'm not mad at you," Noah says after a few minutes of page ruffling.

"You already said that. And I don't really care anymore." Which is kind of true, kind of not. At the moment I don't care because I'm pissed. But later I'll probably end up caring a lot.

Noah keeps talking. "And if I *were* mad at you, I wouldn't ignore you. But I'm not, so it doesn't matter."

"Okay, good." I keep reading, skimming an article about how to make an apron out of an old sheet. It's actually pretty complicated and involves a glue gun, which I guess you should already have, otherwise you should probably just go out and buy an apron.

We read our articles in silence for a few minutes, and then Noah slams his magazine shut. "Can I talk to you outside for a second?" he asks.

"Why? There's no one here except for me, you, and Judge Judy." I fold my hands and look at him expectantly, waiting.

"Never mind," he says, this time sounding annoyed.

"*Fine*," I say, rolling my eyes, "We can go outside." I'm suddenly nervous. Going outside to have a talk? That sounds serious. And hot. Like, temperature-wise, I mean. "Well, we can talk. But can we go to the cafeteria or something? I'm thirsty and it's too hot to sit outside."

So we leave instructions with the triage nurse to tell Lacey to text us when she's done. (The triage nurse is this older woman who couldn't believe we would text each other such important information—I didn't have the heart to tell her that about five people I know have been broken up with by text message, and that it's how one girl I know found out her parents were getting divorced.) Then we head up to the hospital cafeteria. I grab an orange juice from the cooler and a turkey club out of the case, and plop them onto a tray. Noah gets a peanut butter and jelly sandwich, which is kind of funny. And a chocolate milk, which is even funnier.

"You're getting chocolate milk and peanut butter and jelly?" I ask as we wait for the cashier in a line behind two middle-aged doctors I'm hoping aren't in charge of Lacey. That's because while they're waiting in line, one of them shuts his beeper off without even looking at it. Which definitely cannot be good. I mean, what if there's some kind of surgery or something only he's qualified to do? And he misses it because he's too busy enjoying his roast beef sandwich? I know doctors have to eat, too, but still.

"Yeah." Noah looks down at his tray. "What's wrong with that?"

"Nothing," I say. "If you're seven."

"I don't think that ageism should be applied to food," he says. "I think people of all ages should be allowed to enjoy peanut butter and jelly. And Boost."

"Boost?"

"Yeah, you know, Boost? Like Ensure? It's a meal supplement old people take. It makes a very good after-workout protein shake."

"I wouldn't know," I say, "I'm not seventy." I'm trying to be haughty since he *did* ignore me all day, but inside, I think it's kind of cute. While most guys would be all macho and drink something like Muscle Milk, or whatever it's called, Noah's drinking Boost after his workouts. After his workouts, when he comes home all sweaty, his muscles bulging under a tight tank top. Not that I've ever seen Noah wear a tank top, but he probably wears them to work out, right? A tight one that stretches across his stomach and—

"Seven ninety-five," the cashier says, yanking me out of my daydream. Which is probably a good thing, since it was headed in an R-rated direction. I dig into my wallet and hand her my debit card.

We find an empty table in the middle of the cafeteria, away from the evening sunlight that's streaming through the windows. I take the seat across from Noah, careful to keep my tray from touching his and my legs on my own side of the table. I don't need any of my body parts accidentally brushing against his, thank you very much.

"So," I say as Noah opens his chocolate milk. "What do we need to talk about?" Please let it be something about work, please let it be something about work, please let it—

"Look," he says, sighing. "I don't want to make a big deal about it, but I don't think it's a good idea if you and I hang out." He's watching my face carefully for my reaction, but all I say is "Oh," mostly because I don't know what else to say. Honestly, I'm a little bit shocked. I never thought he would just come out and say it like that, like "you and I shouldn't hang out anymore." I mean, I knew something was up, but . . .

"Do you mind telling me why?" I ask before I can lose my nerve.

"I just . . . I don't know if it's a good idea," he says. "I guess it kind of freaked me out that I asked you to lie to Ava last night." He shakes his head, then unwraps his peanut butter and jelly sandwich and takes a bite, his face thoughtful.

"Yeah," I say slowly. "But why did you do that?" I take a sip of my drink. "I mean, who cares if Ava knows me and you were hanging out. She's the one who told you to look out for me, remember?" But even as I'm saying that, I know it's different. Like, Ava wanted Noah to make sure I was getting out of bed every day. I don't know how she'd feel if she knew he was taking me out to concerts, where there was fun and beer and lots of stomach flipping whenever Noah got close to me.

"Because of our problems," he says. He looks down at his tray, an embarrassed look on his face.

"Our problems?" I ask. "But we don't have any problems." Well, besides the fact that every time he's close to me, I feel like I want to pull him closer.

"No, not *our* problems, me and you, our problems, me and Ava."

Oh. Right. Of course he didn't mean that we were an "our." We're not an our, we're just Noah and Hannah. Noah and Hannah. That kind of has a nice ring to it, in a weird, biblical sort of way. Not that I'm religious or anything, but everyone knows about Noah and the Ark, and I'm pretty sure Hannah is some kind of religious name. Which is funny when you think about it, since my mom is, like, the least religious person ever. Actually, I might be thinking of the name Sarah. I wonder if there's a Sebastian in the bible.

"Wait a minute," I say. "What problems?"

"The problems Ava and I were having," he says. "You know, the reason she went away to camp for the summer?" He must be able to tell by the blank look on my face that I have no idea what he's talking about. "She didn't tell you?"

"Ava told me she was going away because her mom's friend needed a last-minute replacement," I say. I pick up my sandwich and force myself to take a bite, not sure how I feel about this bit of information. Noah and Ava were having problems? Why didn't she tell me?

Noah nods. "She probably didn't want you to hate me."

"Probably," I say, even though it's not true and Ava could probably care less if I hated Noah. In fact, if Ava really *was* having problems with Noah, she would definitely want me to hate him. "So do you want to tell me what's going on?" I try to act nonchalant, looking away and picking at an imaginary piece of lint that's supposedly on my shirt.

"I don't know," he says. He takes a sip of his chocolate milk and another bite of his peanut butter and jelly sandwich. "Ava probably wants to tell you herself."

"Probably," I say, knowing it's not true. If Ava wanted to tell me, she would have done it already. "But if you and I can't hang out, and if you want me to lie to her about where we were last night, don't you think I have a right to know what's going on?"

"I guess." He looks uncomfortable, but I can tell he's about to crack, and for some reason, this makes me feel a little panicked. I mean, let's take a minute to summarize the situation, shall we?

1. I am at the hospital waiting for my friend with Noah. Which is a very couple-like thing to do. All you have to do is watch any teen drama—anytime one of the characters is close to death and/or in a coma, the boyfriend/girlfriend teams always end up at the hospital together.
2. We are eating together. (Another coupley thing to do.)
3. We are talking about my best friend, his girlfriend, and their secret problems that she somehow neglected to tell me. Which means that Noah is the one telling me secrets that even my best friend won't.
4. I like it. All of it. Being here, eating food, telling secrets, everything.

This definitely needs to stop. I need to finish this illicit sandwich and get out of here ASAP. I shouldn't even have come to the cafeteria in the first place. I should be downstairs waiting for Lacey. I came here to be with *Lacey*, not to be eating food and sharing secrets with Noah, who ignored me all day.

But before I can put an end to all this madness, Noah starts to talk. "It all started a couple of months ago," he says.

"I was hanging out with my friends a lot and Ava didn't like that."

"Ava didn't like that?"

"No," he says. "Which was totally understandable. I mean, I wanted to spend time with her, she was my girl-friend." He realizes his mistake, that he's referring to Ava in the past tense and quickly corrects himself. "*Is* my girlfriend. But the problem was, she didn't really want to do the same things I did."

"Like what?" I ask, thinking about his comment the other night that Ava was going to end up marrying some rich doctor.

"Well, like shows for one."

"She didn't want to go to shows?" I say. "But that was so fun!"

"I know," he says. "But they're not really Ava's thing, you know?"

"True," I say. Ava doesn't like crowds and being hot and getting sweaty. Which is why it's weird that she went away to work at a summer camp.

"So we started getting into fights a lot. I would always invite her to things, but she didn't want to go. And then, finally, one night I didn't feel like dealing with a fight." He takes his straw wrapper and plays with it, twisting it around his finger. "So I lied to her about where I was going. And she found out. Two days later, she told me she was leaving for Maine."

"But you guys aren't fighting now," I point out. "You guys are still talking all the time."

"I know," he says. "That's the thing. She never said specifically she was going away because of what happened. I never even got the *feeling* she was doing it because she was mad. She just . . . I feel like she kind of wanted to punish me." He leans back in his chair and runs his fingers through his hair. "Does that make sense?"

"No," I say. "But yes."

"No, but yes?"

"No, it doesn't make sense, but yes, I could see Ava doing something like that." I could, too. Ava's very passive-aggressive like that.

"I just wish that sometimes she would talk more, you know? It's like she shuts down every time something comes up. I just . . . It's so frustrating."

"Yeah, I can definitely understand that." I kind of want to ask him why he's even with Ava if he's so frustrated with her, and more about why she went away, and if he's mad that she just left, but there must be something in my tone that makes him realize what I just realized a few minutes ago — that we're here, sharing sandwiches, and talking about things his girlfriend doesn't want me knowing.

Because all he says is, "Yeah, well, I'm sure it will all work out. She'll be home in a few weeks anyway."

"Totally," I say, forcing myself to smile. My cell phone beeps then. Lacey.

"Where r u?! Turns out it was just hives!! Have Benadryl & m ready 2 go home!!!"

"Lacey's ready," I say. "It was hives and she wants to go home."

Noah smiles, then picks up his tray and mine, dumping the rest of our sandwiches in the garbage on the way out of the cafeteria. I follow behind, feeling like, even though we're talking again, things are even worse and more complicated than they were this morning.

The First Day of Senior Year

After Ava slaps me, she stands up and walks out of Cooley's, leaving me sitting at the booth by myself, both of our plates of food still on the table. I'm so shocked that I don't move for a second. I take a couple of deep breaths, and turn to look at myself in the mirrors that line the wall behind the booths. There's an angry red splotch on my cheek where Ava hit me, and I reach up and touch it. It doesn't really hurt, but it stings a little. And seeing it, thinking about it, the shock of it and what it means, makes me eyes water.

"What was that about?" Cooley asks, walking by. He's wearing his trademark white pants with a red silk shirt that's unbuttoned to midchest, and three heavy gold chains with huge Cs on the end. "Did that girl just heet you?"

"Yes," I say. "She did just hit me."

"Wowiee wow wow wow," he says. He starts clearing away our dishes, which is the first time that I've ever seen Cooley bus a table. Which is a sure sign that he wants gossip. "You should have kicked her ass, Hannah," he says.

"This isn't the UFC, Cooley," I say, sighing. Cooley loves the UFC. He orders the pay-per-view fights on the TVs at the diner so he can write them off as a business expense. Which I'm pretty sure is illegal.

"Who was that girly anyway?"

"That was Ava," I say.

"Ava, your best friend, and Ava, Noah's girlfriend?" Cooley's eyes widen and he shakes his head. I guess he's been paying attention after all.

"Yes," I say.

"You better," Cooley says seriously, "warn Noah. Because that girl is not going to be too happy. She might heet him too." He takes the dishes and heads back behind the counter, shaking his head as he goes.

I sigh and put my head down on the table, not even caring if it's gross. Worst. Day. Of. School. Ever.

Of course I have no ride back to school, so I pull my phone out and text Lacey.

"911 cll me immediately"

Five seconds later, my phone rings. "What's wrong?" she asks immediately. "Is it Ava? Are you okay? Where are you?"

"I need you to pick me up," I say.

"From class? Okay," she says. "I'll see you after the bell. You're in gym, right?"

"No," I say. "I'm at Cooley's."

"At Cooley's? What the hell are you doing *there*?"

"I can't explain right now," I say. "Just come and pick me up, okay?"

Ten minutes later, her car is pulling into the parking lot. "If we hurry, we can get back before fifth," she says as I hop in. "Now tell me what the hell you were doing at Cooley's. And how the hell did you get there?"

"Ava wanted to go," I tell her. "She, uh, needed to talk to me about something." I look out the window as Lacey pulls her car out of the parking lot, wondering if maybe Ava is lurking around somewhere, getting ready to jump me or something. But I don't see her. Or her car. She must have gone back to school. Or maybe she went home.

Shit. I have to tell Noah that I told her. Don't I? I pull my phone out of my bag and scroll down until I find his name in my contacts list. I run my hand over the send button, not sure what to do. Warn him? Or let him deal with it by himself, the way he's been letting me deal with it by myself all morning?

"About what?" Lacey asks. "Her new teeth?"

"What?" I look up from my phone.

"What did Ava have to talk to you about that was sooo important she had to pull you out of school on the first day?" She says it like she can't possibly imagine Ava would have anything to tell me that could be important enough for me to skip class. Well. She's in for a shock.

"She had to tell me," I say, "About how her and Noah broke up."

"*What?*" Lacey screeches. She's so excited she almost

runs through a stop sign. The car jerks as she slams on the brakes. "They broke up?! Did you have any idea?"

"No," I say. "Not until she told me."

"Wow," she says. "I can't believe he didn't tell us he was planning to break up with her! I hope I don't sound like a complete bitch, but I'm kind of glad. Noah is way too cool for her. No offense, I know she's your friend." She looks at me out of the corner of her eye, checking my reaction, like she's afraid I'm going to be mad.

But I'm not. I'm just sad. I look out the window and try not to cry.

"What happened to your face?" Lacey asks.

"What?"

"You have a big red mark on your face." We're at a stoplight, and Lacey reaches over and grabs my chin, tilting it up to look at my cheek. "What happened?"

"I . . . I don't know," I say, pulling away from her. "It's nothing, I don't want to talk about it."

"You don't want to *talk* about it?" she says. "You leave school in the middle of the day, then ask me to pick you up, which I do without any questions, and then you show up with a big red mark on your face and tell me you don't want to talk about it? You're talking about it. Now." She waits, and the fact that she didn't even sanitize her hands after touching my face makes me realize this is serious.

"Fine," I say. "You're . . . you're probably going to find out anyway. Ava slapped me."

"She did *what*?" The light turns green, and Lacey slams on the gas, her car flying through the intersection. "I'm going to kill that girl!"

"No," I say. "It's fine, we . . . we got in a fight, and she just got carried away. It didn't hurt or anything." Which is actually true. It didn't hurt all that much. Mostly I was just shocked, but the actual slap wasn't even that bad.

"She can't just go around hitting people!" Lacey says. "What were you guys fighting about?"

"It had to do with Noah," I say slowly. "Ava thought that something was going on between us this summer."

"That's ridiculous," Lacey scoffs, and I'm glad my face has a red mark because suddenly I feel hot. She glances at me out of the corner of her eye. "Isn't it?"

I hesitate. I know I should tell her the truth. I know I should tell her about what happened last night between me and Noah, how it was building all summer, how I couldn't stop it, how I didn't *want* to stop it, how I wish now that I could take it back, how I'm so confused I can barely think straight.

But the reason I couldn't tell Lacey what was happening over the summer is the same reason I can't tell her now. After the situation with her, Riker, and Danielle, she has a zero-tolerance policy for cheating, especially for hooking up with your best friend's boyfriend. (And she *should* have a zero-tolerance policy; *everyone* should have a zero-tolerance policy when it comes to those things, including me.) So if she finds out what happened, she'll probably never speak to me again, and right now she might be the only friend I have left. So I lie.

"Yeah," I say, rolling my eyes and hoping she believes me. "So ridiculous. Nothing is going on between me and Noah."

"I can't believe she would even think that!" Lacey rages. "You would never do something like that. And then to hit you! Who does she think she is?"

She rants the whole way back to school, and once we're in the building she walks me to my locker so I can get my stuff for fifth period.

"Are you okay?" she says. "Do you want to just go home? I can take you."

"No," I say. "I'm okay, really." Going home sounds tempting, but to do that would be taking the easy way out. And I kind of feel like I deserve to be punished. "Listen, I'm going to run to the bathroom before fifth. I'll text you later?"

"You sure?" she asks. "I could go with you. Or I could cut out with you, I don't mind, seriously."

"I'm sure," I say, and give her hand a squeeze. "I promise." I leave Lacey and head to the second-floor bathroom to wait for the bell to ring, signaling the beginning of fifth period.

My eye makeup is running down my face, the same way it did that night at Jenna's party, and it almost drips onto my first-day-of-school shirt. I rip some paper towels off the roll and try to clean myself up. The bell rings as I'm doing it, and the door to the bathroom flies open. A few freshmen trail in and chatter about their classes and how much homework they have already.

I fix my face as best I can, take a deep breath, and head out of the bathroom. And when I do, I bump right into Noah. Again.

"Hey," I say.

"Hi."

I expect him to keep moving, to push past me and go walking down the hall the way he did earlier, but he doesn't. Instead, he stops and looks at me awkwardly. "So, um, how—"

"Listen," I say, cutting him off before he can say anything else. "I have to tell you something."

"Okay." He shifts his books to his other hand, and his features arrange into a look of concern. Which is actually good. He should be concerned.

"I told Ava what happened between us." We've moved a little bit out of the way, standing over to the side by a row of lockers, while kids go rushing by us. Kind of a weird place for us to be having a potentially life-changing conversation, but what choice do I have? Actually, now that I think about it, probably lots of potentially life-changing conversations take place in this hallway. I mean, isn't high school just a string of life-changing moments interspersed with football games, proms, and homework?

"You what?" Noah asks. "*Why?* Why would you do that?"

His tone is halfway between annoyed and disbelieving, like he has no idea how anyone could be so stupid.

"Because I thought she had a right to know," I say, suddenly indignant. Why is he so concerned about Ava knowing anyway? If he broke up with her, it's not like he has anything to lose. It doesn't make any sense, unless he wants to make sure that he comes out of the breakup looking good. The thought fills me with rage. "And besides, who cares if I told her? You guys broke up, didn't you?"

"Yeah, but . . ." he trails off and looks at me. "Hannah, I never wanted you to wreck your friendship with Ava because of me." His tone is suddenly softer, and almost sympathetic.

I stare at him blankly. "What are you talking about?"

"I just mean that what happened last night . . . I never meant for you to tell Ava about it, to ruin your friendship over me."

My mouth drops open. "I didn't ruin my friendship with Ava over you," I tell him. Which is true. I didn't tell Ava because I somehow thought Noah and I were going to be together. I told Ava in a fit of weird anger that somehow led me to tell her, for reasons that had nothing to do with Noah and everything to do with the dynamic that Ava and I have built up over years and years.

"Okay," he says. But he doesn't sound like he really believes it.

I can feel the white-hot wave of anger start in my toes and slide all the way up my body. "I wouldn't just end my friendship with Ava because of you," I say. "That's ridiculous."

God, what an asshole. Noah apparently thinks he can just have sex with me, and then, the very next day, tell me that he doesn't want me to ruin my friendship with Ava because of him? He should have thought about that before he got me naked last night. I turn around and start marching down the hall, my strappy black first-day-of-school shoes making loud noises on the floor.

I turn the corner, not even sure where I'm going. I'm so enraged that I can't even remember what period it is. *Fifth*, I tell myself. *It's fifth period.* I pull my schedule out of my bag, and my hands are shaking. Physics, room 341. Which is on the complete other side of the school and one floor up.

I take a deep breath, trying to calm myself down. I feel like I'm going to throw up. My stomach has been churning ever since I was at the diner with Ava. I try to relax my body.

The sound of footsteps comes from behind me, and I turn around, hoping it's Noah and hoping it's Ava, not caring which one of them I explode on.

But it's not Noah. Or Ava. Or even Lacey. It's Jemima, the girl who hit my car this morning. The girl who hooked up with Sebastian.

"Oh, hi, Hannah," she says. "I was looking for you. Uh, I just wanted to make sure that you had my cell number. I actually think maybe I wrote it down wrong. I just got a new phone, you know? And I can never remember the new number." She rolls her eyes, like, *Oh ha ha, isn't this so funny? I'm such a flake.*

I stare at her, not able to comprehend that this is now my life. I've slept with my best friend's boyfriend, who I think I am probably in love with, and it turns out that he most certainly does not love me. My ex-boyfriend cheated on me and broke my heart, and now the girl he cheated on me *with* is following me around school because she hit my car. How can everything go from being completely okay to completely and totally fucked within the span of a few months? Or even one day! I mean, as bad as things were this morning, they were way better than they are now.

"Sorry," I say to Jemima, giving her a bitchy smile, just because I feel like it. "I don't think I really need your cell number. It's probably better that we go through the insurance, since you really messed up my friend Lacey's neck and she might need to sue you." I force my smile bigger, and then shrug, as if the whole thing's completely out of my control. Jemima, having no idea that this is so not about her, drops her mouth open in shock. But I just shrug, like *sorry, what can you do?* then turn around and run down the hall and up the stairs to physics.

The Summer

After that night at the hospital, Noah and I don't talk for two weeks. Lacey starts picking me up in the morning before work, which is fine, except for the fact that she doesn't bring coffee like Noah did. Lacey uses coffee strictly as a way to get caffeine into her system, and therefore doesn't think that coffee from Dunkin' Donuts or Starbucks is any different than the cheap stuff we have at the diner. (Of course, that didn't stop her from drinking it when Noah would bring it.) Lacey also has a hard time getting up in the mornings, so by the time she gets to my house, we're almost always cutting it close, with no time for morning coffee runs.

But I'm doing okay. I'm not upset about it or anything. I'm actually trying not to think about that, or anything else, and it's also definitely helping that Sebastian hasn't tried to contact me ever since the day he showed up at the diner a couple of weeks ago.

But then one night in the middle of July, I'm in my room writing in my journal, when I'm hit with such a wave of loneliness that I feel like I can't breathe. It comes out of nowhere, and suddenly, I'm missing Sebastian. Which makes no sense because, like I said, ever since that day at Cooley's, he hasn't tried to contact me, and I've really been doing a good job of not thinking about him.

I'm just about to go into my mom's room and look for some of her Ambien to help me sleep, but before I can, I hear her car pulling into the driveway. Shit. I completely forgot that she was coming home before work. She must have gone to the library after her classes, and now she's here, about to come into the house and prevent me from raiding her medicine cabinet. And maybe even wanting to talk. Shit, shit, shit.

I shove my journal into one of my desk drawers, jump into bed, and bury my head in the pillow just as the front door opens. I hear her footsteps on the stairs, echoing through the hallway, and then there's a knock on my door. I squeeze my eyes shut and pretend to be asleep, even though I'm lying in a very uncomfortable position and all my sheets and blankets are in a tangle on the floor.

"Hannah?" she whispers, cracking the door. "Are you awake?"

I force myself to breathe deeply and consider adding in a snore, but decide that would definitely be taking it too far, especially since I'm really bad at fake-snoring. I tried to do it at a sleepover once so I wouldn't have to play truth or dare (I had a crush on this kid named Jacob Heinz and

I didn't want anyone asking me about it), and everyone totally knew I was really awake.

My mom walks into the room, the floorboards squeaking under her sneakers. God. Does she have no respect for my privacy? She can't just come barging into my room without even, like, asking me. Good thing I put my journal away. I mean, really.

"Hannah?" she tries again, and when I don't answer, she picks up the sheet that's on the floor and drapes it over me, then gives me a kiss on the forehead. Okay, so that's kind of sweet, actually.

I sigh and then open one eye. Just because I'm having a bad night doesn't mean I have to be a total shit to her.

"Oh, hi," I say, blinking up at her, trying to look confused and like I just woke up. "I guess I fell asleep after work."

"Hannah, your screen saver's not even up," she says. I glance over to my laptop, which is open to my Facebook page. I was reading through the old messages from Sebastian and using them for inspiration as I wrote in my journal. I know, pathetic.

"Oh," I say. "Well, I fall asleep really fast these days, it's all my long days at work." I give a yawn for good measure.

"Uh-huh." She totally doesn't believe me, which actually makes it even nicer that she pretended to think I was sleeping. God, I'm a horrible daughter. "So now that you're awake, do you want to go to the diner with me?"

"Cooley's is closed," I say automatically.

"Cooley's isn't the only diner in town," she says. "There's IHop, Pepper Pot, Two Trees . . ."

The last place I want to be is a diner after spending all day at one. And I know my mom is going to ask me how I'm doing with the whole Sebastian thing, and it's so not the time to be asking me that.

"I don't really want to be at a diner right now, Mom," I say, turning over so that I'm facing the wall. "I've been at one all day."

"Okay," she says. "Then do you want to come downstairs and join me for some French toast?"

"With banana sauce?" I ask hopefully.

"Yes."

"Fine," I say, turning back over and kicking off the sheet. "But I am *not* talking about Sebastian." And I hope she knows I mean it.

"It's just, I mean, I don't know if I ever even liked him that much," I say, forking up the last piece of French toast, and then dragging it through the brown sugar-banana almond sauce. Yum.

"I thought you didn't want to talk about it," my mom says. She's been listening to me go on and on for the past half hour. It was like, as soon as we sat down, I just cracked and started talking about everything.

"I *didn't* want to," I say. "Well, I thought I didn't. But it's making me feel better. That and the French toast."

"Look," she says. "For whatever reasons you did or didn't like Sebastian, or how much you did or didn't like him, it doesn't make the loss any easier."

"It doesn't?"

"No," she says. She shifts in her chair, then reaches over and takes the tea bag out of her tea. "Do you want my opinion?"

"Yes," I say, even though I know she's probably going to say something totally smart and I'll be annoyed for not thinking of it myself. But I've gone on and on for half an hour, I should at least give her a chance to speak.

"I think you liked him because it was easy."

I stare at her incredulously. Has she totally forgotten what my relationship with Sebastian was like? Tension and anxiety were, like, the basis of our relationship. And my mom was there to witness the whole thing. "It was not easy!" I say. "He was never returning my phone calls, he never returned my texts, I never knew if he even liked me."

"Exactly," my mom says. She stands up from her chair and starts clearing the table, bringing our dishes to the sink. I consider stopping her and asking for another piece of French toast, but I'm sure that late-night carb sessions aren't the best for my waistline. Especially since I've eaten ice cream almost every day this week. "And that's why it was easy. You never had to worry about actually falling for him, because all your energy was put into worrying about if he was going to text you or call you or show up when he was supposed to."

197

I stare at her, my mouth dropping open. "That's true," I say. "All my energy did go into that stuff. But then why do I feel so horrible?"

"Because it still got taken away from you," she says. "You liked the thrill of the chase. The drama was exciting. And now that's gone." She returns to the table and fills my glass back up with milk. "And I'm sure that's not *all* it is. You did like Sebastian, you guys had a lot of fun times together."

"True," I say, although our fun times aren't really in proportion to how I'm feeling. Some parties and some dates and some makeout sessions don't a basket case make. I don't know. It's all so confusing. I think about telling her how I've been feeling about Noah, but I really can't make myself go there. It's too . . . I don't know, raw and emotional. And definitely not something that can be solved in half an hour over banana French toast. But I'm suddenly kind of nervous. I mean, if I only liked Sebastian because it was easy, and liking Noah is going to be anything *but* easy, what does that really mean?

Later, when I'm back in bed upstairs, my stomach full of French toast, I reach over and grab my cell.

"Hey," I say when Ava answers. "Were you sleeping?" I can hear a bunch of commotion, and for a second I think maybe she lost service or something (Seriously, the reception in Maine is horrible — I know it's the middle of nowhere, but you'd think the cell companies could do *something* about it. I mean, even astronauts have cell reception.), but then I can hear her telling someone in the background that she'll be right back.

"Hannah?" she asks. I can hear the other voices fading into the background. "What's going on, what's wrong?"

"Nothing," I lie. "I just really miss you."

"I miss you too," she says. I know she does miss me, but it's hard to feel like it when it's one in the morning and she's obviously out doing something fun, probably with Lulu and all her amazing new camp friends, and I'm at home in my bed, needing to go to work in a few hours, and missing her so much it hurts. "Now tell me what's wrong."

"I've just been thinking about Sebastian," I say. And Noah.

"Sebastian?" she asks. "That asshole? Why are you worried about him?" Since Sebastian never called me like he said he would, Ava's back to calling him an asshole and saying I can do better.

"I'm not *worried* about him," I say. "I just . . . Why do you think I'm not over it yet? I mean, I really thought I was and now . . . Do you think I was addicted to the drama?" It sounds lame when I'm saying it, and now I'm not sure it's true. I feel like my heart has betrayed me or something, making me think I was fine and then hitting me with this out of nowhere.

"It's only been a little over a month, sweetie," Ava says. "And no, I don't think you were just addicted to the drama.

You liked him. Although you liked the drama, too."

I smile. "I know, but I don't even want him back," I say. It's true, I don't want him back. *You know this has nothing to do with Sebastian,* a voice in my head says. *You know you're really upset about Noah.*

There's noise on the other end of the phone, and then I hear a guy's voice say, "Ava, are you coming back? We need to get the fire started!" There's a bunch of laughter, and I can tell Ava's covering the phone because she says something back but it sounds all muffled.

"Listen," she says, when she's back on the line. "Why don't you come and visit me?"

"Seriously?" I sit up in bed, suddenly excited. "Okay! When?" Ohmigod! Yay! It will be so fun! Hanging out in Maine, getting close to nature. Maybe we can go for a hike or do yoga or commune with the trees or something. Lulu can teach me how to meditate, and maybe we can even work on our flexibility and do some Pilates. I'll come back refreshed, invigorated, and totally clearheaded, like people who come back from those spiritual retreats to India. Like that one woman in *Eat, Pray, Love.*

"Not this weekend but next?" she asks. "Does that work?"

"Totally!" I say. "I'll ask for the time off of work. I just have to figure out a way to get to Maine." I wonder if I can rent a car. Probably not. I think you have to be, like, twenty-one or something. But there has to be a bus or a train. I grab my laptop, getting ready to Google.

"You can ride up with Noah," Ava says. At the sound of his name, my heart twists, and my hands stop, poised over the keyboard.

"Noah?"

"Yeah, that's the weekend he's coming. It was supposed to be romantic, but honestly how romantic can you get being out in the woods?" She laughs. "So you can come too. It'll be great, you guys being here at the same time. We'll have so much fun."

"Oh," I say. I lean back on my bed, and trace around the lining of my comforter with one finger. Is Ava crazy? Why would she invite me along on some kind of romantic getaway with her boyfriend? And okay, it's not a *getaway* exactly since, you know, she's already away. But she definitely said romantic. I wonder if this has anything to do with the problems Noah was talking about a couple of weeks ago.

"Um," I say, "I don't want to be the third wheel." Not to mention how weird is it going to be riding up to Maine with Noah? Three hours in a car with him? When we're not even really talking, besides "hi," "how are you," and "those people want their home fries really crispy."

"You won't!" Ava says. "I told you, there's no way we're going to get to do anything romantic, I have a cabin full of eleven-year-olds to watch. I can't even sleep out overnight anywhere."

I take a deep breath, wanting to ask her about her and

Noah, but I'm a little bit afraid. Finally I decide to just go for it. "Is everything okay with you guys?" I ask.

"With who?" Ava's tone is suddenly sharp, and I wish I could take back the question. But it's too late.

"With you and Noah?"

"Yes, things with me and Noah are great," she says. "Why?"

"No reason," I say, "It's just weird that you would want me to come up and visit you on a weekend when you should be getting some." I want to add that it's also weird that she's obviously out somewhere where there are guys around, specifically one guy who's calling her name and asking her when she's coming back to the party or the festivities or whatever it is she's doing. In fact, I think I can hear him now, calling her Queen of the Fire and trying to get her off the phone. Being called "Queen of the Fire" definitely sounds like something inappropriate and scandalous might be going on.

There's a pause, and then Ava starts laughing. "Trust me," she says. "There's nowhere to get it on, unless we want to do it in the woods and get poison ivy. So it's all settled. I'll tell Noah when I talk to him tomorrow. I can't wait, it's going to be so fun!"

"I don't know if we'll both be able to get the time off of work," I say in a last-ditch effort to keep me from having to go.

"Of course you will," she says. "Just beg."

"Okay," I say, deciding to play along, even though I know

there's no way I'm going to go. It actually won't even be that hard to get out of it since Noah probably already asked for the time off, like, weeks ago. He's just that type. Cooley will say that I can't have the time off too, and then I'll have to call Ava, and she'll be sad, of course, but I'll have already warned her so it won't be, like, that big of a surprise or anything. Then she and Noah can have a nice, romantic time together. *And you can stay here by yourself,* the voice in my head whispers.

"Ava," I start, deciding to tell her how much I miss her, how weird everything's been, how I need her, how I don't know if I can get through the rest of the summer without her.

"I have to go," she says. I can hear the same guy in the background calling her name again. "I'm at this party and my friends are waiting for me."

Her friends are waiting for her. Friends I don't know. Friends who are partying with her, friends who are maybe cute guys, friends who know nothing about me, friends who are girls that might want Ava to be their best friend. Friends who are going through things with her that I'll never be a part of. And I'm here, going through things that Ava will never be a part of.

"Okay," I say.

"I'll call you tomorrow," she says. "And we'll figure out the details for the trip."

She hangs up, and I lie back on the pillow. I stare up at the ceiling and it's two more hours before I fall asleep.

❀ ❀ ❀

Pebbles, or something, hitting my bedroom window. I'm half-asleep, so at first I think it's a branch or maybe there's a storm going on outside, and I start to have a dream that I'm out in the storm, clinging to the branch that's slapping against my window. But once I'm awake and my thoughts are coherent, I realize something really *is* hitting my window. I kneel on my bed and look outside, but it's raining and too dark to really see anything. I see a flash of someone, or something, go flying across the lawn and then there's a thunk on my porch.

Is it . . . an animal maybe? The people next door have this super annoying Goldendoodle named Tobias, who they're always letting run around late at night. They think since it's the middle of the night it's okay, but Tobias loves to tear up my mother's tomato plants no matter what time it is. But would they really let poor Tobias out in the middle of a thunderstorm? Not that dogs probably care, but—

Ding dong. The doorbell rings, and I scream. Okay, Tobias definitely cannot ring the doorbell, which means it's some kind of rapist or crazy person or . . . ohmigod, ohmigod, ohmigod. I reach for my phone and dial Lacey. She doesn't answer. I think about calling 911, but what if it's nothing? What if it's just some drunk guy who got lost or something? What if they call my mom, and she comes home and—

My phone rings in my hand and I jump. Noah! Noah is calling me! Maybe he's the one outside.

"Hello?" I say.

"Hey," he says. "Uh, sorry to call so late."

"That's okay," I say, my heart pounding. "What's going on?" I peer through the blinds as the doorbell rings again. "That's you, right? Ringing the doorbell?"

"No," he says. "But I'm about to pull into your—oh my God," he says. "It's *Sebastian*. He's on your porch."

"Sebastian?"

I run downstairs and peer out the window. I can see Noah's car in the driveway, the rain falling and making sheets of water that are illuminated by his headlights. And I can see Sebastian standing on the porch, ringing the doorbell over and over. Then he knocks and says, "Hannah! Hannah, wake up!"

I fling the door open. "What are you doing here?" I ask.

"Hannah," Sebastian says. "I need to talk to you." His hair is dripping wet, droplets sliding down the strands and onto his thin T-shirt, making the white fabric even thinner.

Noah's car door slams and in an instant he's on the porch. "Leave her alone," he says to Sebastian. "She doesn't want to talk to you." For a second, I think maybe they're going to finish what almost happened in the diner that day. But Sebastian just turns around and looks at Noah.

"I have to talk to her," he says. And he sounds so sad, and I remember how it felt to kiss him, and he looks desperate, and I just . . . I don't know. I want to talk to him. But most of all,

I want to prove to myself that I don't care why Noah's here, at my house, at one a.m. And I want to prove it to Noah, too.

"She doesn't want to talk to you," Noah says, and I see his hands clench, becoming fists at his sides.

"It's okay," I say. "I'll . . . I'll talk to him."

"You will?" Noah sounds shocked.

"You will?" Sebastian sounds shocked.

"Yes," I say. "But we have to go inside." We're on the porch, but the boys are both soaked just from their walks up the driveway. Sebastian gives Noah one last long look over his shoulder and then ducks into my house. I cross my arms over my chest, suddenly aware that all I'm wearing is a thin T-shirt and a pair of cotton shorts. "Do you, uh . . . Do you wanna come in?"

I want to ask him what he's doing here, why he's outside my house at one in the morning, why he didn't tell me he was going to visit Ava in a few weeks, why I can't figure out what I feel about him. And for a second, I think maybe he's going to tell me that he can't figure out what he feels about me either, but that he wants to figure it all out together.

But finally, all he says is, "No." And then he turns around and walks back toward his car. I watch him go, then step back inside and shut the front door, ready to deal with Sebastian.

"What was *he* doing here?" Sebastian asks.

I'm in the kitchen, making us a pot of coffee, and Sebastian's sitting up on the counter, looking pretty cute with his hair all wet and his T-shirt soaked through. It's clinging to his biceps and I can see every single muscle.

I pull the can of coffee down and measure out enough for four cups, wondering how to answer that question. Something tells me "I don't know" isn't really going to cut it, even though it's the truth. But in this case, saying "I don't know" seems almost worse. I mean, if you don't know why someone is showing up at your house at one in the morning, then it's almost definitely for a nefarious and/or scandalous purpose.

"Ava's having drama," I say, rolling my eyes. "And she wouldn't answer her phone when Noah called, so he was coming over here to see if I knew what was wrong with her."

Sebastian nods, accepting this. "You got any Sugar in the Raw?" he asks.

"Yeah." I reach up into the cupboard and pull it down. I don't use Sugar in the Raw, but Sebastian loves it, and when we were dating, I always had it around. God, when we were dating. Was that only a month ago? It's weird, having him here now, when in the past I wouldn't think anything of it. He'd be here, hanging out with me for hours, watching movies or playing Wii, and then maybe going up to my room to make out if my mom wasn't home.

Sebastian dumps a bunch of sugar packets into his coffee, and I dump some into mine, too. I probably shouldn't be drinking coffee this late, especially since I'm having trouble sleeping already, but I need something to warm me up.

"Since when do you like Sugar in the Raw?" he asks.

"Since it's the only thing we have in the house," I tell him. "I've been getting Starbucks most mornings, or having coffee at Cooley's."

"With Noah?"

"Um, sometimes." I take a sip of my coffee. "Or Lacey."

He nods, then jumps off the counter and comes over to me, wrapping his arms around my waist. Whoa. That's . . . unexpected.

"What are you doing?" I ask.

"I miss you," he says into my neck. And it feels good. Him talking into my neck, I mean. If I was just addicted to the drama, it wouldn't feel this good, would it? I can feel the beginning of a five o'clock shadow (can you have one of those at one a.m.?) on his face, and it tickles me, and sends heat all through my body.

"I miss you, too," I say honestly, suddenly really, fiercely missing him so much. Or at least missing how simple things were before we broke up. Yeah, I worried sometimes about how we were getting along, and what he was thinking, but it wasn't anything like the things I'm worrying about now. He tries to kiss me then, and I let him for a second, but then my brain flashes a picture of him in the pool with that girl, followed by a picture of her car in his driveway.

"Wait," I say, pulling back. "We can't just . . . We can't just make out."

"Why not?" He's still close to me, and I'm not sure, but I think I smell alcohol on his breath. Which would make sense since sober people don't usually show up at your house at one in the morning. Although Noah didn't appear to be drinking. Noah doesn't really drink. Why am I thinking about Noah? Sebastian is here, in my kitchen, begging me to take him back. Okay, maybe not begging. And he hasn't really said anything about us getting back together, but isn't that where this is going?

"Because we need to talk about what happened." I duck away from him and lead him out onto the covered part of the deck, where I purposely sit in a chair. He takes the chair across from me and scoots it closer, so that he's facing me, and our knees are touching. Which is actually worse than if we were sitting next to each other. Much more intimate. The rain's still falling, but slower now, and the drops bounce off the roof of the deck, sliding down to the ground below, the air thick and humid around us.

"So," I say, tracing my finger around the rim of my coffee cup. "What did you want to talk about?"

"You're the one who said you wanted to talk," he says. His hand is tracing a line on my collarbone, and I shiver and move away. "I just want to be with you."

"Yeah, but . . . what does that mean?" I ask. "Do you want to get back together?"

"Yes." He says it so simply, almost like it *is* that simple, and for a second I almost believe that it would be. That I could just say, "Oh, okay" and we'd go upstairs and maybe do Everything But, and everything would be back to normal and Ava would come back in a few weeks and we'd all start our senior year and it would be just amazing. But then I think of that damn girl in the pool again. And Noah, although I push him out of my thoughts immediately.

"Have you been drinking?" I ask.

"What does that have to do with anything?"

"It has a lot to do with anything. If you've been drinking, you might not be in your right mind, and you might wake up tomorrow morning and regret this whole thing."

"I know what I'm saying," he says, giving me a slow grin. Then he leans in again and kisses me on the lips.

"But Sebastian," I say, pulling my eyes up to his. "You cheated on me."

He sighs, like he was hoping that wouldn't come up, even though it's, like, the most important part of the whole conversation. "It wasn't really cheating," he says. "We just . . . got carried away."

"We?" I raise my eyebrows. No way I want him referring to himself and the sophomore who does it better as a "we."

"I," he quickly corrects. "*I* got carried away. It was the last day of school, and she . . . she just jumped on top of me." He shrugs. "And then later, I went to find you and I couldn't, and someone told me you'd been making out with Jonah Mancuso."

"Why didn't you call me?" I ask, not willing to let him off that easily. He's still close to me, so close that our faces are almost touching, and I can see the plumpness of his lips and remember how it felt when he kissed me just a moment ago.

"I wanted to," he says. "I really, really wanted to."

"If you wanted to," I say, "then you could have."

"I was afraid."

"Of what?"

"Of losing you, of you breaking up with me, of having to hear those words." I want to believe him. I think about how easy it would be to believe him, to just slip back into the relationship and have everything be the same. Sebastian could even come with me when I go to visit Ava in a couple of weeks. Me, Ava, Sebastian, and Noah hanging out, just like old times. Not that we ever hung out that much, but we did sometimes. And yeah, there would still be some weirdness between me and Noah, but I'm sure it would fade as time went on. Ava would come back, and everything would be the same. Exactly as it always was.

But first I have to ask Sebastian a question. "So it was only that one time?" I say. "That you guys hooked up? That night in the pool, it was just a blip?"

I hold my breath. If he tells me the truth, admits that she was over that day, and comes clean, I might, *might* think about taking him back. Sebastian's dark eyes flicker for a second, and then focus on something over my left shoulder. Then he slides his eyes back to mine, and says, "Yes, Hannah, I swear. It was only that one time."

And just like that, I have my answer.

The First Day of Senior Year

When the bell rings at the end of fifth period, you couldn't have paid me five million dollars to tell you what the class was about. I mean, I know it was physics, and I've somehow acquired a physics book (I'm assuming from the teacher, who according to my schedule is named Ms. Beasley, but I seriously could not tell you anything about her, like what she looks like or what she was wearing or anything she said), but other than that, I'm lost. I hope there wasn't an assignment or anything, because I definitely will not be doing it.

I stop off at my locker and drop off my physics book (for a book I don't remember getting, it's ridiculously heavy — seriously, the thing weighs about twenty pounds which I really hope doesn't correlate to the amount of work the class is going to entail) before I head to my sixth-period social media class.

I signed up for social media at the suggestion of my guidance counselor, Mr. Davies, because I had a free period and he said it would look good on my college apps. But now that my life is falling apart, I'm cursing myself for not taking a study hall instead, so I decide to head down to guidance and persuade Mr. Davies to let me drop the class. Then I can huddle up in the library and feel sorry for myself until this nightmare of a day is over.

I'm congratulating myself for coming up with such a brilliant plan, but when I get to the guidance office, there are a ton of people waiting to see their counselors (probably a lot of people's lives are falling apart — I mean, it *is* sixth period, which means people have had six whole periods plus a homeroom for their lives to turn to shit), and the line snakes out the door. Not that I mind. I'm not in a hurry. But surprisingly, the line moves fast and after only a couple of minutes, I'm standing in front of the secretary, Rosie, who's kind of a pain in the ass.

"Hello, Rosie," I say, because I heard somewhere that if you use a person's name when you speak to them, they're way more likely to give you what you want.

"Name?" Rosie asks, not sounding all that friendly.

"Uh, Hannah Kaplan," I say. "I just really need to talk to Mr. Davies. Is he around?"

She looks at me over the top of her super chic Chanel glasses. Rosie's only about twenty-five and has DD-cup boobs, which plays into pretty much every secretary cliché. She's also a total fashionista, and wears designer stuff all the time. I think she must have some kind of rich family, and only took this job because she thought it would be easy. Ava's theory is that Rosie has a rich, older boyfriend. This is because one time we saw Rosie out at a fancy restaurant, and she was with a man who had gray hair and was wearing a smoking jacket. I think it was her father, but Ava insists on the more scandalous theory. Ava. I swallow at the thought of her, then do my best to focus on the task at hand, aka getting past the Guidance Nazi.

"Are you crazy?" Rosie asks. "Of course Mr. Davies is around, it's the first day of school and he's a guidance counselor!" Rosie looks like she should sound like a Valley girl, but in actuality she has a very posh voice. It kind of sounds like someone who's spent some time in England, but hasn't quite mastered the accent. You know, like Madonna when she's trying to sound British?

"Thank you, Rosie," I say, then start walking toward the chairs in the corner.

"Stop right there!" she says. "Where do you think you're *going*?"

"I'm going to sit over there," I say, pointing to the chairs against the wall. "And wait for Mr. Davies."

"Mr. Davies cannot see you," she says. "Mr. Davies is very busy. In case you haven't noticed, it's the first day of school."

"But it's an emergency!" I wail.

"What sort?"

Something tells me "I need to drop my social media class

so that I can sit and veg out in study hall because I slept with my best friend's boyfriend last night and then told her about it" isn't really going to get me what I want.

"It's a personal problem," I say, lowering my eyes and hoping I look like the kind of girl who has a shameful secret. Which, actually, is true. I do have a shameful secret. Well, I guess it's not really a secret anymore, since I already told the one person I didn't want to find out. But either way, it's still shameful.

"What kind of personal problem?" she asks.

"It's *personal*." Duh.

"Fine," Rosie relents. She looks me up and down and then smirks, probably because she likes it when people are miserable. Maybe she broke up with her rich, older boyfriend and now she wants everyone else to be upset, too. Although she *is* wearing a Gucci sweater, so I'm assuming her wishing bad things on others is just a personality trait.

I plop myself down on one of the chairs in the corner, across from a girl wearing a pink miniskirt and a boy who's sleeping. The good thing is that it appears most of the kids trying to get into guidance are getting turned away by Rosie the Guidance Nazi, so there are plenty of chairs for those of us somehow deemed good enough to make it past. Hopefully the wait time won't be that long, and I can sneak out of here and get to the library in time to spend study hall alone. God, this is really the worst first day of school ever. *Only four more periods to go,* I tell myself, *and then I'll be out of here.*

I decide to pull out my iPod and see if I can get away with secretly listening to a few songs while I wait. I'm thinking no, but then again, there is a boy sleeping over there. Maybe that means Rosie gets drunk with power at the door and then doesn't really care what goes on inside. (Right now she's in the process of making a freshman girl almost cry because the girl's somehow been scheduled for three sections of gym, something Rosie apparently thinks is totally acceptable.)

Still. I don't want to take any chances, so I look down and try to covertly rummage through my bag and then slip in my ear buds without anyone noticing. Which is why, at first, I don't notice the shoes: the beat up, black boots that Sebastian always wears. Followed by the black jeans he always wears. Followed by the black T-shirt he always wears.

"Hey," he says.

"Oh," I say. "Um, hi." Before this morning, I hadn't talked to Sebastian since that night in July, the night he came over, the night he told me he wanted to get back together. After I caught him in the lie about Jemima being a one-time thing, I kicked him out of my house. He tried calling me a bunch of times after that, but I refused to answer.

"What are you doing here?" he asks, sitting down in the seat next to me like it's the most natural thing in the world, like the last time we talked he wasn't at my house at one in the morning, maybe drunk and trying to make out with me, the whole time lying about his cheating being a one time thing. And if he's wondering why he couldn't find me this morning after homeroom, he doesn't say anything.

"Trying to add a study hall," I say.

"Me too," he says, grinning.

"Really?" I remember how Sebastian and I met in study hall, how the first time I saw him he was reading *Pride and Prejudice*, and how I thought that was really sexy. Of course, I would come to find out later that it was the only book he'd read, like, ever, and the only reason he was reading it was to impress some college girl he'd met at a party the weekend before. That should have been a sign that maybe he and I weren't going to be the best match.

"Yeah. Maybe we'll be in the same one."

"Maybe."

There's an uncomfortable silence, and I look up and catch the girl who's sitting across from us trying to listen in on our conversation. Probably she's a sophomore. Probably she's friends with Jemima. I remember how I threatened her just a little while ago. Definitely not my best moment. Although she did kind of deserve it for hooking up with my boyfriend. And besides, it's not like I'm really going to sue her or anything.

Sebastian notices the girl too, so he opens up his binder to a fresh sheet of paper, then takes out a pen and writes, "I still really miss you."

I don't say anything, because I'm not sure what to do. And then Sebastian reaches over and takes my hand. I want to pull away, I *know* I should pull away, but I don't because for just one second, it feels nice—safe and secure, even though it's a false sense of safety I know won't last. But right now Sebastian's really the only person who wants to be around me, who actually misses me, who's actually trying to be nice.

I close my eyes and enjoy the feel of his hand around mine just for a second. And then I open my eyes and pull my hand away. But it's not fast enough. Because when I look up, there's Noah, standing in the doorway of the guidance office, right in front of Rosie's desk, watching me and Sebastian.

The Summer

"What did he want?" Noah asks the next morning. He's standing in my driveway at five a.m., a full hour before we have to be at work. Not that he was supposed to pick me up anyway, so it makes no sense that he's here. The only reason I'm even up at this hour is because after I kicked Sebastian out last night, I couldn't fall asleep. I was tossing and turning until I finally gave up and spent the rest of the night writing in my journal and messing around online.

My head was a complete and total mess. I couldn't stop thinking about why Noah was at my house at one a.m., about what he wanted to say, about what he was thinking. I wasn't even thinking that much about Sebastian. And at about four this morning, I decided I definitely need to stay away from Noah because nothing good can come out of the situation. Although my new plan to stay away from him isn't off to a very good start since he's, you know, in my driveway.

"What are you doing here?" I ask. I'm standing on the porch, barefoot and in my pajamas, because when I heard

Noah's car pull up, I ran outside, not even bothering to put on shoes. Now he's standing halfway out of his car with the door open, and a song I've never heard is playing through his iPod.

"What did he want?" Noah asks again.

"To talk," I say.

"So why'd you let him in?"

He sounds angry, which makes *me* angry, and the next thing I know, I'm yelling. "You know, you have a lot of nerve showing up here at five in the morning questioning my choices," I say. "Newsflash, Noah. I can talk to whoever I want, whenever I want." I stop and take a breath. "And besides, what were *you* doing here at one in the morning? And what are you doing here now? I thought we weren't supposed to talk ever again, remember?"

"I never said that," he says.

I turn around and open the front door, so done with this.

"Where are you going?" he asks.

"I have to get ready for work," I yell over my shoulder. "Not that it's any of your business."

"Okay," he says, sounding amicable. "I'll just wait here for you."

"No, thank you," I tell him. "Lacey will be here in an hour." Or an hour and fifteen minutes, or whenever Lacey feels like she can finally pull herself out of bed. But Noah doesn't need to know that.

"No she won't," he says when I'm almost out of earshot. "I told her not to come."

I whirl around. "You what?"

"I texted her and told her that I would pick you up." He shrugs and then lopes up the cobblestone walk after me, checking his watch. "Starbucks is open," he says. "Do you want to go with me?"

So half an hour later, against my total and complete better judgment, we're standing in line at Starbucks, which is surprisingly busy for five-thirty in the morning. I mean, what are all these people *doing* here? I guess they're all on their way to work. And some of them look really perky. A few of them are even in workout clothes, which is just wrong. Although, now that I'm back on the market maybe I should start thinking about working out a little more. Or, you know, a lot more since right now I don't work out at all. It never hurts to get in shape.

"The usual?" Noah asks when we're almost at the front of the line.

"No," I say, mostly because I'm annoyed with him and in a cranky mood. He still hasn't told me why he showed up at my house last night. And the way he says it, the way he just *asks* me if I want the usual, it's almost like he *wants* me to order the same old boring thing. So I decide to shock him and get something completely different. "I'm going to have a soy latte."

"A *soy* latte?" he looks at me skeptically.

"Yes," I say emphatically. "A soy latte. I've decided that I'm limiting my intake of diary products."

"You do realize that ice cream is a dairy product, right?"

I ignore him and shuffle forward with the line. But he's kind of persistent. "Do you even know what soy is?"

"Of course," I say, rolling my eyes. Which isn't really true. I mean, I know that soy milk isn't dairy, and that people who are vegan drink it. But I don't know exactly where it comes from or why it's supposed to be so good for you. "Do you have some kind of problem with soy?"

"No," he says. "It's just surprising, that's all."

"Why?"

"Because usually the only people who drink soy milk are, like, thirty-year-old hippies who are into being green."

"I'm into being green," I say. The line moves forward again. "And I might just become a hippie. There's a lot you don't know about me."

"So your ageism when it comes to food is limited to peanut butter and jelly?"

"I don't eat things," I say, looking him right in the eye, "that are childish. I'm very mature for my age." Which is a total contradiction, since that's actually a very childish thing to say.

When it's our turn to order, I'm so excited about my soy latte that I step right up to the cashier and blurt it out, "One large soy latte." I almost add, "with cream and sugar" but

223

then remember that if I'm limiting my dairy, I wouldn't be adding cream. Plus, I'm not sure you can even add cream to a soy latte, since I'm not sure how that would taste. Is it like mixing Splenda with regular sugar? Or worse?

"You mean a Venti," Riker Strong says from behind the cash register, giving me a smile and punching in my order. I didn't realize he was the one taking my order, otherwise I wouldn't have been so cheerful when I gave it. I would have given him the cold shoulder that he deserves.

"What?" I ask

"A Venti," he says. "That's what we call larges here. You know that, Hannah."

"Well, whatever," I say, my bad mood deepening. "Whatever you call them, that's what I want." They should just call them larges. How stupid.

"And what can I get for you, Noah?" Riker asks.

"I'll have a Tall caramel macchiato with extra whipped cream."

I raise my eyebrows at him. "Isn't that kind of girly?"

"Oh, so now you're sexist when it comes to food as well as ageist?"

I glare at him, then take my drink from where Riker has slid it across the counter, and march over to the condiment station where I dump four sugars and a bunch of cocoa and cinnamon into it. Since I have no idea what soy milk tastes like, I figure it's probably wise to mask the taste as much as I can. I take a small sip. Not bad, although not as good as real milk. Not even close.

Up at the counter, Noah's holding his Grande-Venti-caramel-whatever while he and Riker hold up the line and joke around like they're good friends. What a jerk. I mean, you'd think that Noah would show a little more respect. He shouldn't be palling around with some guy that stalked Ava and cheated on Lacey.

I can't even watch this ridiculousness, so after another minute I stomp over to a table in the corner and sit down.

"Hey," Noah says a few minutes later. "Are you ready?"

"Yes." I walk out the door and head toward the car. "I was waiting for you. And why were you talking to him anyway?"

"Who?" Noah asks.

"Riker!"

"Why wouldn't I talk to him? Because of what happened with him and Ava?"

"Yes!" Seriously, is he that stupid? Probably. I mean, if there's anything I've learned about teenage boys in my (admittedly very limited) experience, it's that they're pretty oblivious.

"I don't care that he broke up with her," he says, shrugging. "Ava's over it, so shouldn't I be, too?"

"He didn't break up with her." We're at the car now, and Noah unlocks the doors. I slide in, being careful not to spill my latte. I wait for Noah to get in, and as soon as he does I say, "*She* broke up with *him*. And then he totally stalked her for, like, ever."

Noah sighs, then shifts the car into gear. "No, he didn't.

He broke up with her, and Ava was really upset about it."

I look at him. "No, he stalked her." But there's a weird feeling in my stomach because, when I really think about it, I never saw any evidence of Riker stalking Ava. I mean, she told me that he was sending her five million emails and texts a day, and she told me that she caught him following her to the mall and driving by her house. But I never saw any of these alleged texts or emails, and anytime I saw Riker around Ava, he seemed perfectly nice. But I just thought that's what made him more creepy—you know, that he would be nice when he saw her, like nothing weird was going on.

"No, he broke up with her. Ava was really upset about it for a couple of weeks, but then she met me and got over it," Noah says. He glances at me out of the corner of his eye.

"Ava told you this?" I ask incredulously.

"Yeah," he says, and shrugs. "So wait, she told you that *she* broke up with *him*?"

"Yeah," I say. "And that he was stalking her."

"Why would she say that?"

"I don't know," I say. "Probably because it's the truth." But I can also think of another reason. She was probably embarrassed that she got dumped.

The thing is, I've always looked up to Ava when it comes to boys—the easy way she blows off their phone calls, the way she doesn't obsess about them, the way she always has that perfect comeback for some guy that's being a douche. I, on the other hand, am a complete disaster when it comes to boys—trying my best to keep them close, falling apart in bathrooms after they cheat on me, thinking I might have a crush on my best friend's boyfriend. . . .

Ava loves being the one I look up to, the one who has it all together. It's our dynamic, and one we're both comfortable with. But if she couldn't even tell me that Riker broke up with her, then what does that say about our friendship?

We're pulling into the parking lot at work now and I turn to Noah, getting ready to ask him about all of this, and about why he was at my house last night, when Lacey comes running out of Cooley's, her face flushed and her hair a mess. "You guys," she says. "You have to get inside. Now. Danielle's here and she will *not* go away."

"What do you mean she won't go away?" I ask.

"I mean, she's, like, refusing to leave." Lacey bites her lip and glances over her shoulder toward the diner fearfully.

"Okay." I sigh and get out of the car. "Come on." I can't believe it's only six a.m. and there's already been this much drama.

The First Day of Senior Year

Noah looks at Sebastian. Sebastian looks at Noah. Noah looks at me. I look at Noah. Noah opens his mouth, like he's thinking about saying something, but then he turns around and walks out of the guidance office. And before I can stop myself, before I even know what I'm doing, I'm running after him.

"Excuse me, young lady," Rosie yells after me. "Once you're in guidance, you *stay* in guidance. You cannot just start *prowling* the halls; you need to—"

But I ignore her and keep going. Noah's far ahead of me already, his long legs giving him a head start.

"Noah!" I yell. He doesn't turn around, he just keeps walking, not varying his speed, but his long, quick strides carry him down the hall and away from me.

I run to catch up with him.

"What's your problem?" I say, stepping in front of him so that he can't go anywhere.

He looks at me like he can't believe I would even ask

such a question. "What's my *problem*?" he says. "You were in the guidance office, holding hands with Sebastian, and you ask me what my *problem* is?"

"I'm surprised you care," I say, shifting my bag on my shoulder and crossing my arms over my chest. "Seeing how you told me that I shouldn't have told Ava what happened last night."

"That's not what I said."

"It *is* what you said."

"No, I said that I never wanted you to ruin your friendship with Ava because of me."

"That's the same thing!" I'm almost yelling now, and we're about one step away from getting yelled at by a teacher, which would not be good, especially since I don't even have a pass to be here or in guidance or anywhere. Technically, I'm supposed to be in social media, and that's where I'll be sent if we get caught.

Noah must realize we're getting loud, because he takes my hand and pulls me around the corner to an alcove under the stairs that lead up to the science wing. It's a small space, so we're forced to stand close, our chests almost touching. "Look," he says. "After what happened last night, for you to be in there holding Sebastian's hand is inexcusable."

"I wasn't holding his hand!" I protest. My heart is beating so hard I'm afraid it might pop right through my chest. It doesn't help that I can see Noah's face up close, the curve of his lip, the stubble on his cheeks that tells me he didn't shave this morning, the way his hair flops over his forehead.

"That's what it looked like to me," Noah says.

"*He* took *my* hand," I say, hoping that will make a difference. But it seems to make Noah mad.

"You let him," he says.

"Not really," I say.

"Hannah." He looks at me, the same way he looked at me last night in the diner, with longing and sadness, and it's like everything I'm feeling I can see in his eyes. I want to kiss him so bad it hurts, but I know I can't. So instead, I tear my gaze from his and look down at the ground.

"Don't be mad," I say.

"I'm not." He takes a breath and lets it out slowly, then runs his fingers through his hair.

"You're not?"

"No," he says. "Not at you." He seems like he's thinking about something for a second, and then, before I can stop him, he's leaving the alcove and walking back toward guidance. Oh, Jesus. What the hell does he think he's going to do? Go into guidance and fight Sebastian? That's the worst plan *ever*, especially since when you get in trouble for fighting, guidance is where they send you. So starting a fight in guidance is like going to a police station to commit a crime.

"Noah," I yell, running after him down the hall. "What are you doing?"

"I'm going to end this," he says.

"Noah! You can't just barge in there and start threatening

him." I'm struggling to keep up, my bag banging against my hip as I go.

"Oh, I'm not going to threaten this time," Noah says.

"No," I say again, stepping in front of him. But before I have to worry about how I'm going to stop Noah, who's twice my size, the bell rings and the hallway fills with kids. It's like the noise and traffic breaks the spell, and suddenly Noah's face changes.

For a second I think he's going to reach out and take my hand, I *want* him to reach out and take my hand, I want him to pull me close to him right here in the hallway and tell me everything's going to be okay, that we'll be together, that whatever happens with Ava, we'll figure it out together.

But before I can see if any of that is going to happen, there's a hand on my shoulder and someone's whirling me around. Hard. For a second, I think it's going to be Ava, back to finish what she started in the diner and kick my ass. But it's not. It's Lacey.

"Hey, Lace," I say, trying not to let my voice betray what's been going on for the past few minutes. Then I realize I don't have to worry about that because Lacey doesn't look like she's in the mood for a chat. Her green eyes are flashing, and I forget about Noah instantly.

"Is it true?" she asks.

"Is what true?" I'm a little confused and having trouble moving from one conversation to the next, and, honestly, so much crazy stuff has happened this morning that I really have no idea what she's talking about. Still, the tone of her voice makes me really nervous, and my stomach flips into an anxious tangle.

"That you slept with Noah." She's talking a little louder now, and a couple of girls in our class turn to stare, then completely stop and huddle over by the wall, watching us.

"Lacey," I say quickly, grabbing her arm and trying to steer her down the hall. "Let's get out of here, let's go somewhere and talk about—"

"No," she says, wrenching her arm out of my grasp. "Is it true? Tell me. Now."

"Who told you that?"

"Ava," she says. "Ava told me." Figures. Now that Ava's pissed at me, she probably decided she would tell Lacey and ruin my friendship with her, too. They probably sat together at lunch or in class, bonding over what a horrible person I am. I picture the two of them becoming best friends, wearing matching sweaters and going on double dates, filling up each other's Facebook walls with private jokes. Suddenly the room is spinning and my face is really hot, and I feel like I can't control my thoughts. But I know, at least, that there's no sense in lying, so I take a deep breath and say, "Yes, it's true."

I wonder if Noah's still behind me, watching, if he's okay with me telling people what happened, if he's mad that Lacey is probably going to hate him now, too. And I'm not sure if it's my imagination, but I think I hear the two girls who are watching the drama gasp.

"How could you?" Lacey asks.

"Lacey, I didn't mean to, it wasn't—"

"You didn't *mean* to? Hannah, I don't like Ava, but she was your best friend! You know that exact same thing happened to me with Riker, and now you . . . you just did it to someone else." Her eyes are filling with tears, and for some reason, I have a feeling that this might be hurting her even more than it hurt Ava.

"Lacey—" I start.

"No," she says. "Don't ever talk to me again."

And then she's gone. And when I turn around, Noah's gone, too.

The Summer

"So what's she doing in there?" I ask, walking toward the diner, Lacey ambling along behind me.

"Just sitting." Lacey chews on her lip. "And she's insisting that we talk. Like, really insisting. She won't take no for an answer." She frowns. "It's kind of scary, actually."

I turn around and look at Noah, who's out of the car now and a few feet behind us. "Would you mind going inside and starting to open?" I ask. "Lacey and I will be in in a second."

"Sure," he says, and rushes toward Cooley's. He actually looks a little relieved, probably because he doesn't want to get too involved in the drama. Guys get all weird when it comes to things like this. They have a hard time comprehending things like feelings and talking things out and sorting through problems. They just want to fistfight and get it over with. That's probably why so many relationships have issues. Guys just don't know how to resolve conflict in a way that makes sense to girls, i.e. marathon phone conversations and lots of crying.

"Now," I say to Lacey. "We cannot stay out here."

"Why not?" she asks.

"Because she can see us through the window." Lacey turns around to look, and there's Danielle, sitting at one of the booths by the window, peering out at us with a pissy look on her face. "Don't look!" I say. Lacey averts her eyes immediately. "What is she doing here so early anyway? Shouldn't she be in bed?"

"She has a new job working overnights at an answering service," Lacey says. "So she got off work and came here. And she says she's going to come back here every day until I talk to her!" Lacey looks like she really might lose it. I hope she brought her Xanax.

"Okay," I say, squaring my shoulders and looking Lacey in the eye. "Listen. We are going to walk back in there, and you are going to tell her that you have to go into the back to take care of something, something very important and work-related. Then you and I are going to go into the storage room and make a plan."

"Okay," Lacey says, but she doesn't seem that certain. I wouldn't be either, if I were her. I mean, all you have to do is look at my love life, and you'd be able to see that I'm definitely not to be trusted when it comes to making plans and dealing with interpersonal relationships. Not to mention, I have no idea what kind of plan I'm going to come up with.

But I guess she really has no other choice, because she follows me inside and tells Danielle that we have to take care of something in the back, just like I told her to.

"Okay," I say once we're in the storage room. "Tell me everything." I pull up an empty bucket that we use for mopping the floors, flip it over and sit down.

"Well," Lacey says, "She came in here and I said 'sorry, we're not open yet, you'll have to wait outside' you know, all mean-like." She looks proud of herself.

"Good for you," I say, nodding. "She shouldn't feel like she can just show up here before we're even open."

"I know!" she says. "It sucks the way people are just always showing up here! I mean, who cares if it's a public place? It's our place of business, and they should respect that. And it was really hard for me to tell her we weren't open yet, you know? Because I was sooo afraid I was going to break out in hives again. The doctor said stress could bring them on."

I just nod, not pointing out that if she *does* break out in hives again, it would be fine, since the doctor gave her a cream and told her she could take Benadryl. They think the hives were probably caused by stress, or maybe an allergic reaction to something, which, of course, is driving Lacey completely crazy since she has no idea what she might be allergic to. It was all I could do to keep her from throwing out all her clothes (it could be something in the fabric) and quitting her job (it could be something in the air).

"And what did Danielle say to *that*?" I ask.

"She said 'Lace, I really need to talk to you.'"

"She calls you Lace? I thought I was the only one who called you Lace!" Not that I call her that very often. But still. I don't want Danielle calling her that, too.

"You are." She walks over to the sink in the corner and starts washing her hands, which probably means she's really nervous. When Lacey starts getting nervous, she goes on a mission to get rid of germs. "Well, you're the only who calls me 'Lace' that I'm speaking to, at least. So it doesn't matter what Danielle calls me, because really, she shouldn't be calling me *anything*."

"I guess," I say glumly, until I remember that this is about her, not me. "So then what?"

"So then you guys showed up and I said 'excuse me, I have to go tell my co-workers something very important,' and then she just plopped down in a booth like it was completely okay for her to be here!"

"Did you tell her to leave?" I ask.

"No," she says.

"I thought you said she wouldn't take no for an answer?"

"Well, she wouldn't," Lacey says. "I mean, it wasn't what she said exactly, it's *how* she said it. And the way she sat down in that booth made it clear she was not going to move anytime soon."

I sigh. "So what did she do exactly? You know, to cause this whole fight?"

Lacey looks at me like she can't believe what I'm asking her. "She stole Riker right out from under my nose!"

"No, I know that," I say. I try to figure out how to put this delicately, without upsetting Lacey, especially since she's already upset. And who knows, maybe her hives really are stress-induced. "But what did she *do*? Like, exactly. Was it just one night at a party, like it was with me and Sebastian?"

"No," Lacey says. Her green eyes fill with tears, and she turns away.

"It's okay," I say quickly. "You don't have to tell me, the details don't really matter."

"No, it's . . . it wasn't a one-time thing. They'd been sneaking around for months." She shrugs, then pulls a paper towel out of the dispenser, drops it in the garbage (the first one is too germy for her), and takes the next one and uses it to gently dab at her mascara. "It was pretty simple, actually. One morning I drove to Riker's, because I'd left my work shirt over there, and Danielle was coming out of his house. Riker came out behind her and he was all disheveled like he'd just woken up, and he didn't have a shirt on, and he kissed her and then walked her to her car, which was parked behind the house in the wrap-around driveway. I guess so no one would see."

"Did you confront her?"

"Yeah," she says. "She admitted it, but only because she'd been caught. I mean, what else could she do?" Her eyes dart to the closed door. "And now she's *out there*." She says "out there" in a whisper, like Danielle is a deranged serial killer, waiting for Lacey to come out so she can attack her with a meat cleaver.

"Okay," I say, standing up. "You are going to go out there. And you are going to tell her that you guys are not going to be friends. Ever, ever again." I shake my head emphatically. "What she did to you is inexcusable! She should be ashamed of herself." My face gets a little hot, thinking about Noah picking me up this morning, about how he asked me to lie to Ava about the night we went to the concert, about how he was at my house at one in the morning for some reason. The guilt washes over me in a huge wave, and it's almost unbearable. And the next thing I know, *my* eyes are filling with tears.

"Hannah, are you . . . Are you crying?" Lacey asks, peering closely at my face.

"No," I say, even though I kind of am. "Well, sort of. God, I must be getting my period or something, I don't know, I'm a mess." I swipe at my tears with the back of my hand.

"You're not a mess," Lacey says, bending down and giving me a hug. "You're just upset for me. Which means you're a good friend. No, a *great* friend." I hug her back, feeling guiltier than ever.

Danielle's sitting in her favorite booth, the one she poured the glass of water all over that day. Cooley's is open now, so there are a couple of older men sitting at the counter drinking coffee and reading the paper. They're regulars, the grouchy, old kind of regulars, and I'm not sure they're going to be too pleased if Lacey and Danielle start getting into a ton of teenage-girl drama in front of them. And if they happen to tell Cooley about it, he's *definitely* not going to be too pleased.

"Take her outside," I tell Lacey. She looks panicked at the thought of what taking it outside could turn into (let's face it, when you say "let's take this outside" usually nothing good happens once you get there), but nods. I watch as she goes over to Danielle, says something to her, and then follows her out onto the sidewalk.

"What's going on?" Noah asks. He's behind the counter, brewing up a fresh pot of coffee and refilling the cream pitchers.

"Danielle showed up here wanting to talk," I say, shrugging. "So they're talking. Don't worry, I gave Lacey a pep talk."

"What do you mean, a pep talk?" Noah asks, looking worried even though I just told him not to be.

"A pep talk," I say. "You know, a talk of pep? A rally call? What they give you in sports to get you all riled up?" I reach behind the counter and pull out the big stack of menus, then grab a towel from the counter. You'd be surprised how disgusting and sticky the menus can get. It's like everyone who orders pancakes is pouring syrup all over them or something. That would be a good trick for Danielle to learn. She could go from pouring water on tables to pouring syrup on menus.

"But you told her to listen to her, right? To what she has to say?"

"To what who has to say?"

"Danielle!"

"No, I did not tell her to listen to what Danielle has to say," I say, shocked. "Danielle did something really heinous to her, which I will not get into right now since I'm not sure Lacey wants me discussing it with you." He rolls his eyes at me, like I'm making a big deal out of nothing. "Don't roll your eyes at me," I say. "You haven't been cheated on, so you can't talk. "

I think about the male voices I heard the other day on the phone with Ava, and wonder if maybe Noah *has* been cheated on. Who knows what the hell Ava's been up to. I remember one time, a while ago, before she met Noah, Ava said if you hook up with a guy in another area code, it doesn't count as cheating. Of course, we were in seventh grade then and neither one of us had boyfriends, much less guys in other area codes we could cheat on them with, but still.

"I already know what happened," he says. "Riker cheated on her with Danielle."

"Yes," I say. "But you don't know all the horrible details. And you know what? It doesn't really matter. All you need to know is that her boyfriend cheated with her best friend."

"And Lacey's not even going to talk to Danielle about it? She's not even going to give her a chance to explain?"

"What's to explain?" I ask, wiping down a menu and trying to ignore the uncomfortable feeling I keep getting in my stomach, the feeling that keeps reminding me about how Noah came to my house last night at one a.m., and about how we haven't even talked about why he was there. I wonder if

I'm afraid to bring it up, and if I'm not afraid, why I don't. Maybe Noah was up late talking to Ava, and she told him it was fine if we hang out, that he should make up with me. But then why didn't he just talk to me at work this morning? Why would he come over to my house in the middle of the night?

"So Lacey doesn't even want to hear Danielle's side of the story?" Noah asks. He takes the now-full coffeepot, sets it on the warmer, and gets to work making another batch. The guys at the counter really take this whole "bottomless cup of coffee" thing to another level. With the kind of coffee we serve here, I'm surprised they still have any stomachs left.

"Her side of the story?" Suddenly, I'm furious at him. "What could her side of the story possibly be? 'I wanted to have sex with your boyfriend, so I just did'?"

"No," he says. "Sometimes people do things that are complicated. For complicated reasons."

"Right," I say. "Like showing up at someone's house at one o'clock in the morning." Noah turns around and looks at me, a stricken look on his face. I've never seen him look that way, not even when he caught me reading his screenplay that day. But he doesn't say anything, just turns around and goes back to making the coffee, which enrages me even more. "Or like if someone's writing a screenplay and doesn't want anyone to know about it."

The muscles in his arm flex as he puts the pot on the

burner and his mouth tightens as he turns back around. "That's not fair," he says.

"Why not?" I ask. Suddenly, I feel like I want to take everything out on him. The fact that Ava lied to me about how she and Riker broke up, the fact that Lacey is outside right now talking to a girl who did something horrible to her, the fact that Sebastian cheated on me. And most of all I want to punish him for the fact that I could be as horrible as Danielle, because every second, ever since that night at the concert, every time I'm around Noah, all I want to do is kiss him.

"Because you don't know what you're talking about," he says. "And you shouldn't talk about things you know nothing about."

"Guys!" Lacey says, running into Cooley's, her face all flushed. "I did it! I told her to leave me alone and that I don't want to be friends anymore!" She twirls around. "I finally stood up to her!"

"Good for you, Lace," I say, shooting Noah a pointed look.

He doesn't say anything for a beat, but then finally, he looks at Lacey and says softly, "Yeah. Good for you."

The First Day of Senior Year

I can't afford to miss another class, which means I have to go to seventh period world history, even though I'm a mess. I decide take a seat in the back, and hope I don't have a total and complete breakdown in front of everyone. Although if I did, no one could really blame me. I mean, I've ruined everything. My whole entire life! And for what? Some dumb boy?

Everyone knows that you should never wreck your life for a boy, and especially not one that you meet while you're in high school. Seriously, *everyone* knows it. You never hear someone say, "Oh, wow, you're seventeen and you really like him? That's great, you should do whatever it takes to get him, even if it means wrecking your whole life." The only people who would even come *close* to saying something like that are the people who are actually dumb enough to do it, right before they end up wrecking their whole lives. And then they realize how stupid they were for doing it.

A tear falls down my cheek and onto my notebook,

making a splotch on the cover. Great. I hate when the covers of my notebooks get splotchy! Of course, a splotchy notebook cover is really the least of my problems at this point.

And then a problem I forgot all about comes waltzing into the room and sits down in the seat next to me. And that problem is named Jemima Marshall.

"Hey," she says, softly. I don't say anything, because I am so not in the mood to deal with this right now. She fidgets around in her seat, then scratches at a mosquito bite on her elbow.

"What are you doing in this class?" I ask finally. "I didn't know sophomores could take world history."

"It's an elective," she says. "And I needed another history credit." Great. Now I can be reminded every day of what a mess my life is. Maybe if I'm really lucky I'll fail, and she'll get an A and end up going to Yale because of it or something. Not right away, of course. She's only a sophomore.

"Good for you," I say, annoyed. I contemplate picking up all my stuff and moving a few rows over, but the room is filling up now and that would look really obvious. People would talk about it. Which they're probably going to do already, but no sense adding fuel to the fire.

"Why are you crying?" Jemima asks.

"I'm not."

"Yes, you are," she says, but not in a mean way, more just matter-of-fact. "Your eyes are all red and your notebook is all splotchy."

"My eyes are all red? How red?" Not that I really care

how they look (who do I have to impress?) but I'm pretty sure the rumors are already flying about my showdown in the hallway with Lacey, and if people know I'm crying, that will be even more humiliating. God, I really wish I could go home. Only two more periods to go, and then I'll be out of this hellhole. Of course, I'll have the next ten months to deal with, but I'll worry about that later.

"Not that bad," Jemima says, but she says it the way you tell someone they look fine after they've put on a bunch of weight. She reaches into her bag and pulls out a mirror, a concealer stick, and a bottle of Visine. "If you do it quick, no one will notice," she says.

"Thanks." I accept the items gratefully, then use a few drops of Visine and dab some concealer under my eyes. A quick look in the mirror lets me know that even if it's not perfect, it's a lot better. And I feel a little better, too.

"So listen," she says. "About—"

"Look," I tell her. "I'm sorry I said that thing earlier about suing you. No one's going to sue you. Lacey's fine." Just saying Lacey's name makes me sad, and it gets stuck in my throat for a second before I can push it out. It's also kind of a lie, since Lacey definitely isn't fine. Ohmigod. What if her hives came back? And it's all because of me? Or what if her acid reflux gets going? That's the new thing that happens to her now when she gets stressed. "I'll find out how much it's going to cost to get my car fixed, and then I'll let you know, okay? And we can go from there."

"Okay," she says, then scratches the bite on her elbow again. "But that's not what I wanted to talk to you about."

"What did you want to talk to me about?"

"Sebastian," she says. "And that night at the party."

Oh for the love of God. I glance at the clock on the wall, willing the second hand to move faster so the bell will ring, class will begin, and this conversation will end. "We don't need to talk about that," I say, forcing a smile onto my face and hoping she buys it.

"Yes," she says. "We do." She takes a deep breath. More scratching of her elbow. "Look, I want you to know that I didn't know he had a girlfriend."

"You didn't know he had a girlfriend?"

"No," she says.

"You didn't ask him?"

"No," she says, surprised. "Why would I? Some guy was flirting with me and then tried to kiss me in a pool. I assumed he was single. Did you ask him if he had a girlfriend when you first met him?"

"No," I say, then shift on my chair uncomfortably. She has a point. Also, I kind of like that she gave me a little bit of attitude. I mean, she's obviously super apologetic and she knows it's a horrible situation, and she's definitely nervous I might flip the fuck out on her, but she doesn't seem embarrassed. It's more like she thinks shit happens, and I should deal with it. I can respect that.

"Anyway, I wanted to say I'm sorry. It doesn't make it right, it just . . . makes it what it is."

The bell rings then, and I turn around in my seat, thinking I agree with her, that it is just what it is. And not just the situation with Sebastian. But I still wish I knew how I could make it right. How I could make everything right.

The Summer

Noah and I aren't talking again. Not for the rest of the day. Not for the rest of the week. It's probably for the best, because I'm actually able to kind of forget about the whole, uh, situation with us. Until one day, a week or so later, when Lacey and I are eating Chinese food at the mall food court. We've spent the past two hours trying on ridiculously expensive prom dresses we will never wear, and have decided to reward ourselves with General Gau's. We even splurged and got wonton soup to go with it. (I figured an extra two dollars for soup is the least I can do for myself—plus I'm so close to having enough money for my car that I decide it's okay to treat myself) when my phone rings. Ava.

"Ava," I tell Lacey, and she wrinkles up her nose and makes a face.

"You better answer it," she says, slurping up another spoonful of soup. "Otherwise she's just going to keep calling. I'll go get us some more crispy noodles."

"Hey," I say into my phone as Lacey leaves the table. Even though Noah and I haven't been talking, Ava and I have actually been in almost-constant contact. I think now that the summer is getting closer to being over and she's been at camp so long, she's getting more homesick and missing me and Noah more.

Not that I know anything about how much she's talking to Noah. She doesn't bring him up, and when she does, it's to tell me how she just got off the phone with him, or to ask if I know whether or not he's still at work. I'm assuming she doesn't know that he and I aren't talking, since she hasn't brought it up. I'm not sure what's going to happen when she comes back and we all have to be in the same room together. But I guess I'll cross that bridge when I come to it.

"How's my little Lewis and Clark?" I ask her.

"Ugh, stop calling me that," she says, but she's laughing. Ever since a couple of weeks ago when Ava got her campers lost on a hiking trip, I've been calling her my little Lewis and Clark. She always tells me to stop, but I know she secretly likes it even though it's not the most witty, as far as nicknames go. Also, it doesn't really make much sense, because Lewis and Clark were two people, not one.

"I miss you, Aves," I say.

"I miss you too, Hans," she says. "But only three more days until I see you!"

It takes me a second to realize what she's talking about, since she's not supposed to come back for another few weeks. And then I remember. The trip. That I'm supposed to go on. With Noah. To Maine. To visit her. She doesn't think that's still happening does she? We haven't even talked about it again since that first day she brought it up to me. But that's Ava for you, just assuming something's a plan when it's not. Obviously I *cannot* go to Maine since Noah and I aren't even speaking, much less able to sit in a car together for three hours and then spend a whole weekend hanging out with Ava. I mean, holy freaking crap.

"Yeah," I say slowly, wondering how I'm going to break this to her.

"I'm sooo excited," she says. "You guys are gonna love it here!"

"The thing is, Ava," I say. "I'm still not sure I can get the time off of work. Weekends are our busiest time, and usually I have to work both days, otherwise—"

"That's the best part!" she says. "I talked to Cooley!"

"You talked to Cooley?"

"Yup! And I got him to give you the time off."

My stomach drops. "You got him to give me the time off?"

"Yeah," she says. "Well, Friday and Saturday at least. It turns out he needs to hire some new people when you guys go back to school, and this will give them a chance to do a trial run. You know, work out the kinks." I don't say anything. "Hannah? Are you there?"

"Yeah," I say. "I'm here, I'm just . . . I'm shocked." And

a little pissed that she went behind my back and talked to my boss, but I don't say that. I take a sip of my water.

"I knew you would be," she says. "That's why I hadn't brought it up in so long, I wanted it to be a surprise. We're gonna have so much fun, we can—Oh, shit! Hannah, I have to go, one of my campers is puking." The sound of someone getting sick comes through the phone, and then it goes dead.

Lacey returns to the table, holding a huge bowl of crispy noodles. "Hey," she says. "Everything okay?"

"Yup," I say, forcing myself to smile, and then reaching out and grabbing a handful of noodles. "But we're definitely going to have to stop for ice cream after this."

Later that night, I stand on Noah's front porch, my palms sweaty and my heart racing. But I don't really have a choice. I have to talk to him and figure out what we're going to do about our trip. Should I go? If I *don't* go, will Ava be suspicious? Is Noah maybe going to refuse to drive me? What will we tell Ava? Can I fake an illness? Will she believe it? Does she know something is going on with me and Noah? *Is* something going on with me and Noah? Maybe we can say that I can't get off work after all, that at the last minute one of the new people got sick and I had to cover.

God, I really should have just called. I didn't want to take the chance that Noah wouldn't answer, and then I'd have to spend the whole night wondering if he wasn't near his phone or if he just didn't want to talk to me. Plus, I definitely thought this was the kind of convo you should have in person. But now I'm thinking I should probably just go home and maybe send a text or —

The door flies open, and there's Noah, standing behind the screen. He has on a pair of track pants and a T-shirt, and he's holding one of those shaker cups full of a thick brown liquid. Probably a protein shake. Or a Boost.

"Hi," I say.

"Hey," he says. I wait for him to say something else, but he doesn't. I shift on my legs, which suddenly feel all wobbly, although that could be from the walk over here, which is about two miles. But what else could I do? I couldn't ask Lacey to drive me, she would have asked why I was going to Noah's. She picks me up for work without asking too many questions, because she just thinks Noah got sick of getting up so early, and at work Noah and I are cordial so she doesn't get suspicious. But driving over to his house at night? She would definitely know something's up.

I want to tell him that we need to talk, but that sounds so . . . serious and stereotypical, and besides, I'm not really sure we need to have a big talk about it. But before I can say anything, Noah says, "Do you wanna go for a ride? We could . . . talk?"

I nod, not trusting myself to say anything. "Do you mind waiting while I take a shower? I just got back from the gym." I shake my head no, and he holds the screen door open. "Do you want to come in?"

I shake my head again. "I'll stay out here." I sit down on the porch and take in deep breaths of the late summer air, and before I know it, before I'm ready, Noah's back at the door.

He's changed into a pair of khaki shorts and the T-shirt that he got at The Spill Canvas concert that night. He bought it from one of the opening acts, a band called Treaty of Paris. The shirt says I HELPED TREATY OF PARIS GET TO THEIR NEXT SHOW with a picture of a tour bus. I try to calm my heart again unsuccessfully. Did he wear the shirt because of me? Is it some kind of sign that everything is going to be okay with the two of us? That we're going to be friends?

I follow him to his car, and we drive, not saying anything, me not even knowing where we're going, until finally we're at Monsumet Beach. The sun is dipping down, with only about an hour or so before it sets completely. Most everyone has gone for the day, but there are still a few people hanging out on picnic tables enjoying a late dinner.

We don't say anything as we walk through the sand toward the water. Finally, we stop, and Noah spreads out the towel he grabbed from his trunk so we could sit without getting all sandy. I'm happy to keep up the whole silence thing we have going on, but as soon as we're settled, Noah says, "So should we talk about what's going on with us?"

"Okay." I swallow. "Um, should we talk about the trip first, or our fight?"

"Our fight?" He frowns, his eyebrows knitting together in confusion.

"Yeah, our fight. You know, the fight we got into the other day?"

"I didn't know it was a fight."

"You didn't? We said kind of mean things to each other."

"I didn't say anything mean to you."

I think about it. He's right. He didn't say anything mean to me. "Well, I said something mean to you. About how you lie about your screenplay." I leave out the part about him showing up at my house at one in the morning, not quite ready to go there.

"I do lie about my screenplay." He shrugs, like it's not a big deal to call someone out on their lies. "Well, not really lie," he says. "More like, don't tell people. Which I guess is a lie by omission." I shift on the blanket, wondering if he's thinking of how we're both kind of lying to Ava by omission.

"Why?" I ask.

"Why what?"

"Why do you lie by omission? I mean, how come you don't tell people you're writing it?" I'm not sure why I'm asking. I guess because I want to know why he decided to tell me about his screenplay when he hasn't told any-one else. "I mean, I know you don't want people to ask you about it and bother you about it, but couldn't you just tell them not to do that?"

"Writing a screenplay is a really big fucking deal," he says.

"I know," I say. "Which is why I don't understand why you wouldn't want people to know."

"What do you think most people would say if I told them?"

I think about it. "Probably they would ask to read it."

"Exactly."

"But I didn't ask to read it."

"I know," he says. "For some reason, I knew you would get that it's cool just that I'm writing it."

"But what if I *had* asked to read it?"

"Well, I would have had to say no because I don't want anyone reading it."

"Because you don't know if it's good or not?"

"Yeah," he says. "And if you said it was good, I would think you were just saying it because you're my friend. And if you said it wasn't good I'd probably be crushed. So it's a no-win situation."

I nod. We sit there for a few minutes not saying any-thing, just enjoying the cool air and the breeze, watching the seagulls dip down over the water and the families on the beach pack up their sand pails and shovels. After a few minutes, I shiver from the breeze that's now blowing off the water, and Noah reaches over and hands me one of the sweatshirts he brought from the car. It smells like him, and I look down at my hands, trying to figure out what to say.

Finally I settle on, "So. We're friends?"

"What?"

"You just said that if I liked your screenplay, you wouldn't believe me because we're friends."

"Yes," he says, looking me right in the eye. "We're friends. Right?"

"Right," I say, hoping my voice sounds stronger than I feel. Because the truth is, Noah and I aren't friends. You can't be friends with someone who makes you feel the way Noah makes me feel, you can't be friends with someone who makes your head all cloudy when he gives you his sweatshirt, you can't be friends with someone who shows up at your house at one a.m. for a mysterious reason, and you can't be friends with someone who tells you about their screenplay which nobody else knows about. But you also can't be *more* than friends with your best friend's boyfriend.

"So," I say. "About the trip . . ."

I trail off, because even though I've been dreading it, suddenly I want to go. I want to go to Maine, partly because I want to spend time with Noah outside of work, and partly because I want to see Ava. Maybe if we're all there together, I can prove to myself that nothing really is going on between me and Noah. I'll see them together, and it'll be like it was before.

257

"I'll pick you up Friday?" Noah asks. "At, like, around seven?"

"Sounds good," I say, hoping I sound like I mean it. We sit there for a little while longer, then head back to the car.

That night, when I check my email, I have one from Noah. And attached to it is his screenplay.

The First Day of Senior Year

Between seventh and eighth periods, I remember something horrible. Something I can't believe slipped my mind, something I should have remembered way before, but I guess I didn't because I had too much other stuff going on.

And it's that ninth period, the last period of the day, I have ceramics. Which in and of itself isn't that big of a deal — ceramics is an art elective, and it's supposedly pretty easy as far as art electives go. The teacher, Mr. Guthrie, is super laid back, so you spend most of your time throwing bowls and then glazing them. They only offer one section of it per semester, since there's only one pottery wheel, so unless you're a senior, it's almost impossible to get into.

And at the end of last year, Ava, Sebastian, Noah, and I all signed up for it. We figured it'd be an easy A, it would get our art elective over with, and it would guarantee that we'd all have at least one class together. Unfortunately, that means that at the end of the day, we're all going to be together. In one class. Not even sitting in desks, but at those long tables that are in all the art rooms, the kind that allow people to mingle and talk and maybe even get into fights. When I remember all of this, I realize there's no way we can all be in the same room together. So I have no choice but to go back down to guidance.

"Oh, hi," I say to Rosie when I get there, giving her an embarrassed grin. "Sorry about that before." I roll my eyes, like, *wow, who hasn't been in a situation like that, wasn't it crazy?*

But Rosie's not having it. "You mean when you ran out of here and caused a big disturbance in the hall that would have constituted me writing you up if I weren't so busy in here?" she asks.

I want to tell her that (a) she doesn't have the authority to write people up, that only teachers can do that, (b) she doesn't really look that busy, since it seems like she's been spending most of her time turning people away, and (c) she really shouldn't mess with me, because I'm definitely not in the mood.

But instead I just smile sweetly and say, "Yes, well, I'm obviously in need of some guidance." When did I become such a smartass? I have no idea. I think I've been pushed to my brink. Normally I wouldn't dare say that to someone. Ever. Secretary or not.

"Obviously," she says.

"So can I see Mr. Davies?"

"No," she says. "You had your chance. You blew it."

I don't even bother listening to her. I just march over to a chair in the corner and sit down. Again, I don't know where this is coming from. Until today, I've never been in trouble at school. I hardly ever even skip class. I seriously might have really lost my mind. Like, for real. Not that anyone could blame me.

"What are you doing?" Rosie asks, sounding aghast.

"Waiting for Mr. Davies." I cross my legs and fold my hands on my lap primly.

Rosie looks at me for a second, then reaches over and buzzes Mr. Davies on the phone. "I have Hannah Kaplan in here," she says. I guess she knows my name after our little interaction earlier. Which I'm not sure is a good thing. "She's *insisting* on seeing you, and being very belligerent, not to mention that scene she caused in the hall earlier. Shall I write her up and send her back to class?" She listens for a second, and then her lips purse up and she replaces the receiver without saying goodbye. Judging from the dirty look she gives me, I'm assuming Mr. Davies said he'd see me. She turns away and then starts typing something into her computer, probably updating her Facebook page with something about how she can't deal with the little snots that go to this school. I've seen her write similar things on there before. She has her page set to private, but Sebastian knows ways around that.

After about twenty minutes, Mr. Davies calls me in. Which is no good. I haven't missed ceramics yet, and I realize that, in my panic, I've made a huge tactical error. I should have come here *during* ceramics. But now that I'm already here, I can't just leave and decide I'm coming back later. Especially with Rosie out there. Which means I'm just going to have to convince Mr. Davies that I need to drop ceramics. Immediately.

"Hi, Mr. Davies," I say as soon as I'm in his office.

"Hello, Hannah," he says, pushing his glasses further up his nose. "What can I do for you today?" Mr. Davies looks exactly the way you'd expect a guidance counselor to look, with a trim little mustache and glasses. He's always wearing sweater vests, even when the weather is super hot, and he's never without a cup of coffee.

I pull my schedule out from under the cover of my math book and slide it across the desk at him. Better make this quick, hit him before he has a chance to realize what I'm doing. Not that he could have any idea of my real motives. "I need to drop ceramics, so can I have a drop slip?" Wow, I've really gotten very aggressive today. It's kind of making me uncomfortable, if you want to know the truth.

"Now, Hannah," Mr. Davies says, looking down at my schedule. "Why would you want to drop ceramics? That's a very hard class to get into."

"I know," I say. "But, um, . . ." I wrack my brain, trying to think of an excuse. I really should have planned this out better. "My hands are just . . . I mean, I've been having arthritis or Carpal Tunnel or something, and it's really not good for me to work with clay."

Mr. Davies frowns, and I don't blame him. It sounds lame

even to me, and I'm the one who made it up. "That doesn't sound right," he says. "Listen, why don't you give it a shot for a couple of days, and then if you still want to drop it, come back here and we'll talk, okay?"

"No!" I almost scream. "I mean, I can't. It . . . It will only take a few minutes of working with the clay to set off my hands." I try to contort my face in a mask of pain, then reach my fingers up and flex them at him.

Mr. Davies frowns again, his bushy eyebrows knotting together over the top of his glasses. Then understanding dawns on his face, and he looks at me. "Does this have anything to do with what happened in the hall earlier?"

"What do you mean?"

"The scene in the hall? Between you and Lacey and Noah?"

"Nooo," I say. "It doesn't have anything to do with that." I try to sound offended, like high school dramas have no bearing on the decisions I make, even though we both know that making decisions based on high school dramas is, like, the basis of your teenage years.

"Hannah, running away from your problems isn't going to change them. Now, let me write you a pass back to Western Civ." God. Does he have to be such a guidance counselor? Seriously, guidance counselors are always putting the fact that they're supposed to be guiding us above treating us like human beings. It's really kind of annoying.

And that's when it happens. I lose all my self-respect.

I literally throw myself across his desk. "Please!" I say. "Please, you don't understand. I cannot be in that ceramics class. Please, Mr. Davies."

He looks at me and for a moment, I think maybe, just maybe, he's going to change his mind. He's going to say that even though he doesn't believe in running away from things, that it's okay this one time, that he's going to make an exception, that he trusts me to know what's best for myself. The indecision flickers over his face, but the next thing I know, he's signing the pass for me, sending me back to Western Civ.

"Hannah," he says. "Please return to class. And next period, I'll expect to hear that you're in ceramics."

So what can I do? I take the pass. Which means that next period, I'll be in the same room as Ava. And Noah. And Sebastian. I leave guidance, and I don't think it's my imagination that Rosie smirks at me as I go by.

The Summer

"Okay," Noah says when I open the door at seven a.m. on the morning of our trip. "Are you ready to rock 'n' roll?"

I stare at him blankly. "First of all, no one says 'are you ready to rock 'n' roll?' anymore."

"They don't?"

"No. And second, do I *look* like I'm ready to rock 'n' roll?" He takes in my hair (a mess), my clothes (the T-shirt and shorts that I slept in), and the space in the hallway behind me (a tangle of suitcases, bags, and clothes, with a stray curling iron and some makeup thrown in for good measure).

"No," he says. "You don't. What is all this mess?"

"Packing," I say, walking toward the pile and almost tripping over the cord to my hot-roller set.

"We're only going for two nights."

"I know," I say. "But I've never been to a summer camp before. I don't know what to wear."

"You don't know what to wear to camp?" Noah looks

perplexed, like it should be obvious. But it's really not.

"Yeah," I say. "I mean, I know I need mostly casual clothes, like shorts, T-shirts, stuff like that." I point to my open suitcase, where a bunch of those items are shoved into one corner. "But will we be going out at all? Like on Ava's time off? Will we go out to dinner? If so, I should probably bring regular clothes. And what if we decide to go to a nice place? Then I should probably bring a nice sundress or something. And what if she wants to go out both nights? Then I need two. And what if it rains? Do I need sneakers? Are we going to go hiking? How messy will I get? Are there showers? I want to bring my hair dryer, but are there even outlets?"

"I see what you mean," Noah says, nodding mock-seriously. "There are very important decisions to be made here."

"Life-changing," I agree. "Or at least trip-changing."

"I vote for three T-shirts and pairs of shorts, one nice pair of jeans, a nice shirt, two sundresses, and all your hair dryers and stuff, just in case. Also, wear your sandals in the car, but pack your sneakers in case of a hike."

I stare at him in awe. "That was an amazing amount of distillation."

"Yeah, well, I'm an amazing distiller."

He grins, and I grin back, then gather up all the stuff he told me I would need, place it in my suitcase, and zip it all up. I hurry upstairs, run a brush through my hair, change into a pair of jean shorts and a tank, step into my sparkly black slides, and run down the stairs. "Ready," I say.

When we get in the car, Noah pulls out his iPod and plugs it in. "I made a new playlist," he says.

"You made a playlist for us?" Then I realize how that sounds, and so I quickly add, "I mean not for us, I know not for *us*, but for the trip?"

Somehow the babbling makes it even worse, and Noah looks uncomfortable for a second and then he says, "Yeah, a lot of The Spill Canvas and some stuff you haven't heard before."

"Cool," I say, sliding my seat belt over my lap. "How long does it take to get there?"

He checks the GPS. "Two and a half hours," he says.

"Yay, road trip!"

Three hours later, we've gone twenty miles. There's some kind of horrible accident on the Mass Pike, and we've been stuck in traffic forever. We can't even get off the highway, because the shoulder's closed and there's nowhere to go. "I should call Ava," I say. "And tell her that we're going to be late."

"Good idea," he says. I can't believe neither one of us thought to call her earlier, but honestly, sitting in traffic with Noah hasn't really been all that bad. We've been talking and listening to music, and the time has just flown by. The only thing we haven't talked about is his screenplay, which I *do* want to talk about, but haven't brought up because:

a. I don't know what to say about it. I mean, I read it three times and it was amazing and well-written and I loved it, even though I have some ideas on what he could do to sharpen some of the girl's dialogue and the romance between the two characters. But I don't know how to bring it up, since it's obviously a big deal for him to show it to anyone, and I really don't want him to think that I'm saying I like it just because I feel I have to.

b. I don't know what it means that he showed it to me. Sometimes (okay, a lot of times) late at night when I'm in bed, I think about how no one else, not even Ava, has read it, and how that has to mean something. And then I hope I'm right, while at the same time hoping that I'm wrong. Because if I am right, and it does mean something, then what does that mean? And if I'm wrong, and it doesn't mean anything, well, then . . . that would kind of break my heart a little bit.

I push all that stuff out of my head and dial Ava's number. "Hi," I say when she answers.

"Hi!" she says. "Are you almost here? Just pull around to the south parking lot, you'll see a big sign that says 'visitors.' I'm in the dining hall, but I can—"

"Actually, we're not almost there," I say. "Not even close. We got stuck in traffic, we've been sitting on the Pike for, like, three hours." Silence.

Then, "Well, how far away are you?"

"We're only about twenty minutes from home," I say. "And to tell you the truth, it doesn't seem like it's going to be breaking up anytime soon."

More silence. Then, "Oh."

"Oh?" I ask. "Are you mad?"

"Not mad," she says. "It's just kind of rude of you not to call me before this."

"I know," I say. "I'm so sorry, we just lost track of time." Next to me, Noah is going through his iPod, scrolling through songs until he settles on one. "Ohmigod!" I say as the first notes come out of the speakers. "This is Sting! I recognize his voice."

Noah reaches over and gives me a high-five. "There might be hope for you yet," he says.

"Excuse me?" Ava screeches.

"Oh," I say. "Nothing, sorry, I just . . . I got excited because I recognized a Sting song Noah put on."

"So?"

"So he thinks I have horrible taste in music, and he's been trying to expand my horizons."

"Oh." It's just one word, but something about her one-word responses are really packing a punch, if you know what

I mean. It could be my imagination, I could just be feeling guilty, but I don't think so.

"So we'll be there really soon," I say brightly. "And I'll call you when we get close."

"Okay," she says. "Hurry up." And then she hangs up on me.

I slide my phone back into my bag. "She said to hurry up," I say. I don't tell him that she hung up on me, but I think he knows, since I never said goodbye. Yikes.

An hour more into the trip, I crack. I can't take it anymore. So after we've stopped at a McDonald's drive-through for strawberry-banana smoothies and chicken nuggets, I wait until we're back on the highway and then I blurt, "So I read your screenplay."

Noah doesn't say anything for a second, then reaches over and turns down the music. He takes a slow sip of his smoothie, then shifts on his seat. "Oh?"

"Yeah."

"And?"

"Honestly?" I say. "I really, really loved it."

"Of course you did," he says, looking straight ahead with a wry smile. At first I think he's pretending to be arrogant in that fake-macho way guys do, but then I realize he thinks I'm saying I like it just because we're friends. But I'm not just saying it. I really did love it. So to prove it, I pull the script out of my bag.

"What's that?" he asks.

"The copy of your script I printed out and made notes on," I say. Suddenly, I feel like kind of a dork. *The copy of your script I printed out and made notes on?* I mean, that's kind of pathetic. "Not a lot of notes," I rush on. "I mean, I didn't read it a ton of times or anything, it was just some, you know, overall thoughts." I've read it three times and given it a thorough line edit, but Noah doesn't need to know that.

"So you really did like it," he says, looking over at me and grinning.

"I really did," I say, flushing at the thought that me reading his script could make him so happy. "But, um, I, ah, had some ideas on how you could make it better."

"You did?" He sounds interested, so I forge ahead.

"Yeah," I say. "Mostly with the girl's dialogue. Girls don't usually say things like 'homes' and 'tricked out'."

He laughs. "Point taken."

"Also, the . . . the romance. I didn't really buy that he's so in love with her that he would give everything up throughout the movie. His family, school . . . He busted his ass for that."

"I didn't know girls said things like 'busted his ass'," he says, but he's teasing, so I say, "This girl does."

"So you didn't think the ending paid off?"

"No, it . . . I mean, I got that he liked her a lot, but he just let her leave at the end, after he'd risked everything. I felt like if he loved her, if he really wanted her, he would have fought for her. At least, that's what I would do if I really loved someone."

"That's true," he says. "I guess it's hard to write when you've never really felt that way about someone, you know?"

"Oh," I say, flipping through the pages of the script and suddenly feeling uncomfortable. "You don't . . . I mean, what about Ava?"

"Oh, of course I love Ava. I'm just talking about the kind of love that's in that screenplay. You know, like, an epic love story."

"You and Ava aren't an epic-love-story love?"

"Ava is amazing, don't get me wrong," he says. "She's funny and smart and when I came to school, she really went out of her way to be nice to me." *So did I*, I want to say, but don't. "But I'm only seventeen. I'm not sure that's old enough for epic-love-story love." He laughs, and then turns the conversation back to me. "How about you?" he asks. "Is Sebastian your epic love?"

"No," I say.

"Did you think he was?"

I consider the question. "I guess not," I say. "Maybe for, like, a second. But I don't think that seventeen is too young for epic love. And you shouldn't either. I mean, the characters in your screenplay are seventeen."

"Yeah, but that's a screenplay."

"Right." I hesitate, and then I say, "But don't you kind of want that?"

"Epic-love-story love?"

"Yeah," I say.

He looks at me out of the corner of his eye, and I hold my breath, wondering what he's going to say next. "Of course," he says. "I'm just not sure I'm ready for everything that comes along with it."

Ava comes flying out of the dining hall after we pull into the parking lot. She got extensions in her hair, and it's halfway down her back, all straight and smooth and gorgeous. Her legs are tan from spending so much time outside, and she actually has muscles. She's wearing a pair of khaki shorts and a navy blue tank. I jump out of the car and she throws her arms around me before she even looks at Noah.

"Hans!" she yells.

"Avs!" I say. I am so, so happy to see her, my stomach is all excited and it hits me how much I missed her. It's almost enough to get me all teared up. "I missed you!" I pull back and look at her. "Look at your hair, it's amazing!"

"They're clip-ins," she says, reaching up and smoothing them down. "There's a beauty supply store a couple of miles away, and since it's one of the only places there is to go around here . . ." She smiles and then looks at Noah, who's still sitting in the car. Their eyes meet and her smile gets wider, and then Noah's out of the car, hugging her.

She grabs onto him for a long time, and when she finally pulls back, she says, "I missed you."

"I missed you, too," he says. I look down at the ground and drag my toe across the sand and gravel, feeling like an outsider. Which is weird, since I know Noah way more now than I did before the summer, and I never used to feel that way when Noah and I would hang out with Ava before. Or when Ava and I would hang out with Noah, I mean.

"So let me give you guys the grand tour," Ava says. "I signed out the guest cabin for us, so we'll all be able to stay in there together, although I think Brooke Wilkins is having friends up, so they'll probably be in there, too." She wrinkles up her nose.

"Brooke Wilkins?" I ask as Noah walks around to the back of the car and hefts our bags out of the trunk.

"Oh, right," she says. "I never told you about her. She's this really annoying girl from Cali who, like, constantly talks about all the girls she's hooked up with. It's just so freshman year, you know?"

"What is?"

"Bragging about how you've hooked up with girls."

"We never did that."

"No, but everyone else did. Remember Sonya Fullmer?"

"Oh, right," I say. "She was always kissing girls to get guys interested in her."

"I remember her," Noah says, grinning.

"Figures," Ava says, grabbing his arm. But he has both our suitcases in his hands, and they're banging against Ava's leg so she lets go of him, and it makes me happy to think that Noah wouldn't have picked up both our suitcases if he was thinking about holding Ava's hand.

"So here's my cabin!" Ava says a few minutes later, opening the door. It's small, with six bunk beds pushed up against the walls. "No one's here right now, obviously. The girls are at their swimming lesson."

"Who's watching them?" I ask.

"No one's watching them, Hannah, they're not here to get babysat." Ava rolls her eyes. "They're being supervised and taught by the swimming instructor and Carrie, my co-counselor."

"Cool," I say, deciding to let her snarky remark go.

We drop our bags off in the guest cabin, and then Ava shows us the lake and the dining hall before we head back to Noah's car so we can drive into town and get something to eat. I stop at the passenger side, and almost climb in before I remember that Ava will sit in front. She holds open the door and I reach down to push the car seat forward, then slide into the back behind her.

We have lunch at a place called The Seaman, which Noah decides is the best name for a restaurant he's ever heard. Once we're inside, I suddenly wish that I'd changed my clothes, since everyone here is kind of dressed up. Well, not really dressed up, they're just more, like . . . preppy. Ava fits right in with her tan skin and her long blond hair and her crisp khaki shorts, but I'm still wearing the same clothes I wore on the drive, jean shorts and a tank top.

"I thought you said this place was casual," I say as I slide into the booth across from her and Noah. The waitress gives us menus, and I glance down at the specials. All seafood and steak. Which means expensive. Oh, well. After working so hard all summer, this is like my vacation. And on vacation, you should be able to treat yourself. Plus, last night I checked my bank balance, did some googling, and found this super-cute red Honda that I can actually afford. I emailed the guy who's selling it, and as soon as I get back, I'm going to take it for a test-drive.

"Did I say it was casual?" Ava says, looking confused. "It's not, really. They get more of a wealthy crowd here, the vacationers who come up on their boats to spend time in their summer homes." She *knows* that she said the place was casual, and I look at Noah, waiting for him to back me up. But he just keeps his eyes on his menu, which makes me annoyed at both of them.

"Now," Ava says. "I want you guys to order whatever you want. My treat."

"Your treat?"

"Yes," she says. "I get a big bonus at the end of the sum-mer. And besides, we're celebrating. Me, you, and my boy-friend." She kisses Noah on the cheek, and he smiles. *Me, you, and my boyfriend.* God, that really sums up my life. Only I'm the "you." *Me, you, and my boyfriend.* That sounds like the title of a really horrible, heartbreaking movie. Or a really bad porno.

When the waitress comes over, we order steamers to start.

"You like steamers, right?" Ava asks.

I shrug. "I dunno," I say. "I've never had steamers." Steamers seem like the kind of thing you don't just all of a sudden start ordering. They're steamed clams and you dip them in butter and the whole thing just seems super compli- cated.

"You've never had steamers?" Noah says. He looks at me incredulously.

"Really?" Ava says, laughing. "Well, you're going to love them."

I feel even more annoyed with both of them, but some- thing tells me I can't afford to show it, that if I do show it, there's going to be a lot of bad things that happen, a lot of horrible things that are going to come up. So I bite my tongue and hope that when I talk I won't sound passive-aggressive, even though it's how I feel.

"That's me," I say, giving them a smile. "Totally sheltered. And I'm sure I'll love steamers." And then I order the Surf 'n' Turf, not because I love it that much, but because Ava's paying.

After lunch, Ava insists that we hit the grocery store so she can stock up on some stuff to bring back to camp. "The food at the dining hall is so disgusting," she says, rolling her eyes. "Like, even the pizza is inedible. And they used to have a salad bar but they shut it down when a couple of camp- ers got food poisoning." She rolls her eyes again, like the thought of shutting down the salad bar is just way too horrible to comprehend.

I don't understand the point of going to the grocery store now, when Noah and I are here (shouldn't we be doing something a lot more fun than grocery shopping?) but I know better than to say anything. So I just follow Ava around the store, listening to her chatter away. Noah splits off from us and roams the aisles by himself, picking out snacks for us to eat later once we're back in the cabin.

"I'm sooo glad you're here," Ava says as we look at the packages of cookies and candy. "Honestly, Hannah, the girls here are just so . . ." She wrinkles up her nose.

"What about Lulu?" I ask. I pick up some Junior Mints and add them to the basket, wishing we had a way to keep things cold. I could really go for some Butterfinger ice cream right about now. I wonder if there's a good ice-cream stand around. You'd think that with all the summer vacationers, Maine would have excellent ice cream.

"Lulu's cool," she says. "But she's not you." My insides start to thaw out a little bit. "Oooh, Double Stuffs," she says and drops them into the cart.

"And we have to get Bugles," I tell her. Bugles are these really disgusting corn-chip-type things that are in the shape of, what else, bugles. Ava's mom used to buy them constantly when we were younger, even though we hated them. We still eat them now sometimes, because they remind us of middle school.

"Oh, definitely Bugles," she says. "I'm going to get the sour cream and onion kind." She drops them into the basket she's holding.

"Good idea," I say, happy to be joking around. "And while we're at it, why don't we get some dip for them?"

"Better yet," Ava says. "Let's skip the Bugles and just eat dip." We both collapse into giggles, doubled over in the chip aisle. But then, suddenly, Ava's face changes completely. She stops laughing and straightens up, her mouth set in a tight line.

"What's wrong?" I ask, turning around, expecting to maybe see her camp archnemesis, Brooke Wilkins. Not that I know what Brooke Wilkins looks like. I know her type, though, so I bet I could spot her. But instead of an annoying looking girl, there are just two guys, around our age, both wearing green T-shirts that say CAMP IGOOANA.

"Hey, Ava," the taller one says, stopping in front of us. "What's going on?" He's cute, with a lean swimmer's body and dark hair.

"Nothing," she says, her voice strained. "What are you guys doing here?"

"Well, it's a grocery store," the shorter one says sarcastically. "So probably the same thing you are." He peers into our basket, his eyes falling on the Bugles. "Although maybe not exactly."

I stand there, waiting for Ava to introduce me. But she doesn't. Awwwk-ward.

"Well," Ava says, twirling a strand of her newly long blond hair around her finger. "Enjoy your day."

"Will I see you tonight?" the taller one says. And something about the way he says it sounds very . . . cozy. It isn't like, *oh, will I see you tonight at the student council meeting?* It's more like *oh, will I see you tonight when I ravage your body and get you naked in my bunk?*

"Uh, no," Ava says. "I have a friend up." I notice that she doesn't say "friends" multiple, and since I'm obviously standing right there, it leads me to believe she doesn't want them to know about Noah.

We all hover there for a second, still waiting for her to introduce us, and her still not doing it. I'm this close to introducing myself, but something tells me Ava really wouldn't like that. So I just look down at the ground and after a few more seconds, the boys say goodbye and disappear down the aisle.

Ava and I just stand there, and then finally, I reach down and pick up the sour cream and onion bugles. "So," I say. "Should we still get these? Or would you rather have barbeque?"

"Those," she says, forcing a smile. But I can tell it's not real.

I follow her to produce where she picks out some bananas, and then up to the registers where she picks out some bottles of water from the front coolers.

"Hey," Noah says, joining us in line. He holds up a pack of Boost. "Hannah, look what I found!"

"Ohmigod," I say. "I have to try it!"

"Right now?"

"Yes, right now." I tear open the cardboard package and pull out a Boost. "Uh oh," I say. "It says Boost Plus. What do you think that means?"

"It means," he says, "that you need to drink it immediately. Boost Plus is, like, even better than regular Boost. More vitamins for the buck. Or the Boost."

I grin, and Ava looks at us like we're crazy. Which, now that I think about it, we probably are, since we're opening up a can of Boost in the middle of the grocery store.

"What are you guys talking about?" she asks.

"Come here," I say. "You should have some." I hand her one of the red plastic bottles.

"Yeah," Noah says. "Come here, you need to try one too. See, one night when Hannah and I were at the hospital waiting for Lacey—"

"Wait," Ava says. "Why were you at the hospital waiting for Lacey?"

"Because she had an allergic reaction and broke out in hives," I say. "So we were waiting for her in the cafeteria."

"You never told me about that," Ava says, looking at Noah accusingly.

"It wasn't a big deal," Noah says. "We weren't there

for that long, but we did have dinner in the cafeteria."

"And Noah ordered a peanut butter and jelly sandwich," I say.

"And then Hannah said that was only for seven-year-olds."

"So then *Noah* said I shouldn't be ageist when it comes to food, and then he told me about how he drinks Boost." Ava looks completely lost, and hearing the story out loud makes it sound so ridiculous that I start giggling. "I know," I say. "It's so stupid."

"I guess," Ava says. Another register opens up next to us, and the cashier calls for the next person, so Ava goes over and starts loading her items onto the belt. I open up the red container and step out of line, letting the little old couple behind us go ahead of me. "You ready?" I ask.

"Yes," Noah says.

"One . . . Two . . . Three." I tip the container all the way back, taking a huge chug of Boost. It's warm and gritty and tastes a little bit like cardboard. I try to make myself swallow, but it's so not happening, and I end up spitting it out all over the floor. I look at Noah. Noah looks at me.

"Clean up in aisle two," he says. Which makes no sense because we're not even in aisle two. In fact, we're not in an aisle at all. We both burst out laughing.

"So I guess you didn't like it," he says.

"It's disgusting!" I say. "I have no idea how you can drink this stuff." I look at the package. "Twelve ninety-nine! How can they charge twelve ninety-nine for something that tastes like milk mixed with crushed up wood particles?"

"Hannah," Noah says, pretending to be offended. "Be careful what you say about Boost. And keep in mind that each bottle is its own meal replacement. So it's like getting six whole meals for thirteen dollars."

"You can get six whole meals for thirteen dollars at Taco Bell," I say. "And they taste a lot better."

We rejoin the line and pay for our Boost and the rest of the stuff that Noah picked out, but when we're done, we can't find Ava. I peer through the plate-glass windows at the front of the store and see her in Noah's car, sitting in the passenger seat with her sunglasses on, staring straight ahead. "I guess she got bored of waiting for us," I say.

We walk out to the car, and Ava leans forward so I can climb into the backseat, and suddenly, I'm in a good mood. I mean, I'm actually having fun. Everyone is joking around, Ava was really glad to see us, and I was really glad to see her. For the first time all summer, I start to think that maybe everything's going to work out and be okay.

"Ohmigod, Avs," I say, pulling my seatbelt across my lap and buckling it. "I spit the Boost out all over the floor. It was totally disgusting, you should have tasted it. I really don't think you should let Noah drink them anymore."

But Ava doesn't say anything. Noah's outside, loading all the groceries he bought into the trunk. I hope he doesn't have too many perishables in there. Our dip probably already went bad in this heat.

"Hey, listen," she says finally, turning around. "Do you mind if Noah and I spend some time alone?"

I swallow. Hard. "Um, no," I say, fiddling with my seat-belt. "I mean, I figured you guys would want to be alone at some point." It's a lie, of course. I didn't figure that, because Ava told me specifically this wasn't going to be a romantic weekend, that it was fine if I was here, that she wanted me here and didn't *need* to spend time alone with Noah.

"I'm sorry," she says, pulling her sunglasses off. "I just haven't seen him all summer. And it wouldn't be for long, I promise. Just a couple of hours."

"Of course." I force myself to smile.

When Noah gets in the car, Ava reaches over and turns on the music. "So we're going to bring Hannah back to camp," she says. "She thought it would be a good idea if we spent some time together. You know, alone." I want to say no, I didn't say that, but mostly I want Noah to say no, that we're not dropping me off, that we drove all the way up here for us to spend time together, all of us, so that's what we're going to do.

Our eyes meet in the rearview mirror. "Is that okay, Hannah?" he asks.

"Yes," I say brightly. "Of course!"

And then I blink back the tears until they drop me back off at camp.

❈ ❈ ❈

They don't come back until late that night. They just leave me. Both of them just leave me in a cabin full of people I don't know, including the aforementioned Brooke Wilkins, who, it turns out, *does* have a lot of friends up visiting. Friends who ignore me when they come in and change into their bathing suits to go down to the lake. Friends who ignore me when they come back from the lake, seemingly inebriated. Friends who ignore me when they change into going-out clothes and totter down the stairs, off to some club in Portland. (I know they're going to Portland not because they invited me, but because they were so loud that by the time they left, I knew a lot of stuff about them, their lives, and their plans. Including one girl's brush with Chlamydia, which was definitely TMI.)

Ava and Noah don't even call to tell me where they are, and I sure as hell don't call them. By the time Ava gets back to the cabin at around ten o'clock, I'm furious.

"Hey," she says. "I brought you the snacks. We left them in the car. Of course, I wouldn't eat the dip." She giggles.

"Thanks," I say sharply. "How nice of you to think of me."

"What's your problem?

"My *problem*," I say, "is that you left me here all day!" I gesture around the room. "With nothing! No friends, no idea where I am, nothing! You didn't even call to tell me when you'd be back! And you didn't even apologize." I wave the book I'm holding in her face. "I've been reading this ridiculous book on critical thinking someone left under one of the beds!"

"Hannah, don't be such a drama queen," Ava says, plopping down on the bunk across from me. She pulls off her sandals and rubs her feet, then flops back on the bed like she's had a long day. Which she probably has. A long day of having fun and completely ignoring me. "You could have gone swimming. Or you could have taken a walk by the lake, or gone on a hike, or used a kayak."

"By *myself*?"

She sits up. "Hannah," she says. "Noah is my boyfriend. I wanted to spend some time with him. I'm really sorry I left you here, but we just lost track of time."

I'm about to start yelling at her again, but I wonder how much of me is really mad about them leaving me, and how much of me is really mad that she was with Noah. Alone. So I close my mouth.

"Where's Noah?" I ask.

"He had to sleep in the guys' cabin," she says. "I was going to sneak him in here, but the camp director found out and said no way." She lies down on the bed and closes her eyes drowsily. And a second later, she's asleep.

In the morning, Ava acts like nothing's wrong. She's up early, singing happily while she showers in the stall in the corner. The air in the cabin is cool but not cold—more of a late summer morning kind of cool—and I can hear birds chirping outside.

"Hannah!" Ava yells. "Are you awake?"

"Yes," I yell back, stretching lazily in bed, extending my arms over my head and flexing my toes.

"Oh, good!" she says. "I want to go to breakfast, just you and me. We don't have to worry about Noah, he'll be sleeping until at least noon."

I snuggle back under the covers, glad we'll be hanging out alone, even though I'm still kind of mad at her for what happened last night. She steps out of the shower, a fluffy yellow towel wrapped around her body. "I got you some papaya shampoo last time I went into town," she says. "You know, the kind you like from Sephora? It's in my shower caddy."

"Really?" I ask, sitting up. "Thanks, Avs." The papaya shampoo I love is, like, thirty dollars a bottle, but it makes my hair smooth and shiny.

"No prob," she says, then dances over to the cubby where she's keeping her clothes. "I'm kinda faded but I feel alllrigghhht," she sings, swaying her hips. It's an old song that we used to sing in junior high, and I can't help but laugh. She looks so silly dancing around in her towel.

"Thinking 'bout makin' my move tonight," I join in, getting out of bed and twirling around the room. We keep singing as I get in the shower, and by the time we're both dressed and ready, what she did yesterday is forgotten.

Ava and I have a great time at breakfast, talking and gossiping. We eat veggie omelettes with Swiss cheese, and she tells me about camp and I tell her about work, and it's almost like we haven't missed a beat.

Later, we meet up with Noah, and spend the day poking around in T-shirt shops, buying crappy souvenirs, taking a boat tour on Sebago Lake, and eating lobster rolls and ice cream from a little seafood shack on the main drag.

When it's time for me and Noah to head back to Boston, Ava hugs me tight. "Bye Hans," she says. It feels different now, hugging her, since I can feel the muscles in her arms and her shoulder blades are more prominent.

"Bye, Avs," I say. I inhale the smell of her perfume one more time, and hold on tight. Then, I turn around and get in the car. I keep my eyes down and pretend to be looking at my phone, not watching as she and Noah say goodbye, not wanting to know if they kiss, if they say how much they're going to miss each other, if they make plans for what they're going to do when Ava gets home.

By the time Noah gets in the car, I'm thinking again about how they left me alone yesterday. And I don't feel like talking. At all. So I turn toward the window, pull the travel pillow I brought with me out of the backseat, and pretend to be sleeping the whole two and a half hours home.

The First Day of Senior Year

Mr. Davies writes me a pass back to my eighth-period class, but since I never went there to begin with, no one will be expecting me, so I ditch the pass and decide to hide out in the cafeteria, where I plop myself down in a corner. Literally, in a corner. Not even a corner table. I go right for the floor.

I don't even care that it's probably really gross, or that I'm wrecking my first day-of-school outfit. The first day of school is bullshit anyway. It's supposed to be about new beginnings, but really all it does is wreck your life. And set you up for failure. And make you realize everything is completely and totally fucked.

I bury my face in my knees and decide to sit here for a long time and feel sorry for myself. I wonder if I can get away with skipping ceramics next period, but I know that if I do, I'll definitely get written up. Mr. Davies is totally on to me. He knows I want nothing to do with the pottery wheel. Not to mention, Ava and Sebastian and Noah will all know exactly what happened, that I chickened out of facing them.

I sit there for a few minutes, feeling like I want to have a good cry, but not really being able to find any tears. And then I hear a voice say, "Hannah? Are you okay?"

I look up to see Riker Strong, of all people, standing there with a concerned look on his face. "What are you doing here?" I ask. "Shouldn't you be in class?"

"Shouldn't you?" he asks. Which is a good point.

He sits down at the table near me and sets his books down. "Don't you wanna get up? It's probably dirty down there."

"You're one to talk about being dirty," I say.

He sighs. "So you hate me, huh? Because I broke up with Ava? Come on, Hannah, even Noah's over that."

"No," I say, looking up at him. "And I still don't know if I believe you broke up with Ava." The whole thing is very sketchy in my mind, and despite everything that's happened today, I'm still having a hard time believing Ava would lie about something like that.

Riker sighs. "I broke up with Ava," he says. "Trust me." He reaches into his back pocket and pulls out a sandwich. Tuna fish. Riker has a tuna fish sandwich in his back pocket. In a Ziploc bag. He pulls out one half and offers it to me. "You want some?"

"No, thank you," I say haughtily. "And it almost doesn't matter if you broke up with Ava, because either way, you cheated on Lacey." Not that Lacey and I are friends anymore. But still. It's the principle of the thing.

"Now that, I did," he says, nodding before taking a big bite of his sandwich. "But I heard that you had sex with Noah, and isn't that just as bad?"

"As bad as maybe breaking up with Ava and then cheating on Lacey? No."

"Not 'maybe breaking up with,'" he says, exasperated. He reaches into his pocket, the same pocket that held the tuna fish sandwich, and pulls out his cell phone. He scrolls through, then shows me something on the screen. An email. From Ava.

I know we can work it out. Just give me one more chance.

"You made that up," I say. "That's so not real, who saves their emails from ten months ago?"

"I save all my emails," he says, shrugging. "Don't you?"

"Well, yeah, but . . ." I trail off. Because the thing is, I believe him. Which means Ava's been lying to me this whole time.

"Whatever," he says, shrugging. He slides his phone back into his pocket, picks up the rest of his sandwich and stands up. "And Hannah?" he says. "Don't beat yourself up too much. You know, about the whole Noah thing. Sometimes it happens."

The Summer

The next two weeks are horrible. In fact, they might even be the most horrible days of my life. It's kind of a weird, cruel joke when you think about it. I mean, I traded being heartbroken over one guy for being completely heartbroken over another. And I didn't even get to have any fun in between. No relationship, no sex, not even a good make-out session.

"So are you going to come tonight?" Lacey asks. It's the last day of work before school starts tomorrow, we're getting ready to close up the diner, and Lacey is trying to convince me we have to go to Jenna Lamacchia's party tonight.

"Lacey," I say, wiping down one of the counters. "You do understand that the last time I was at Jenna's house something horrible happened, right?"

"Which is *why*," she says, "you have to go tonight. So you can create a new, better memory to replace the old one."

"But I don't want to." She's lucky she got me to go into the city a few days ago to get a haircut and buy school clothes. And really, the only reason I did that was because I wanted a chance to drive my new car, which I picked up last week. It totally decimated my bank account, and put a serious dent in my back-to-school shopping money, but it was so worth it. But there's no way I'm going to a party. Replace the old memory with a potentially crappier new one? No thank you.

"But then you'll never be able to get over your old memory, and you'll never be able to go to a party at Jenna's again."

I shrug. "Fine with me."

"Noah," Lacey yells into the kitchen. "Will you please tell Hannah that it's ridiculous not to want to go to Jenna's party tonight?"

"Why don't you want to go?" Noah asks, popping his head through the divider.

"Because I don't," I say. "I'm tired. And I'm cranky. And I want to go home and go to sleep." I don't tell him the real reason I don't want to go is because I know Ava will be there. She's coming back from camp tonight. And they'll be together, and it will be like . . . I don't know, like something awful. And that's the other problem. Who am I supposed to hang out with at the party? Ava or Lacey? Lacey or Ava? They hate each other.

"You have to gooo," Lacey says.

"She doesn't have to," Noah says. "If she can't handle it, she can't handle it."

I turn around and glare at him. Nothing really *bad* has been going on between me and Noah—he still picks me up in the mornings, we make small talk on the way to work, he buys me coffee, etc. But we don't get personal, we don't talk about music, and we definitely don't talk about his screenplay or the reason he was at my house that night. We don't talk about what happened in Maine, or how pissed off I am at him for leaving me all alone that day, or how we both know I was just pretending to sleep on the ride home.

"I think I will go after all," I tell Lacey. "Pick me up at nine?" I just really hope it's not a mistake.

This was a complete mistake.

"Now, when we get in here, if you see Danielle, don't even look at her," Lacey instructs. "And if you see her before I do, don't, like, try to tell me or anything, because then it will be obvious that I care." She pulls up the top of her black strapless sundress. "I don't want her to know that I'm even *thinking* about her being here."

"Okay," I say, following her up the steps and wondering if there's going to be a lot of alcohol here, and if so, what kind. I'm thinking it might be time to get drunk, and fast. The good thing is, Ava and Noah won't be here after all— Ava decided to stay in Maine to have dinner with her camp friends, so she's not getting back until late tonight. I tried to tell her she'd be exhausted at school tomorrow, but she didn't want to listen.

When we get into the party, I start to have some kind of horrible flashback. Seriously. It's like I have PTSD or something. I'm walking through Jenna's living room, and suddenly my head feels all light, and I can't really even see where I'm going. The music's on, and there's that familiar smell of Jenna's house—pot and beer and cologne. And then the room starts spinning a little bit, so I pull on Lacey's hand and lean into her and say, "I'm sorry, I . . . I have to get out of here."

"Wait, what?" she says, but it's kind of like I'm underwater or in a dream or something and I can't really hear her.

I stumble back through the front door and onto the sidewalk, and I can hear Lacey calling my name, but I'm running down the street, all the way home. When I finally get there, I suddenly feel very calm.

And then, before I even know what I'm doing, I get into my car and drive to Cooley's.

I can see him in there, mopping the floors, staying late so Lacey and I could go to the party. On my cell, I have a bunch of texts and missed calls from Lacey, freaking out about where I am and if I'm okay, so I text her back letting her know I'm fine.

And then I open the door and walk into the diner.

He doesn't seem that surprised to see me, which is kind of surprising to me, since *I'm* surprised I'm here, so you'd think he would be too.

But he just leans the mop he's holding against the wall.

"Hannah," he says. And it's something about the way he says my name that makes me almost turn around, that makes me almost stop what I know is probably about to happen.

"Why did you come to my house that night?" I ask. "At one in the morning?"

"I wanted to see you," he says, and takes a step toward me. My face heats up and my stomach does a flip, and it's the same thing he's been doing to me all summer, but this time, somehow and in a way I can't explain, it's different.

"Why?" I look up at him, and he hesitates for a second and I'm afraid he's going to take it back, that he's going to stop it, that it's not going to happen.

But then he says, "Hannah," again, and he moves toward me and his mouth is on mine and my heart is racing, but it feels right and perfect and safe.

The First Day of Senior Year

This day has seriously been like some kind of crazy loop. You know, like that movie *Groundhog Day* where the guy keeps waking up and living the same day over and over? Only with me, I keep being afraid to go places. Like this morning when I was sitting in my car, afraid to go into school. And right now, when I'm standing in the hallway of the art wing, afraid to go into the ceramics studio.

"Please tell me you're not in this class," a voice says behind me, and I turn around to see Lacey standing there, her eyes angry and her voice steely.

"Please tell me *you're* not in this class," I say, not to be smart, but more out of weariness and a feeling of disbelief that this is my life.

"I am," she says, then pushes by me and into the room. Great. Now, not only do I have to deal with everyone else who's going to be here, I have to deal with Lacey, too.

I peer into the classroom. I'm one of the first people here, which gives me some hope. Maybe Ava and Noah and

Sebastian all had the same idea I did, only maybe they have different, better guidance counselors than I do, ones who actually let them drop the class. Maybe they're not coming, maybe they're not going to even be here, maybe they're—

Ava goes brushing by me, her face streaked with tears.

Great. There goes that theory. She takes a seat at one of the tables on the right-hand side, so I go in and take a seat near the back and in the middle. Both Lacey and Ava shoot daggers at me from different sides of the room, but I keep my gaze fixed straight ahead as kids start pouring into the studio. Two girls I don't know very well, Luna Marsh and Lilly Peters, sit down at my table. Which is good, because it means there's only one chair left. Hopefully some other random person will sit there. If I can just keep all of us away from each other, maybe I can get out of here unscathed. And then tomorrow I can go back to Mr. Davies, I can tell him that I tried it and that it didn't work, that I really made an effort but that—

Lacey comes over and plops herself down in the chair next to me.

"So," she says. "You want to tell me what happened?"

"Um," I say. "I will. I mean, I want to." I take a deep breath. "Let's get coffee or something after this, okay?"

"No," she says. *"Now."*

Both of the girls at my table are staring at us, along with a couple of other people at other tables. But I have a feeling that if I don't answer Lacey's questions, she's going to get even louder, and then even *more* people are going to start staring, which I definitely don't want.

"Lacey," I whisper, looking nervously over to where Ava's sitting. "Please, can we—"

"No," she says. "Now."

I grab her hand and drag her over to the corner of the room. Everyone's still staring at us, so I lower my voice in an effort to keep Ava, and everyone else, from hearing.

"Well," I say. "This summer, I . . . I kind of started having feelings for Noah."

"And you never told me?"

"No," I say. "I never told you."

She sighs and runs her fingers through her hair. "I can't believe you never told me! I thought we were best friends."

"We were! I mean, we are, I hope. I just . . . I guess I kept wishing it would go away, you know?"

"But this morning, in homeroom and in math, you just sat there, letting me believe everything was fine, that nothing was going on with you guys. You never even told me! And then I came to pick you up from Cooley's, I *left school* to come and get you, and you totally lied to me!"

"I didn't really *lie*. But I know it's just semantics. Lacey gives me a look. "Fine," I say. "I lied."

I look down at my hands, and two tears come streaming down my face. I wipe them angrily away with the back of my hand. Figures. When I wanted to have a good cry in the cafeteria, nothing. And now that I'm here, in front of everyone, it happens.

"Oh, God," Lacey says. "Please don't cry. It's . . . I mean, I understand."

"You do?" I ask her.

"Yeah," she says. "Because, um, I have a secret, too."

Ohmigod. She slept with someone too? I wonder who it could be. The only guys we've really had contact with this summer are the old men who come into the diner and Cooley. Unless . . .

"Oh, God, Lacey," I say. "Please tell me that you aren't in love with one of your doctors."

"God, no!" she says. "I only go to female doctors—they have a lower malpractice rate."

"Oh," I say. "Then who is it?"

"Who's who?"

"Who did you sleep with?"

"Oh, no, I didn't sleep with anyone," she says. "I . . . I've been talking to Danielle again."

"You have?" I'm shocked. Lacey hates Danielle. "But you hate Danielle!"

"I know," she says. "But I just . . . I missed her and she seemed like she felt really bad and . . . I don't know, we've been texting a little bit. I'm not saying we're friends again, but I'm just . . . I'm keeping my options open." She looks at me nervously, like maybe I'm going to be mad at her, but all I do is reach over and squeeze her hand.

"I think it's great," I say.

"You do?"

"Yeah," I say. "People make mistakes."

"It will probably never be the same," she tells me, and I don't know if she's talking about her and Danielle, her and me, me and Ava, or me and Noah. Probably all of the above.

"I know," I say. I smile at Lacey, and she smiles at me, and I know we're going to be okay.

And then, suddenly, Ava's speaking up from her side of the room. "Isn't that nice," she says. "You guys are so cute, becoming BFF while I'm out of town. The psycho stalker —" She looks at Lacey. "And the boyfriend stealer." She looks at me.

"I am *not* a boyfriend stealer," I say. I think about telling her Noah wants nothing to do with me, but I have a feeling that really wouldn't make her feel better.

"Whatever," she says. And her voice is so cold that I'm kind of afraid she's going to hit me again. At least now we're in school, so it would be broken up pretty quickly.

Out of the corner of my eye I see Noah's head snap up from a table. He must have come in while I was talking to Lacey. Our eyes meet across the room, and I want him to say something, to do something, but it doesn't seem like he's going to. "It doesn't matter," Ava says. "You two deserve each other anyway. My ex-best friend the bitch," she looks at me, "and my ex-boyfriend the asshole." She looks at Noah. If he hears her, he doesn't show it.

"Ava," I say. "Please, let's talk about this later, let's—"

"I never want to talk to you again!" she screams. So much for bringing Lacey over to the corner. I am officially and definitely making a scene.

And at that moment, our ceramics teacher, Mr. Guthrie, walks into the room. He sees Ava and me yelling (well, Ava's yelling, I'm standing there with a shell-shocked look on my face) and he says calmly, "You two girls, please go to the office."

I start to protest, but then I realize there's nothing I can do. So I gather my books, and as the whole class watches, follow Ava out the door to the office.

But Ava has other ideas. Besides going to the office, I mean. She leads me out of the school, which we're going to get in total trouble for, since we're not supposed to be leaving school, we're supposed to be going to the office, and they'll know it. Mr. Guthrie would have called down and told them to be expecting us.

"So why'd you do it?" she asks, once we're standing on the side of the building by the basketball courts. "Tell me why you did it."

"Ava," I say. "Please, let's go somewhere after school,

let's go have coffee, you can come over, we can—"

"Fine," she says. "Forget it. Don't talk to me." She starts walking back toward the school, her purple dress swishing around her legs.

"Wait!" I say, taking a few steps. I grab her arm, and she stops and turns back around. "I just . . . I started liking him."

"Are you guys together?"

"No," I say. "We're not together." Saying those words makes me upset, but I force myself to look at her. "We're not together, and I regret it, Ava, I really do, I never meant to hurt you." And in that moment, I mean it. I do. If I could go back, if I could take everything back, I would. Because it's not worth it. Feeling this way, like my heart is completely shattered, isn't worth anything.

"Well, you did hurt me," she says. Then she shakes her head and sighs, leaning her head back against the brick wall of the school. She slides herself down until she collapses into a heap on the ground.

After a second, I sit down next to her. My clothes are already ruined from the cafeteria floor, so there's no way a little pavement is going to hurt me.

Ava reaches into her bag, pulls out a cigarette, and lights it. I look at her incredulously.

"You smoke now?"

She takes a long, slow drag, blows out the smoke and says, "Yeah." I must look shocked, because she says, "You're not the only one who kept secrets this summer. Lulu got me into it." Wow. I guess Lulu isn't as crunchy as I thought.

We sit there, not saying anything for a few minutes and then Ava says, "It's not like I didn't know something was going on, you know."

"You did?"

"Yeah," she says, taking another drag on her cigarette. "You guys with your Boost, and your music, and your dumb private jokes. Plus I could tell by the way he was talking about you all summer."

"He was talking about me all summer?"

"Yeah." She taps ashes onto the ground and then turns to look at me, her eyes sad. "And you guys were spending all that time together." She doesn't say anything for a few seconds.

"Ava," I say slowly. "What was up with those guys in the supermarket?"

"What guys?" But I can tell by the look that passes across her face that she knows exactly what I'm talking about.

"The guys you didn't want to introduce me to."

She opens her mouth like maybe she's going to lie, and then thinks better of it. "The tall one? Alex? We hung out a lot over the summer. Nothing happened," she says. "But we . . . talked a lot."

I don't say anything, because in a way, it doesn't matter. It doesn't matter if she hung out with some guy named Alex, or a bunch of guys, or no guys. It doesn't matter if she cheated on Noah, or if she didn't, or if she thought about it.

All that matters is what I did to her. What Ava did doesn't change the fact that I really, really betrayed her.

"It doesn't make what I did okay," I say.

"I know that," she says. She leans her head back against the wall and stares up at the sky. "Jesus, Hannah, why couldn't you have waited?"

"Waited for what?"

"Until I got home, until we broke up."

"What do you mean?"

"It wasn't working, it . . . it just wasn't." She closes her eyes, and a tear slides down her face. "It's not even that I'm that broken-hearted about him, you know? It's just that it sucks it's over."

"Yeah," I say. I wonder why she's being so honest now, why she didn't think she could tell me about Riker when everything was great between us, and why now she feels comfortable telling me about her and Noah. But maybe it's because now it's wrecked, our relationship is smashed, and we don't have to pretend anymore.

We sit there for a while, not saying anything while Ava smokes her cigarette, and a breeze floats through the trees across the parking lot. Then, finally, without a word, Ava stands up and starts walking back toward the school.

"Avs!" I call after her.

She stops for a second and then turns around. "What?" she says, and she looks small and alone, the breeze now ruffling her hair and her dress.

My voice catches in my throat, and I almost can't speak. "What's going to happen to us?" I ask.

"I don't know," she says. She looks at me for a long moment, then turns around and goes back into school. And once she's out of sight, I sit there for a few more moments, then take a deep breath and follow her.

I decide I'm skipping the office, mostly because there's no way I'm going back to ceramics, and also because I'm just completely and totally sick of this place. If I get in trouble, I get in trouble. I can deal with it tomorrow. But first I head back to my locker to drop off my stuff and get the books I need for my homework.

And when I get there, Sebastian's waiting for me.

"Hey," he says.

"Hey," I say.

"You want a piece of gum?" he asks, holding out a pack.

"No thanks," I say. I open my locker door slowly, then exchange the books I'm holding for the ones I need to take home with me.

"You getting out of here?"

"Yeah."

He nods, even though until today I've hardly ever skipped a class in my entire life. "Me too," he says. "You want me to go with you?"

I hesitate, thinking about how easy it would be to slip back into things with him, to get back together, to maybe forgive him. *Sometimes it happens,* I think to myself, looking at his deep blue eyes and remembering how his stubble used to leave my face all scratchy after a long make-out session. But I really can't ever be with Sebastian again. Honestly, I'm not sure if we ever should have been together in the first place, or if I just liked the excitement and the idea of having someone.

Besides, my feelings for Noah are too strong, and there's nothing I can really do to change that.

"It's not a good idea," I tell him, then slam my locker door shut. "But maybe we can be friends."

"Friends?" He looks confused, then shrugs. "I guess."

"Good," I say. "Because I could really use some."

I text Lacey on the way out of school, and we make plans to meet up at Cooley's in a couple of hours, to talk and try to figure things out. And then I drive to the beach, mostly because I don't want to go home. When I get there, it's pretty deserted and I sit down on the sand right near the water, letting it brush up against my toes. The air has that feel to it, the one that lets you know summer is really over and fall is really coming.

I put my head in my hands and start to cry. It just comes over me, and I'm sobbing hard, my whole body shaking. I'm crying for Ava, for Noah, for Sebastian, for Lacey, for everything I've been through this summer. I'm crying because for some reason everything changes, and there's nothing you can do about it, even though it's really, really hard to accept.

I cry for myself, for what I've done, for how I've behaved. It doesn't matter the reasons, or what kind of problems Ava and I had, or if we even had any problems. All that matters is that I slept with my best friend's boyfriend. I'm the girl who sleeps with her best friend's boyfriend. I imagine people at school knowing about it, about what they're going to say, about how people will talk about it behind my back. How they'll all take Ava's side, how they *should* take Ava's side, how there's no excuse for what I've done.

I cry for a long time, and when I look up, Noah's standing there, looking down at me, his face worried.

"What are you doing?" he asks.

"Crying," I say. "What does it look like?" I start to get up, to leave, to get far, far away from him. I don't want to be around him after he ignored me all day at school. Everything's too much of a mess for me to start talking to Noah.

"I know you're crying," he says. "But why?"

I look at him incredulously. "Are you actually asking me that?"

"Good point."

I'm standing up now, and I say, "Well, I actually have to meet Lacey, so . . ."

"Okay." He shoves his hands in his pockets and looks like he wants to say something else. But he doesn't, so I turn and start to walk to my car.

"Hannah!"

I turn around. "It's not your fault, you know."

"Yes, it is."

"Half of it's mine."

I think about this, but then I realize it's not true. Yes, he cheated on Ava. Yes, he slept with me. Yes, he has half the responsibility for the situation. But my friendship with Ava is one hundred percent mine.

"My friendship with Ava is one hundred percent my responsibility," I say. "I came to you last night, I . . ." I think about last night, how I came bursting into the diner, and my face gets red.

"I know," he says. He takes a step toward me. "But I didn't have to do anything."

"Oh, thanks," I say.

"No, that's not . . . that's not what I meant." He sighs. "Look, can we sit down?"

I want to. I really, really, really want to. But I know I shouldn't. "Please," he says.

So I slide down onto the sand, and he sits down next to me. "I shouldn't have been with you before I broke up with Ava," he says.

"That's your own problem," I say.

"I know," he says. "But what I mean is . . . we shouldn't have done anything until we had a chance to talk to her." And then he reaches over and takes my hand. It feels warm and comforting, and all I want to do is be close to him, to melt into him, for us to be the way we were last night. "I thought I could hold off, I was thinking about you all summer, ever since that night at the show, you were so cute and after that, I couldn't get you out of my head. And when I came to you that night, when I showed up at one in the morning, I realized what would have happened if Sebastian hadn't been there, and I knew I had to stay away from you."

"If it's true," I say, "then why didn't you just break up with her?"

"I don't know," he says. He looks out across the water, squinting in the sunlight, the breeze ruffling his hair. "Probably the same reason you didn't want to tell her. It's not something you really want to get in to over the phone."

"I guess," I say. "Although, looking back, a phone breakup would have been preferable to what went down today."

"I'm sorry about today," he says. "I should have been there for you. You didn't deserve to take the heat on yourself."

"Then why did you let me?"

"I just . . . " he says with a sigh. "I didn't want to be the reason that you and Ava stopped talking. I didn't want to be the reason your friendship broke up. I couldn't do that to you, even if it meant I couldn't be with you."

"You wanted to be with me?"

"Of course," he says. "I told you, all summer, you're all I've been able to think about. But I didn't want to cost you your friendship with Ava, I never wanted to do that to you, Hannah. I knew how much that would hurt you, and so I felt like I had to stay away from you." He sighs. "I just . . . I screwed everything up. I wanted to wait until Ava got home from camp, I thought . . ." He shakes his head and looks out toward the water.

"You thought what?"

"I thought we could talk to her together, that we could explain to her what happened, and maybe she would under-stand."

"But we never . . . me and you never even talked about it, not just today, but the whole summer, you didn't even . . . I mean, I wasn't sure you even . . ."

"I know," he says. "How could I? I couldn't tell you how I felt before talking to Ava, and I felt like I couldn't talk to Ava until she got back. But then last night, there you were, and you looked so beautiful, and I couldn't stop myself any-more. But I shouldn't have done it, I should have stopped it, I should have put you first. I was trying to do the right thing, but all I did was fuck everything up. With you, with Ava, with your friendship . . ."

"You're not the reason Ava and I are having problems," I say. He opens his mouth to protest, but I cut him off. "I mean, you *are* the reason we fought today, why everything exploded. But the problems between me and Ava, those are . . . they go deeper, you know?"

"I know," he says. "But I still should have stopped it." He stares out across the water, and so do I. The wind is get-ting stronger now, and he takes off his sweatshirt and drapes it over both of us, pulling me close. He looks down at me, his eyes searching mine. "I put my own feelings before what was right for you, for us. And I shouldn't have done that. Seriously, I fucked it all up."

I look up at him, my heart in my throat. It's the first time we've been close like this since Ava found out, and I feel something loosen inside me. "You did fuck it all up," I agree. "*We* fucked it all up."

"Can it still be fixed?" he asks. And he's so close I can feel his breath on my face and his cheek against mine, and his arms are around me and his lips are right there.

"I hope so," I say. "I really, really hope so." And then, finally, he kisses me. It's soft and sweet and wonderful, different than the way he was kissing me last night. Last night it felt like we were doing something wrong, like something had to happen before we got caught. Now it feels slow and wonderful and like the beginning of something. I kiss him back, and I wonder why the only time I've felt right all day is now, with him, being close, when it's the very thing that's responsible for all that's happened today.

"So what now?" I ask when I finally pull away. I bury my head into his shoulder, not sure I want to know the answer.

But when I look at him, his face is surprised, like it should be obvious. "Now," he says, "we figure it out together."

We sit there for a long time with our hands intertwined, watching the water lapping up over the sand, over our toes. And then, finally, he takes me to meet Lacey.